"The ____ got me drunk."

Flannery stared at Jack, trying to decide if he was kidding. "You're saying there was a St. Patrick's Day party in the pub?"

He stood up, rearranging the sheet around him. "I suppose you're going to tell me it's now September and I've been sleeping in your bed for six months, like Rip Van Winkle?"

"Uh, no, but—"

"Look, last night at this party," he repeated impatiently, "there was this old guy in a funny green outfit. He kept buying me drinks and telling me about fairies and leprechauns, I think." He raked his hand through his hair. "I wish I could remember. But it's all so fuzzy."

"Leprechauns?" she echoed. She started to have a bad feeling about this.

"No, wait. It's coming back now." Slowly, he opened his hand. "He gave me this," Jack muttered, revealing something small and shiny sitting on his palm.

Flannery closed her eyes. She knew what it was, and she knew where it came from, and she knew she was in deep trouble.

Dear Reader,

It's St. Patrick's Day, with four-leaf clovers and a pot of gold at the end of the rainbow. And this one includes a funny little man in a green suit who calls himself a leprechaun. Julie Kistler brings to you the "luck o' the Irish" in *Flannery's Rainbow,* the third book in A Calendar of Romance—a year-long celebration of love set against the holidays of 1992.

In A Calendar of Romance, you can experience all the passion and excitement of falling in love during each month's special holiday. Next month it's an explosion of springtime flowers and new beginnings with Stella Cameron's *A Man for Easter.*

We hope you enjoy 1992's Calendar of Romance titles, coming to you one per month, only in American Romance.

Happy St. Patrick's Day!

Debra Matteucci
Senior Editor & Editorial Coordinator
Harlequin Books
300 E. 42nd St., 6th floor
New York, NY 10017

JULIE KISTLER

FLANNERY'S RAINBOW

Harlequin Books

TORONTO • NEW YORK • LONDON
AMSTERDAM • PARIS • SYDNEY • HAMBURG
STOCKHOLM • ATHENS • TOKYO • MILAN
MADRID • WARSAW • BUDAPEST • AUCKLAND

This book is dedicated to all of my writing friends, but especially to Linda Jenkins Nutting and Pat Kay, without whom I probably would've committed hara-kiri long ago, and to the Bloomington Bunch—Dixie, Caron, Pat and Sara—for being there and being great

Published March 1992

ISBN 0-373-16429-7

FLANNERY'S RAINBOW

Chapter One

The fog was as thick as an Irish wool sweater—the heavy, hand-knitted kind his Aunt Margaret had given him for Christmas every year when he was a kid.

Jack peered over the steering wheel, trying to decide if visibility was so poor because there were no lights from other cars or if there were other vehicles and he just couldn't see them. Too bad cars weren't equipped with fog horns. Then he might be able to tell if he was really as alone on this godforsaken road as he thought he was.

"I need coffee," he said out loud. "I need a bed. I need to get home. I need to find out where the hell I am."

But the fog yielded no answers. It just kept streaming by, dense and wispy at the same time, mysterious and elusive, as impenetrable as a wall of wet gray wool.

Damnation. He never should have left the airport. If he'd stayed put, he could've been safely in bed by now. It would have been a lousy bed in a fourth-rate motel, but it would've been a bed. And that had to be better than wandering around like a Boy Scout without a compass. As the hour grew late, the roads got narrower and curvier, and the fog rolled in like a tidal wave.

Of course, that's what all the helpful employees at the airport had tried to tell him—that if it was too foggy to get planes in and out, it was too dangerous to drive—but he'd snarled at them and rented a car anyway. *If you can't get me on a plane here, then I'll find an airport that will,* he'd told them. After all, the deal was done, the contract was in his pocket and he wanted *out* of this place. He'd been hanging around hick towns and back roads for two weeks now, and that was too long, as far as he was concerned.

So he'd bolted from the airport, ignoring all that well-meaning advice. At first he'd felt good and in control to be out of the damned airport and heading for somewhere—anywhere. Now he just felt stupid.

"John Patrick McKeegan does *not* feel stupid," he told himself between gritted teeth.

Without losing his grip on the wheel, he switched on the overhead light and tried to shake out enough of the map lying on the passenger seat to figure out where he was or how he'd gotten there. But the fog was blocking out all the road signs and helpful markers, so there was no way to compare the map to where he was. Finally, he had to admit it: he was good and lost.

Impatiently, he turned the light off, shoved the map aside and switched the radio back on. He'd tried it before, to no avail, but maybe some station would come in now and give him a clue as to his location.

"Oh, Danny boy..." the radio sang out in a glorious tenor, and Jack groaned, changing the station immediately.

"I don't care if it is St. Patrick's Day," he muttered. "Doesn't anyone around here—wherever here is—listen to the news? If I hear another version of 'When Irish Eyes Are Smiling,' I'm setting the damn radio on fire."

The new station yielded "The Rose of Tralee."

"What the hell?" He broke off, feeling vaguely uncomfortable swearing on St. Patrick's Day. But why was everyone playing Irish music? His own hometown of Boston was one thing, but it seemed a bit odd here in southern Illinois, where he didn't think the Irish were exactly growing on trees.

If there were trees. At the moment, the fog was obliterating those, too.

Suddenly, out of nowhere, a loud horn blared, slicing through "The Rose of Tralee" and jolting Jack to attention. A car. No, a truck. A set of headlights pierced the thick gloom, blinding him. He had the presence of mind to swerve sharply to the right, narrowly missing the truck, but almost sending his car careering off the road.

Suddenly, a ditch loomed large. Jack hit the brakes and steered left, and the car slammed to an abrupt stop, spinning gravel and squealing its tires.

Still laying on the horn, the truck swept past, until the red pinpoints of its taillights disappeared around a curve or into the fog. It was impossible to say which.

Jack just sat there, stunned. His right front wheel was tipping off the shoulder, while the rest of the car hung out into traffic. He knew he had to move, but at the moment he couldn't think of anything but his near encounter with the Grim Reaper.

And "The Rose of Tralee" played on.

Shaky, he pressed the accelerator and slowly brought the car back onto the road. He now realized that it wasn't just annoying to drive in heavy fog. It was also dangerous.

"I'm stopping," he shouted into the murky night. "I give up, okay? You win, damn you. Anyplace that looks like anything, I'm stopping. I'll get some sleep—I'll re-group. But damn you, I'll be gone as soon as it's light."

As if in answer to his angry surrender, a small sign poked through the ghostly darkness.

It said *Welcome To Inisheer, The Edge Of The World.*

Jack and his car crept up to the sign at a snail's pace, and he centered his headlights on it, trying to decide if he was hallucinating. It looked like an old sign, but real enough.

"Inisheer?" he asked doubtfully. "What the hell is Inisheer?"

He supposed it must be a town, but there were no welcoming lights, nothing that indicated the normal human disarray of gas stations and fast-food places. Still, he crawled on through the night, searching for any hint of habitation, anyplace he could safely spend the hours until light burned the fog away.

But there was nothing there.

Finally, when he had all but given up on finding any-thing in Inisheer, he saw it. It was a two-story white tav-ern, not far from the road, flanked by two huge oak trees in the front. Soft light glowed from an old-fashioned lantern next to the door, barely illuminating the sign that swung out from the overhang. As Jack pulled to a stop, rolling down his window, he could just make out the words Inisheer Pub. Established 1892.

"Good enough," he said under his breath. He would've supped with the Devil himself for the chance to get off the road and out of this impossible fog.

But as he neared the door, painted bright green in contrast to the white frame structure, his resolve weak-ened. It seemed spooky for a pub to appear in the mid-dle of nowhere, just when he needed it. Maybe his mind was playing tricks on him. But the rough wood of the door felt real and substantial enough under his hand, and he met the challenge of the ghostly night, pushing the door open with a hard shove.

Suddenly, everything was different.

Inside the pub, people were laughing and singing, and a fiddler was perched in the corner, whipping up Irish jigs. Jack felt himself relax, even as he stared at the good-natured chaos unfolding around him. The contrast between this carefree party and the lonely, foggy countryside beyond its doors was striking.

Nonetheless, this was a scene he could relate to. In fact, it reminded him a great deal of his grandfather's pub in Boston on St. Patrick's Day, down to the green-dyed beer all the patrons were sloshing around. As he paused through the doorway, a green beer was pressed into his hand, too, and he looked down at it in surprise. The pretty redhead who'd donated the beer went dancing past, her full, old-fashioned skirts swinging.

"Wait," Jack called out. "I didn't order this."

"Oh, but everyone drinks on St. Paddy's Day!" she shouted back over the din in the pub. As she laughed breathlessly, her partner swung her around into some-one else's arms. Before Jack had a chance to reply, she was halfway across the bar, swirling and swaying to the music, obviously having a wonderful time.

"Come in, come in," a voice at his elbow urged him. "Don't be standing on the threshold all night."

The man who'd spoken to him was very short, no more than five-four, and Jack had to look down to find him. Even odder than the rest of the partiers, this funny little man was dressed in green, from head to toe. His outfit included a cutaway jacket, knickers and a top hat with a wobbly felt shamrock stuck in the hatband. He had quaint buckled shoes, and he kept hopping from foot to foot, as if the music were nipping at his heels, forcing him to keep moving.

"Where am I?" Jack asked in confusion.

"Inisheer Pub," his companion responded promptly, bobbing his head in time to the gay tune lilting across the barroom from the fiddler. "Should've been Sully's Pub—that's me, Turlough Sullivan—but it being the only thing in Inisheer, why, we called it Inisheer Pub. Wishful thinking, you see."

"No, I don't see." Jack ran a hand through his hair. "It's your pub, you said?" The little man nodded. "But where are we?"

"Inisheer, I told you."

"Yes, I know, but where is Inisheer?" Jack tried the only way he could think of to determine his location. "What state?"

"Why, the state of celebration," the man in green said with a lively wink. "It's St. Paddy's Day! Drink up, lad, while there's still celebrating to be had."

And then he was gone, jigging in and around the other dancers, leaving Jack alone with his mug of green beer. The icy glass was cold in his hand, and he took a swallow, more to get rid of it than anything else. It tasted wonderful. He hadn't realized how thirsty he was. And, funniest thing, when the beer was sliding down his throat and the fiddle music was spinning through his head, he didn't feel tired at all.

The first beer was replaced by another and then another, and Jack began to feel pretty darned good. The celebration in the pub had begun to blur around the edges, as if the dancers had whirled so fast, they'd spun the whole room out of focus. The thought struck him as funny, and he chuckled to himself, thirstily draining the end of his beer.

The pretty redhead stepped back up to him, tapping him on the shoulder and coyly offering a hand.

"Are you asking me to dance?"

"And what if I am?" She leaned in closer and smiled, showing off a wonderful set of dimples, as well as a substantial expanse of creamy white skin around the low neckline of her blouse. "Will you offer a girl a dance, sir?" she asked saucily.

"It's Jack." He could feel a sheepish grin creep over his face. Although he wasn't sure he knew how to do the complicated footwork the others were happily jigging away at, he was just tipsy enough to try. He squinted down at his feet, still very respectable in their tasseled loafers. They seemed a long way down there.

Could those feet somehow regain their ancestral spirit long enough to manage an energetic little hop? "I guess I—" he began.

"Now, Kathleen, don't be bothering the boy," the funny little man called Sully admonished, swatting her away. With a rueful toss of her flame-red curls, she smiled back at Jack, accepting the hand of a different partner and vanishing into the crowd of dancers once more.

"But I—" Jack started, not at all happy to forgo a go-round with the beauteous Kathleen.

Sully shook his head, wiggling the shamrock in his hatband from side to side. "She's a darling girl, my Kathleen, but she hasn't the sense of a newborn kitten. Anyone can see you're sorely in need of a spot of good Irish whiskey, my boy, and can't be dancing just yet. Am I right?"

"Whiskey?" Jack's brain was already so fuzzy, he was amazed he knew his own name. Should he be tackling whiskey, too, in this condition? Or should he find Kathleen and kick up his heels?

As if in answer to his unposed question, Sully nudged him and offered, "You're looking a little under the weather, young Jack. What you need is a bit of fortification, and quick."

He did feel slightly wobbly. And, actually, now that he thought about it, whiskey was more his style than green beer. Besides, everyone in Boston knew that Jack McKeegan could hold his liquor. "Whiskey," he said with more conviction. "Good Irish whiskey. Lead the way."

Focusing his bleary eyes on the receding back of the small man in green, Jack concentrated on weaving through the dancers, putting one unsteady foot in front of the other until he'd made it safely to the other side. Good thing he hadn't gone in for dancing. With a sigh of relief, he climbed onto a high wooden bar stool next to the one where his new little friend was perched.

His hands found the long, solid surface of the dark wood bar in front of him, and he hung on for dear life. And then he shook his head, hard, to clear away the cobwebs.

When he opened his eyes, he saw a full glass of whiskey sitting on the bar in front of him and the funny little man beaming at him. Sully raised his glass, and it would have been impolite not to reciprocate, so Jack raised his, too.

"To Ireland!" Sully shouted, downing his whiskey in one swift gulp. Around him, the bar patrons responded with hearty cheers, tossing back healthy doses of their own drinks.

"To Ireland," Jack chorused, carelessly swigging down the whole shot, blasting fire down his throat and almost strangling himself.

"Ah, there's nothing like it, is there, boy?" Sully asked fondly, pounding a tiny hand in the center of Jack's back.

Jack tried to breathe again, but it wasn't easy. "Nothing like it," he choked.

"Have another," Sully invited, waving over the solid unsmiling bartender. "Malachy, bring another for my friend."

There was nothing for it but to keep drinking, as Jack's newfound pal kept supplying the whiskey and the conversation. Jack was so tired, and the whiskey tasted so fine, he hardly noticed himself completely losing touch with reality.

"Inisheer!" he said loudly. "What a place! What a night!"

Through the haze in his brain, he pondered the question of what had happened to Kathleen, the girl with the soft white skin and glorious red hair....

He was forced to refocus on his drinking buddy when the old man clapped him on the shoulder and asked, "And what would you be doing in Inisheer this night, young Jack?"

"Drinking to your health," he said smugly, finding himself very witty all of a sudden. He winked at his companion.

"That you are, that you are." Sully grinned like a Cheshire cat. He urged, "Drink it down now. Wouldn't want to waste good whiskey."

Jack complied, downing another shot. Funny, it hardly burned at all on the way down, after you'd had a few, he thought.

"And how did you come to find us tonight?" the tiny man asked, cocking an eyebrow Jack's way. "Where did you come from, young Jack?"

"Out of the fog," he answered with a sigh. "I almost got run over by a truck. Was driving from..." Where had he been driving from? Some airport, but damned if he could remember where. "I was trying to get out of here—to anywhere I could catch a plane."

"In a hurry to be gone, it seems. Not fond of these parts, are you?"

"Oh, I like it well enough. But," he explained slowly, trying very hard not to slur his words, "I'm not from around here."

"Ah." Sully nodded sympathetically. "And I'd never have guessed it, either."

"I'm here on a job." After a quick look around to assure himself no one was listening, Jack continued, "And I just pulled off a deal that would knock your socks off."

His small friend regarded his knee-high green socks doubtfully. "My stockings look right enough to me."

Jack waved that off. "No, no," he said, pulling a sheaf of papers from his inside pocket. These were *the* papers, and he hadn't even trusted them to his brief-case. This deal was so hot he wanted to be able to touch the contract at any given moment. He whispered, "You're not gonna believe what a deal I made."

"And what would you be dealing for?"

"Land." He leaned over, waving the packet of papers under Sully's nose to emphasize his words. "I've got a contract for two hundred acres here. It's going to be the new..." Curvaceous Kathleen went sailing past, and Jack suddenly lost his place in the sentence. He blinked. "What was I saying?"

"A contract for two hundred acres," Sully prompted. "The new . . . ?"

"Oh." He tried again. "The new . . ." He hadn't a clue. He shook his head, and the right word popped through. "Headquarters? That's it—the new headquarters for RuMex International. Ever heard of it?"

"Can't say as I have."

Jack's pride was hurt. Old Sully seemed positively unimpressed. "You don't understand." He slapped the papers down on the bar, waiting until Sully took the hint and began to leaf through them dutifully.

"Very nice. Very nice, indeed," the old man responded, with a barely concealed yawn.

"I swung the deal of the century," Jack insisted. "I found the perfect land—and let me tell you, it wasn't easy. Soil samples and water samples and cow patties . . ."

He shut his eyes against the humiliating memory of John Patrick McKeegan, Seaboard Development's hottest hotshot, tiptoeing through cow pies.

"Anyway, I got it," he went on, banishing the thought, "and it fits all the . . ." He tried twice, but his inebriated mouth was simply unable to get round the word *specifications*. "Let's just say it's perfect. And the price is so sweet they'll probably elect me king back home."

"Proud of yourself, are you, boy?"

"Damn right." Jack drained his glass cheerfully. "Vice president," he proclaimed, tapping himself on the chest. "You wait and see." He chuckled to himself. "Ol' Bucky's gonna spit nails."

"And who might this Bucky be?"

"The competition." Jack glanced around suspiciously, as if ol' Bucky himself might be listening. "I may not be back in Boston yet, which is where I wanted to be to celebrate, but the signatures are on the dotted lines, so who cares?''

"Indeed," Sully returned sourly. "Who cares indeed? A grand Irish lad like yourself, making fancy deals to tear up the good green earth God gave us, and no one the wiser."

"But that's the beauty of it," Jack contended, beginning to get a little miffed. "RuMex wants someplace like this, in the middle of nowhere, so they can grow herbs or spices or whatever the hell they put in all those little pills they sell. The middle of nowhere..."

Jack tried to wink, but it was too complicated for him in his current tipsy state, and he almost fell off his stool. Regaining his balance, he said slyly, "But it won't be nowhere long."

"And what exactly does that mean?"

"Hotels," Jack countered, waving his hands in the air. "Airports, highways, houses—big, fancy homes—for the RuMex brass. There's no limit. We're talking progress here."

"Hotels, and big fancy homes," Sully mimicked. "What a lot of nonsense. And where will a leprechaun be finding a place to bury his pot of gold when your bulldozers start digging up our fields and knocking down our trees? Why, it's a disgrace."

"It's a great deal," he said stubbornly. "And I'm still in a state of celebration. Aren't I?"

"Of course you are," Sully told him, in an odd, shrewd tone that made Jack look up in surprise. "So drink up, why don't you, lad?"

"Right." He tried to focus his blurred vision on the glass in front of him. As if by magic, the thing kept refilling itself, and there it was, not two inches from his right hand. "How does it do that?" he mused.

"It would be the fairies," the little man crooned. And he grinned, with his tiny, bright green eyes twinkling and sparkling. "Did you know the little people invented Irish whiskey?"

Jack laughed out loud. "Did they now?" If he didn't watch it, he'd be slipping into the brogue himself.

"It was back in the days before they were little," his companion confided solemnly. "When Ireland was green with rolling meadows and thick with great, mysterious mists, and the forests grew so tall with oak and hawthorn, and they were nigh to blocking out the sun. Surely they were grand days."

Although it wasn't word for word what he'd heard from his grandfather when he was a boy, it was close enough for Jack to recognize the basic concept. In the stories, Ireland was always greener and taller and bigger and better when the fairies ruled the land.

"The Good People—the fairy folk, that is—weren't little at all, but giants then, and their magic was so potent there was none could best them," Sully continued in a soft, beguiling voice. "There were three things they liked to be doing if they had half a chance. And that would be dancing and drinking and riding with the wind."

"So they already had whiskey then?" Jack eyed the shot glass in front of him. It was full again, and he could swear he'd just downed it. "If they were already dancing and drinking, I mean."

"Oh, my, no," the little man scoffed. "They had a very inferior sort of wine, made from bog berries or some such. No, it was a wily leprechaun, one of my own forebears, who discovered the secret of good Irish whiskey."

Without pausing, the little man launched into his story, something about a drunk leprechaun trying to feed barley to his horse and dropping the grain into a hot spring.

Meanwhile, the fiddler behind them began to pick up speed. The tune sounded familiar, but Jack couldn't quite place it. His attention wandered from Sully's story as the music caught him. The tune seemed to have taken on a spooky, ethereal air. To Jack's ear, it sounded unbearably sweet, high and unreal, and at a breakneck pace, as if the fairies had taken over the bar and were spinning enchanted music to bewitch the St. Patrick's Day revelers.

Jack edged around on his stool, not quite believing what he was hearing. As the fiddler pushed his bow more swiftly, more urgently, and the dancers jigged faster and faster, the whole room seemed to swirl around him in a constant blur of motion and music and astonishing magic.

A sweat broke out on Jack's face and his mouth dropped open. He was bedazzled; he'd never felt so strange in his life, as if he were in slow motion and yet reeling so fast that he was out of control.

"It's fairy music," Sully declared. "You mustn't struggle against it. When the music calls an Irishman, there's no answer for it but dancing."

Before Jack could argue, the little old man had tipped him off his stool and was handing him over to the lovely Kathleen. Jack was so muddled, he hadn't a hope of resisting. And the music, the music was the most beautiful thing he'd ever heard. It was like a magic spell set to a tune. His body moved of its own accord, whirling and dipping and spinning, with Kathleen right at his elbow.

Ah, Kathleen. Had he ever seen a more gorgeous woman? The soft lights shot sparks through her hair and her eyes were as green as...as green as something. He'd felt so poetic there for a moment, before his vocabulary failed him.

He shook his head, but there was no time to clear his thoughts. The music filled his head, and Kathleen filled his arms, and he truly believed in enchantment.

Until he fell down.

"I think you've had enough dancing for one night," Kathleen said with a giggle. As she hauled him to his feet, her green eyes sparkled with mirth, and he decided he was in love. "Granddad, help me with Jack," she called. "He's having a bit of trouble getting his feet under him."

"Ahh, Jack," Sully commiserated. "Dancing can wear you right out, now can't it?"

Propped up on one side by the funny little man, and on the other by wonderful, beautiful Kathleen, Jack was dimly aware of being led up a set of stairs and into a small, shadowy bedroom, lit only by a candle near the brass bed.

"Jack, my boy, it isn't fair what I've done." Sully shook his head, waving the shamrock on his hat back and forth. "Not fair at all. But it's the only way, now isn't it?"

Entranced by the motion of the shamrock, Jack just barely heard the old man's words. "Sorry," he mumbled, as Kathleen gently pushed him backward onto a soft bed, heaped with pillows and quilts. "Didn't catch that. What's not fair?"

"I've stolen your contract," the little man confessed. "And I know it's mischief I'm up to, but it can't be helped."

"My contract?" Jack groped for his pocket. Empty. Even through the terrible fog in his brain, he felt the stirrings of panic. As quickly as he could manage, which was none too quickly, he patted down his other pockets. "Where is it?"

"Why, you handed it right to me down there in the pub," Sully said helpfully. "What was there but to take it? But not to worry. Being a leprechaun, I'll leave you something of equal value."

"A leprechaun?" Jack tried to rise to a sitting position, but he was unbearably dizzy, and he closed his eyes for a moment. Forcing his eyelids open, he concentrated on Sully. "What do you mean, you're a leprechaun?"

"Complete with pot of gold." His small, wizened face glowed with happiness under that absurd green hat. "I hope you realize what an honor it is for me to be telling the likes of you about my pot of gold. It being a secret and all."

"But what does that have to do with my contract?"

"Well, Jack, I decided that you and I had become such grand friends, perhaps I should share my secret with you."

Jack rubbed his head. The music from downstairs was still pulling at him, and he was so damned drunk he couldn't even sit up straight. "I don't understand."

"Of course you don't. You're of the mortal world," Kathleen put in from the side. She leaned over to help him take off his jacket.

As he let her strip off his coat and tie, he realized he'd almost forgotten about her. He smiled. Ahh, Kathleen.

"So, Jack," the tiny man who thought he was a leprechaun added kindly, "I've relieved you of your burden of that terrible contract, and in return, as a symbol of my good faith, I'll be leaving you a piece of my pot of gold." Right in front of Jack's eyes, Sully held up something small and shiny. "Now what do you have to say to that?"

Gingerly accepting the gold coin, Jack held it in the palm of his hand. He gazed down at it for a long moment, unable to fathom what was happening. "My contract," he began, but he couldn't for the life of him remember why it was important. Kathleen was pulling at his shirt, and her hands were so soft and her eyes were so green. "Kathleen," he said under his breath, and she smiled. "Dimples," he told her.

"Yes," she whispered, "I know."

The fairy music was sending ghostly strains through his brain, and behind his eyes Kathleen was dancing just for him. Her skin was glowing and her hair was the color of fire, and then she was taking off his clothes. . . .

Smiling at the lovely visions, letting himself drown in the smell and feel of Kathleen, he closed his eyes and settled down into cool, soft sheets.

"Kathleen . . ." he muttered. And then he fell fast asleep.

Chapter Two

The sign said *Welcome To Inisheer, The Edge Of The World*.

The morning light cast a soft glow around the old sign, and Mary Flannery O'Shea smiled. She had only been gone for a week, but she was awfully glad to see the bright green door of home.

"Thanks for the ride," she offered, hoping her escort would take the hint and drive off.

But, of course, good old Ken would do nothing of the kind. "Geesh," he said, getting out and stretching his long, spindly frame. "That was a long drive. How about a cup of coffee, Flan?"

"Yeah, okay," she said, even as she wondered why she was saying it.

The louse didn't even have the courtesy to offer to carry her luggage. No, good old Ken watched her struggle with both bags and open the back door at the same time.

"Granddad?" she called out, propping open the door to push her luggage through. But there was no answer. She hadn't really expected one. That wily old codger was always off somewhere, gallivanting around, getting into trouble.

Later she would track him down. Right now all she wanted was to get inside her own house, take a long, hot bubble bath, and then maybe sit down with a cup of tea.

But first she'd have to deal with good old Ken, "The Date Who Wouldn't Die."

Not that he was really a date. Even she wouldn't call a botany conference a date, although she had been known to stretch the truth about some other rather staid events just to make herself feel like she had a social life. But no, a week-long botany conference in St. Louis with Ken could hardly be classified as a date, a picnic or anything else the least bit interesting.

This particular conference had been as dry as toast—just like Ken.

As Ken took a seat at her kitchen table, Flannery fished around in the cupboard for the coffeepot, barely able to stifle a yawn. She was exhausted. She might've only been gone a week, but it felt like months.

And there was no telling what mischief her grandfather had gotten into during her absence. Especially since last night had been St. Patrick's Day, and Granddad had been none too pleased she wouldn't be home to observe it. She felt a twinge of unease, wondering what crazy way he'd thought of to celebrate by himself.

"Nah," she muttered. "He probably just went into town and had a few drinks with his buddies. How much harm could he really do?"

"What did you say?" Ken asked, dying as always to be in on whatever didn't concern him.

"Nothing."

She smiled weakly at him, trying not to look as annoyed as she felt that he was still around. Oh well, it was good to be home, even if she did have Ken to contend with. Flannery stared a hole in the coffeepot, willing it to percolate so she could get Ken his coffee and then get him *gone*.

"What time is it?" Ken asked.

She knew very well he had a watch; he referred to it often. Nonetheless, she humored him and glanced at her own. "Almost ten. Why?"

"Still so early," he said, clicking his tongue.

Oh, so that was it. Flannery fumed silently, trying to control her irritation. During the entire drive, he'd been complaining about the ungodly hour at which she'd wanted to leave St. Louis. So she was anxious to get home! Was that a crime?

"Here's your coffee," she announced, splashing it as she set the cup down in front of him. "I'm sorry, Ken, but I'm really tired. If it's okay, I'll just go ahead upstairs—you know, get unpacked and things—and you can let yourself out."

She knew it was *not* okay, that given his druthers, Ken would hang around her kitchen table all day, but she grabbed her baggage and fled up the stairs before he had a chance to whine about it.

"How do I get myself into these things, anyway?" she muttered, lugging her suitcase upstairs. "I don't even like the guy. All I did was accept a ride to a conference. I mean, we were both going, so what was the harm?"

She backed through the doorway into her bedroom, tugging at the heavy bags. "Now he's acting like he thinks he owns me or something," she said under her breath. "How in the world do I get myself into these things?"

There was no answer, just as there was no point in hauling her bags any farther. They were huge and ponderously heavy, so she might as well unpack what she needed for now and leave the rest till later. Just inside the door, she dropped to the floor next to the bigger of the two suitcases, unlatched it and rummaged through long enough to find her bathrobe and the little zipper bag that held her shampoo and toothpaste.

"Honestly," she groused, as she carried her things into the bathroom. "What could I have done differently? Was I supposed to bite his head off every time he spoke to me?"

She perched on the edge of the big, claw-footed tub, brushing out the long waves of her hair, as she started the water for her bath. When the water was steamy hot, she poured in an outrageous amount of wild strawberry bubble bath.

"Wonderful. It smells wonderful." She paused, sniffing at the air from the bedroom. "Unlike the rest of this place."

Now that she thought about it, it seemed unusually musty in her bedroom. And someone—her grandfather, no doubt—had pulled the shades. Dark and stuffy. Flannery frowned as she turned off the taps. She didn't want to come out of her nice, clean bath to a dark, stale bedroom.

"I'll open the window first," she decided, quickly shedding her clothes and slipping into her robe. "Air this place out a little."

Wandering back into the bedroom, she leaned over the dresser and slid the lace curtains out of the way to pull the shade. At first it wouldn't go, but she tugged harder, and it flapped all the way up with a loud crack.

She thought she heard a funny, muffled groan as she shoved open the window, but the old wooden frame was so noisy she couldn't be sure.

Until a voice behind her mumbled, "Kathleen?"

Flannery spun around wildly, clutching together the edges of her robe. There was someone in her bed!

She'd been strolling back and forth between the bedroom and the bathroom for a full ten minutes, and all the while some stranger, some intruder, had been lounging in the bed. How could she not have noticed?

"The shades were down—it was dark," she cried. "The bed's clear across the room. I'm nearsighted. It's not my fault!"

Not that it mattered in the least whose fault it was if she was going to die in the next few minutes at the hands of a crazed intruder. She peered at the rumpled lump in the big brass bed, wishing she had her glasses, wishing even more she had a weapon. She fumbled behind her on the dresser, until her hand closed on a cut-glass perfume atomizer.

"Who are you?" she called out, brandishing the perfume bottle in front of her. "What are you doing here?"

A dark head emerged from the disarray of bedclothes. Even without her glasses, she could see that it was a very groggy, very handsome head.

"Kathleen?" he asked dimly.

Her fear evaporated, to be replaced with righteous indignation. This time, she'd plainly heard the infuriating word that had dropped from his lips. The man had clearly said "Kathleen."

And didn't that just take the cake?

"No, I am not Kathleen," she said fiercely. "Which you would know, if you looked, because I don't look a thing like my idiotic sister."

It probably wasn't kind to call one's sister idiotic, but Kathleen deserved it—and more—for abandoning a stranger in Flannery's bed. Of course, she already deserved a good swift kick for past misdeeds, but that hardly took away from the outrage of this new transgression.

"You ought to be ashamed," she went on, building up steam. "I don't know why Kathleen decided to drop you here—safely out of her husband's range, I suppose—but you did know she was married, didn't you?"

His head lifted a few inches, and his gaze narrowed in her direction. "You're not Kathleen."

"I tried to tell you—"

"Her hair was redder, and she was ... rounder," he interrupted.

Flannery's spine stiffened. She knew very well what he meant by "rounder." Men always loved that particular portion of Kathleen's anatomical gifts.

The stranger muttered, "So who the hell are you?"

"I'm her sister," she said primly. "Flannery. I don't suppose she bothered to tell you she had a sister, or that you were playing your little games in *my* bed?"

"We didn't do much talking," he said grimly.

He began to sit up, and the sheet—*her* sheet, with her initials hand-stitched across the hem—slid down his smoothly muscled chest, pooling around his belly button. He had a very nice torso. It was also a very naked torso. And her initials were sitting in his lap.

Flannery blushed. "Stop right there—don't you dare move!" She held out the atomizer, her hand on the sprayer, ready to blind him with perfume if he flashed one more inch of skin.

Moaning loudly, he shielded his eyes with one hand and slumped back on the bed. "There's no need to shout. My head is pounding."

"Hung over, aren't you?" she asked smugly.

She advanced on him, still aiming the perfume bottle right at his head. With all due care, she leaned in close enough to catch the outside corner of the sheet and tug it back up to the middle of his chest without actually touching him. "You got drunk with my *married* sister and wandered into *my* bed, and now you expect me to bail you out. Well, listen, buster, I'm not making you coffee, I'm not feeding you breakfast, I'm not driving you home, wherever you live, and I'm not doing anything else, either."

"Go away...." he groaned.

"No, *you* go away. Now! Get dressed and get out of here."

Casting dark looks in her direction, the man in the bed roused himself enough to declare, "I'd be glad to."

He sent a quick glance under the covers, and his scowl deepened. It was as if he was only now discovering that he was naked. Well, she had news for him; she'd figured that out a long time ago.

She backed up as far as the door. "I'll go out in the hall while you put your clothes on, but then you have to leave." She pointed the spray bottle at him, "Got that?"

"I'm sure some people are petrified of being perfumed to death," he said coldly. "I'm not one of them. So will you please stop waving that thing around?"

She set the bottle down on top of her suitcase with as much dignity as she could muster. This guy was going to get a serious lecture from her on guest etiquette. As soon as he put some clothes on.

Still glaring at her, he poked around through the jumble of bedclothes, and then leaned over the edge far enough to scan the floor. Sitting back up, he demanded, "Where the hell are they? What did you do with my clothes?"

"I didn't do anything with your clothes," Flannery protested. "I'm sure they're wherever you left them."

She couldn't resist adding, "If you were a little more careful about where and when you jumped out of them, you wouldn't have these problems."

"Could you please hold off on the insults long enough to help me out here?" He ran an impatient hand through the cropped edges of his black hair. "If I can't get dressed, I can't leave. And you seem to want me out of here. So will you help me look, please?"

She considered. "Okay," she said after a pause. "You stay right there. Don't move!" she commanded, as he continued to search the corners of the bed, revealing bits and pieces of a long, lean body that she really didn't want to see.

"I have to move." Grabbing a handful of Irish linen, he wrapped the whole sheet around his body and stripped it off the bed in one swift motion as he rose.

Flannery panicked. "I told you not to move," she managed, feeling for the door handle behind her.

"I can't find my clothes if I don't move," he returned. Awkwardly fastening his sheet in a big lump, he kicked at a quilt that had fallen over the side of the bed. "Where are the damned things?" When Flannery didn't reply, he sent her a murderous glare. "Are you going to help me look or not?"

"I'll get my glasses," she mumbled, finding it absolutely necessary to be out of this room and away from this man.

Before she had a chance to think better of it, she ran down the stairs to the kitchen to look for her purse and her glasses.

"Flannery?" Ken inquired, rising from the table. "What was all that shouting upstairs?"

She'd forgotten completely about Ken. "Nothing," she said hastily. "That is, nothing that concerns you."

Snatching her purse off the kitchen counter, she quickly fished through the contents and pulled out her glasses, sturdy, round tortoiseshell frames that she hoped would make her feel more steady. "I needed these," she told Ken. "Stay here, or leave, but don't you dare come upstairs."

His mouth fell open as he fixed her with a dim-witted stare. "But, Flan—" he started to say.

"I mean it!" she said savagely. She pointed at his chair. "Sit!"

As Ken dropped himself back into his seat at the kitchen table, Flannery turned around and raced right back up the steps to the second floor.

But outside her bedroom door, she paused. Did she really want to go back in there with *that man?* She adjusted her glasses, smoothed her hair and yanked the belt on her bathrobe into a secure knot. But she still didn't feel like venturing in there with *him*.

"Are you decent?" she called out.

"No," he growled, in the nastiest, crankiest voice she'd ever heard. "I don't have any clothes. How in the hell could I be decent?"

"Well, should I come in or not?"

"Of course," he snapped. "It's your room, isn't it?"

Still she hesitated. "Are you wearing the sheet?"

"Yes, dammit. I am wearing the damn sheet. Now get in here!"

His voice rose on his last words, jumping through the door and biting her. "Okay, okay, I'm coming," she told him, sliding around the door with all due haste.

And there he was, swathed in cream-colored Irish linen from the waist down, seething with barely suppressed rage. And for the first time, Flannery got a good look at him.

She swallowed. Suddenly she was sorry she'd put on her glasses.

She swallowed again. She didn't want to stand there in the doorway, gawking at him, but she couldn't seem to move or speak.

Sweet Mary, Mother of God. The man was gorgeous.

It wasn't just his body that had her reeling, although that was impressive enough, slim and tall, strong and smooth, all the right pieces in all the right places, negligently covered in her sheet.

No, it wasn't his body. It was his face that was the stunner. Whoever he was, this leftover lover of her sister Kathleen, he had the face of an angel.

A fallen angel. His features were elegant and sharply etched, almost perfect. He might have been too perfect, if he weren't a little pale, a little strained, probably from his hangover. And he was clearly angry, too. The rigid line of his jaw, the harsh angle of his black brows and the fury in his gaze made him more scary than any remote object of perfection.

And those eyes . . .

She tried to look away; she really did. But his eyes kept calling her back. They were dark blue, Inisheer blue, the smoky, wild, bewitching blue of family legend. Her great-grandfather's eyes had been just that color, and they'd said it was the exact color of storm-tossed waves in Galway Bay, repeated in Great-Granddad's eyes to remind them all of the country they'd left behind.

Damn you, she thought. *Damn you for having the gall to show up in my house, in my bed, with those eyes.*

"Who are you? Where in God's name did Kathleen find you?"

"My name," he said tersely, switching his grip on his sheet so he could offer a hand, "is Jack McKeegan."

She looked down at his hand for a long moment, not sure she was brave enough to touch him. Finally, she had to do it. It would've been rude to just leave his hand hanging there in midair.

"Flannery," she murmured, trying not to notice how warm and strong his fingers felt wrapped around hers. "That is, Mary Flannery. Mary Flannery O'Shea. But I've always been called Flannery."

He shook her hand carefully. "I would say it's nice to meet you, but it's not. As a matter of fact, under the circumstances, it's downright awful."

"Well, excuse me," she returned, hastily retrieving her hand.

"Yeah, well, you and your family have some explaining to do." He frowned. "While you were gone, I think I figured out what happened here last night."

"What do you mean? We already know what happened." Flannery tried not to blush. "You got very drunk and, uh, shall we say, fooled around with my sister."

"I barely know your sister," he said heatedly.

"Oh, I see. And that's supposed to make it better?"

"That's not what I mean."

"Then what do you mean, Mr. McKeegan?"

"That I don't know Kathleen, and I did not sleep with her!"

"Right."

"I didn't," he insisted.

"And I suppose that's why you woke up out of your drunken stupor calling out her name," she said snidely. "Because you barely know her and didn't, uh, *you know,* with her."

He winced. "Could you please keep your voice down?"

She pressed her lips together and said nothing.

"Well, you can believe whatever you want," he muttered, getting down on his knees and peering under the bed. "But I know what happened."

"So do I." Flannery raised her chin as she stalked over to the dresser and made a pretense of looking in her drawers for his missing clothing. "You got drunk last night, so now you have a terrible hangover and can't remember where you tossed off your clothes in the heat of passion. Maybe Indianapolis."

"Indianapolis? Why the hell would I do that?"

"Or wherever you and Kathleen got this little affair of yours going. I don't know why you'd drive all the way down here from Indianapolis. Don't they have motels there? Or did you meet her somewhere else?" Flannery shrugged. "I don't keep up with Kathleen's comings and goings. For all I know, she and her husband don't live up by Indianapolis anymore. Maybe they're back in this neck of the woods. God forbid."

"Look," he said, hitching himself back out from under the bed, "I don't know what you're babbling about. I met your sister here, last night, at the St. Patrick's Day party in the pub. It was an accident, a coincidence. I wandered in because the fog was so bad last night. Remember the fog?"

"Well, no. But I wasn't here last night," she told him slowly, trying to make sense of this.

What was he talking about? Fog was plausible, but a party in the pub? How could that be?

"Well, trust me," he continued with a pained expression. "The fog was worse than soup—it was more like pudding. I almost hit a truck. And the only place I could find to pull in was here, at the pub.'' He clenched his jaw. ''I got here in the middle of the party, and your sister and the old man got me drunk and rolled me.''

She stared at him, trying to decide if he was kidding, but he looked deadly serious. She went back to the beginning. ''You're saying there was a party in the pub? For St. Patrick's Day?''

He stood up, rearranging his sheet, regarding her with a very annoyed look on his face. ''I suppose you're going to tell me it's now September, and I've been sleeping in your bed for six months, right? Like Rip van Winkle?''

''Uh, no, but...'' She shook her head. ''Look, what did you mean, about an old man who rolled you?''

''Rolled me—got me drunk and ripped me off.''

''Ripped you off?''

''Last night,'' he repeated impatiently. ''At the party. There was this old guy, in a funny green outfit. He kept buying me drinks and talking to me, about fairies and leprechauns, I think.'' He raked a hand through his hair. ''I wish I could remember. But I drank so much, and it's all so fuzzy.''

''Leprechauns?'' she echoed, starting to have a very bad feeling about this. *An old man in a green suit talking about leprechauns...* Who else could it be?

''Yeah, leprechauns. And the girl—Kathleen—I danced with her. She was really pretty, had red hair.'' Sighing, he shook his head. ''I was smashed, so the two of them brought me up here and put me to bed. I remember being on the bed and Kathleen was taking my clothes off.''

''Look,'' Flannery interrupted. ''I don't think I want to hear about—''

''No, wait. It's coming back now.''

"I know, but—"

"The old man—he was smiling, and he said something about being up to mischief, that he was taking my contract." A look of horror crossed Jack McKeegan's gorgeous face. "My contract! It was in the breast pocket of my jacket! Where the hell are my clothes?"

"We don't know where your clothes are, remember?"

"Good God!" Jack grabbed her by the shoulders, almost losing his bed sheet. "I have to get my contract back!"

Then he scrambled over to the bed and began tearing through the covers, flinging lacy little pillows and handmade quilts aside in his mad search for his contract. Flannery looked on, openmouthed. She still hadn't dealt with the fact that there was a party in the pub last night, let alone this news about a stolen contract.

As she watched, Jack suddenly stopped in the middle of his crazy quest, slowly turning back to face her. With an unreadable expression, he lowered himself to the edge of the bed, holding one clenched fist out in front of him.

"What is it?" she asked. "Did you find something?"

Slowly he opened his hand. "This," he muttered, revealing something small and shiny sitting on his palm.

Flannery closed her eyes. She knew what it was, and she knew where it came from, and she knew she was in deep trouble.

Chapter Three

"Good God," Jack mumbled. "I remember now. The old man wasn't just talking about leprechauns. He told me he *was* one."

"Oh, I'm sure you must be mistaken."

Jack looked up suspiciously, noting a definite lack of conviction in her voice.

The woman across the room—the straitlaced sister of seductive, dangerous Kathleen—gave an anxious little laugh. She had auburn-red hair, thick and wavy, spilling loosely to her shoulders, and it shimmied slightly in the breeze from the open window. Impatiently, she dashed it behind one ear. She kept fussing with it, as if it bothered her to have her hair down in front of him.

"How could he have said he was a leprechaun?" she asked nervously. "Everyone knows there's no such thing as leprechauns."

He'd barely met Flannery O'Shea, but he felt like they were old pals, or maybe old enemies. Whichever she was, he could read her like a book. In the short time since he'd crawled out of that bed, she'd gone through a whole parade of emotions, each one written all over her expressive face. Right now, she was back at square one— panic.

But the fear didn't seem to come just from being in the same room with him, like before, when she'd threatened him with the perfume bottle or when she'd suddenly felt the need to run off and find spectacles to hide behind.

So if it wasn't him that was scaring her, then it must be the gold piece he'd found in the bed. But what was there in one small coin to be afraid of?

He advanced on her, flashing the gold coin. "You recognize this, don't you?"

"No, no, of course not," she insisted, backing around the end of the bed.

But her face was transparent. And Jack was too good a judge of character not to recognize deception when it stared him in the face.

"Tell me what you know about this thing," he said softly, still advancing, until he had her cornered between the bed and the wall. He leaned in closer. "Tell me."

He saw the quick intake of breath, the fear in her wide green eyes, the flush of hot color stealing over her pale cheeks. The look on her face—she looked petrified.

He gave up. This was like interrogating Bambi.

With a sigh that spoke of relief, she slid past him and into the closet. She left the door open, and when he followed, he could see her in there, rummaging around, sliding things back and forth on the racks.

"What are you doing?" he demanded. "Is this any time to organize your closet?"

"I'm looking for your clothes," she replied, without bothering to turn around. "Kathleen might have hung them up or something."

"Yeah, right."

"Well, you never know." This time she faced him, chin up. "I thought you wanted your clothes and your contract. Standing around shooting the breeze about magic gold coins isn't helping."

"I never said it was magic."

"Oh, and you think you've caught me in some big mistake, don't you?" She took two steps out of the closet, slamming its old-fashioned door behind her, and slamming new waves of pain through Jack's head. "You're the one who brought up leprechauns. Everybody knows they go with pots of gold and magic coins. Do you think I'm stupid?"

"No, I don't think you're stupid." He sat back down on the bed with a thump. "More's the pity."

Maybe if she were a little less clever, he wouldn't have to be dueling for answers. Maybe she'd have spilled all she knew about Kathleen and the old man and the whereabouts of the precious contract. Not to mention Jack's clothes.

He sighed, gazing down at the gold piece in his hand. It was a pretty little thing, but utterly useless. "What am I going to do?"

"About what exactly?"

Jack looked up, catching a spark of sympathy in her expression. She might not be Kathleen, with the redhead's obvious charms, but he found himself liking this sister. Against his better judgment. Maybe they came in pairs, like good cop/bad cop, just to confuse him.

"Well?" And then, in a more skeptical tone, she inquired, "Why are you looking at me like that?"

"Like what?"

"Like I'm so very interesting."

He smiled. "Aren't you?"

She blinked behind her glasses. "Of course not."

His smile widened. Yes, he definitely liked Flannery O'Shea. She was smart, which always appealed to him, and maybe a little shy, a little self-conscious, with enough moxie to brave it out. He liked that, too. He even liked the way she kept clutching the front of her bathrobe together, as if she were hiding secrets under there.

That question intrigued him. What was she hiding under there?

"Why are you wearing a bathrobe?" he asked instead.

He could tell the question threw her. He hadn't meant to fluster her; he was just curious. But on the other hand, flustering her was okay, too.

"I was going to take a bath—I just got home—I was in St. Louis at a conference." She stopped in midexplanation. "Why do you want to know, anyway?"

He shrugged. "Just figuring things out. So you drove home from St. Louis this morning, and you were going to take a bath first thing? Isn't that a little weird?"

"I don't think it's weird at all," she shot back. "I was away from home for a week, and it was a long drive, and I wanted a bubble bath in my own tub. And I fail to see how that concerns you."

"I'm trying to sort out your story, to see if you're telling me the truth."

"Of course I'm telling you the truth! Why would I lie?" She pointed to a door on the other side of the room. "You can check my bathwater if you don't believe me. My bathwater... Oh, good grief."

And then she stomped past him, back around the bed and into the bathroom. She came out with a very grieved expression.

"My bathwater is stone cold and the bubbles are all gone," she said in an accusing tone.

"Yeah, well, I have some problem of my own, like the fact that my clothes are missing, a very important contract went AWOL with them, and I've got to find both and get on the next plane out of here. Except I haven't got a clue as to where to look for either of them."

Silence greeted him.

"Are you going to say anything?" he asked.

"Why should I? You've cornered the market on sympathy here."

"Okay, okay, I'm sorry about your bathwater. But surely you can run a new bubble bath."

"That's not the point!"

Jack sighed. Under other circumstances, he might have enjoyed sparring with Flannery O'Shea and her righteous indignation. But right now, he only wanted out of this nightmare. And that included her.

"Look," he said finally, "let's put your bathing habits aside for a moment, okay? I'm really tired of sitting around in this sheet. Have you got something else I can wear, just long enough to get out to my car and get a change of clothes?"

"Car?" she echoed doubtfully. "You drove here?"

"Yes." The look on her face was making him very uneasy. "Well? What's wrong now?"

"Well..."

"I think you'd better tell me."

"I didn't see a car when we drove in this morning," she said tentatively. "I'm sure I would've noticed. We would've had to go right past it. Unless you parked in a ditch or something."

"No, I pulled in right in front of the pub, just off the road."

He waited, but she didn't respond. She just kept gazing at him, her green eyes round and sad behind her
schoolgirl glasses. He knew he wasn't going to like this.

"A little red car," he told her, hoping for the best. "A
Ford, maybe. It was a rental car."

Still, she said nothing.

He raked his hand through his hair so harshly, he was
afraid he'd pulled half of it out. "Flannery, please don't
tell me the car has disappeared, too."

"The car has disappeared, too," she whispered.

"Damn it all to hell." He struggled not to smash
something. "What did I do to deserve this? My clothes,
my contract, now my car—everything I had with me—is
now gone, vanished, poof, goodbye, no more. No
toothbrush, no driver's license, no credit cards, no
money—"

"Maybe you shouldn't dwell on this," she offered
kindly.

"And what the hell should I dwell on?"

"Well, you're fine, health-wise, I mean. No real harm
done."

"No harm?" he shouted. "No harm?" Jack tried to
clamp down on his rising temper, as the sound of his
own voice ricocheted through his aching head. Out of
necessity, he lowered his voice. "I spend my whole life
in Boston," he said. "Right there in the middle of Urban Crime, U.S.A. And I never so much as get my lunch
money stolen. Now I'm in Nowheresville for ten minutes and I'm stripped down to my skin."

"I'm really sorry, but . . ." She clasped her hands in
front of her robe. "Try to remember this isn't my fault."

"Oh, yeah?" He wondered if steam was going to
come out his ears. "Well, your sister is in it up to her

hips. Not to mention the old man. If he's her grandfather, I assume he's *your* grandfather, too."

"Well, yes," she admitted.

"So where is he? Where is she? They both have a lot to answer for."

"But I don't know where they are," she contended. "I told you, Kathleen and her husband live up by Indianapolis, as far as I know. She hasn't been down here in years. Eight years." She paused, but shook it off, continuing stubbornly, "And my grandfather... Well, I never know where he is. But I don't believe for one minute that they stole your clothes or your contract, let alone your car." Her eyes flashed fire as she warmed up to her topic. "Kathleen may be a bit of a sleaze, but she's no thief. And my grandfather is the dearest, sweetest, kindest man—"

"That's it," Jack said, striding for the door with his sheet flapping. He wasn't going to sit around for one more second of her impassioned defense. "I'm going to call the police. We'll see if we can't get this straightened out."

"No!" she cried. "You can't!"

His head began to pound more viciously every time her voice rose so much as a decibel. Very softly, trying to give her the hint to keep the noise level down for the benefit of his mental well-being, he asked, "Why not?"

"Look, we'll figure it out," she said desperately, pulling on his arm. "Really. But you can't call the police anyway, because there's no phone here. And you can't walk ten miles to the nearest telephone wearing a sheet."

"Ten miles? Ten miles to the nearest phone?" If things could get any worse, Jack couldn't imagine how. He put a hand to his head, right there at the temple, where the throbbing was the worst. "Where the hell are we, anyway? I've never heard of a place with no phone."

"Inisheer," she told him helpfully. "The edge of the world."

"We're in Illinois," he muttered. "Last time I looked, it was right square in the middle of the country. How did that get to be the edge of the world?"

"It's sort of a state of mind."

He sighed. "You really don't have a phone?"

"Well, we used to have one. But nobody ever called, so I took it out."

"My God, I can't believe this," he said dully. He swept back into the bedroom, sat down on the bed, and put his head in his hands. "Why is this happening to me?"

"Maybe because you got so drunk you can't remember what happened."

His head snapped up, and he was immediately sorry he'd moved so fast. "Can we stop the temperance sermon? Why don't you make yourself useful and find me something to wear?"

"Well, okay. I guess that's a good idea." She twisted a long tendril of shiny auburn hair between her fingers, clearly deep in thought. "God only knows what Granddad has lying around, but whatever he has, it's too small for you. I can manage a sweater, but what about pants?" She looked him up and down, gave a little shudder, and shook her head. "No way my stuff would fit you," she murmured.

"Great. Just great. I'm going to be buried in this damned sheet."

"No, wait—I know," she said suddenly. "Ken will have something. If he's still here."

"Ken?" he asked suspiciously. "Who's Ken?"

She fiddled with her hair. "Nobody."

"Then why is he here?"

"He drove me from St. Louis. We were at the same conference."

"And he's been sitting somewhere in this house during all of this? Eavesdropping? Or what?"

"I really can't go into that now," she told him in a rush. "He may have left, and then we won't have any pants." She raced for the door, but turned back at the last minute. "Oh, what size shoe do you wear?"

"You think of everything, don't you?" he asked snidely. But he told her.

"Great. That ought to work just fine." Once again she turned to leave, but hesitated. "Look, why don't you go ahead and take a shower while I round up some clothes? That way you won't have to sit here in the sheet, just waiting."

It was an entirely sensible suggestion, which was probably why it annoyed the hell out of him. As the door slammed shut behind Mary Flannery O'Shea, slicing pain through his headache, Jack fell back onto the bed, wishing he could go to sleep and wake up on a different planet.

"But no little green men," he begged, as he got himself up and walked slowly toward the shower. "Please, no little green men."

"I NEED TO BORROW some clothes," she said crisply, looking Ken right in the eye. "Now."

"What for?"

"For an unexpected visitor whose luggage was stolen."

"Is this a relative?" Ken asked slyly. "A friend? Who?"

"I'm not playing Twenty Questions with you. Can I borrow some clothes or not?"

Ken appeared to be considering the matter, and Flannery felt like kicking him. It wasn't that difficult a question, and anybody but Ken would've said sure in two seconds flat. But he had to ponder all the implications.

"Look, I'll pay you for them, okay? Just a T-shirt and some sweatpants or something." She regarded Ken's skinny frame doubtfully. "The baggier, the better."

"I don't wear that sort of thing," Ken said grandly.

"You don't have even one small article of clothing that would work?" she demanded, losing patience fast.

"Well, I may have a pair of jeans."

"Jeans—perfect."

She led the way out to his car, crossing her arms and tapping her foot as he carefully undid his hatchback and began to neatly unfold every item in his suitcase. Finally, he came up with a very faded pair of Levi's. They looked as if they'd been through a few wars, but they were clean, anyway.

Ken stood there, holding the jeans, looking at her with a sullen expression.

"Well?" she asked. "What are you waiting for?"

"Didn't you say you'd pay me?"

She couldn't believe it, but she reached for her wallet. "How much?"

Ken brightened immediately. "How about twenty bucks?"

He probably hadn't paid that much for them in the first place, but it was worth it to find clothes for the mysterious Mr. McKeegan, to get him and his damn blue eyes out of her house.

With that little bit of extortion out of the way, she and the jeans trooped upstairs, with Ken in tow.

She knocked politely. "Are you decent?"

"Why do you always ask that?" he said fiercely, wrenching the door open.

Flannery looked him up and down, still not quite believing the sum total of Jack McKeegan. He was wet, and every bit as grumpy as before, except now he was wearing a towel instead of the sheet. If anything, this was worse, revealing long, strong legs and a flash of hip when he stalked back into the room.

"Oh, my," she said. That was all she could manage.

"Clothes?" he prompted, and she held out the jeans. "I'm supposed to wear a pair of jeans and nothing else?"

"Nothing else? Oh, my."

Mechanically, she crossed to her dresser and opened the sock drawer, tossing a pair of one-size-fits-all crew socks over her shoulder at him. Next she fussed around on the floor of her closet, pulling out a big box of old shoes and finally retrieving a very worn pair of black canvas high tops.

"I keep meaning to get rid of this stuff," she murmured absently. "Goodwill or something."

Jack held up one large sneaker. "Definitely not your size, sweetheart. Whose are these?"

She retreated to her sweater drawer, where she turned her back on Jack McKeegan and his impertinent questions. After poking through a pile of greens and browns, she pulled out a big, bulky sweater. A blue sweater. She tried to ignore the fact that it was the same moody blue as his eyes.

"Here. I think this will fit."

Jack held it up against his torso as Ken ventured into the room, peering at them with curiosity.

"This must be Ken," Jack said evenly.

Flannery clenched her jaw. "Right."

"Your boyfriend?"

"No," she said emphatically, as Ken chimed in with, "Yes!"

"No," she repeated, giving Ken a dirty look. "Ken, weren't you just leaving?"

"Oh, no," he interjected. "I couldn't possibly leave you alone with this person. I'd never forgive myself."

"Try," she said firmly.

"Don't worry, Ken, old man." Jack clapped him hard on the back and began to steer him toward the door. As Ken coughed loudly, Jack pushed him out into the hall. "Flannery's not staying much longer, either, unless she wants to watch me get dressed. Which I doubt she does."

"She doesn't," Flannery snapped.

"But—"

"Then it's all settled," Jack said, smiling serenely. And he shut the door in Ken's face.

A few more "buts" wafted through the door, but they both ignored it, until the sound of Ken's voice finally died out. There was silence for a long beat, followed by the pounding of footsteps descending the stairs.

As she listened intently, she heard the sound of a car coughing to life outside the house. Dashing to the open window, she was in time to see Ken's small hatchback grind its way out of her driveway.

"Yes!" she exclaimed. "He's gone. He's really gone."

Leaning back against the door with a satisfied expression, Jack announced, "I don't think I like your boyfriend, Flannery."

"He's not my boyfriend."

"Then it's a good thing I got rid of him, isn't it?"

"You're actually enjoying this," she said in disbelief.

He was standing there smirking, with a look on his face that spoke of primeval male forces and infantile behavior. She imagined a stag would look like that, after he and his antlers had just crashed and bashed a rival out of his forest.

What in God's name did she think she was doing, alone in her own bedroom with a stranger, conspiring to get rid of the only person within shouting distance that she was sure was safe?

He interrupted the crisis in her thoughts by asking, "What about underwear?"

"Underwear?" She took a shaky breath. "What do you mean?"

"Underwear," he repeated. "The jeans and the sweater are fine, but I'd be happier, and I'd feel a lot safer, if I had some—"

"Underwear. Right."

Flannery tried not to blush. She had no intention of finding out why he was so hell-bent on undergarments. The whole idea conjured up images of this man zipping himself into too-small jeans with nothing on underneath, and she absolutely, positively, wasn't going to think about that.

"Well, I could hardly ask Ken for spare underwear," she said sharply. "And I really doubt you'd want to wear it if I did."

"Right on that score. But don't you have a pair of gym shorts or anything?"

She couldn't help lashing back with a snide remark. "You sound like you've had a lot of practice coming up with alternatives. Misplace your undies often?"

He smiled, and she didn't like the look of that smile. "You'd be surprised."

"I doubt it," she muttered, but she suddenly realized that she had exactly what he needed, on a shelf somewhere in the recesses of her very own closet. "Wait right here," she said quickly.

"Where would I be going?"

She ignored that as she stood on tiptoe to reach into the very back of her closet, coming out after a few minutes with a flat white box. Of all the people to have to share this particular box with... The indignity was galling.

"Now, don't say anything," she commanded, as she opened the box.

Jack leaned over and pushed aside the tissue paper. Wide-eyed, he held up a pair of boxer shorts by the green-patterned waistband. "These have shamrocks all over them. Shamrock boxer shorts? Where did you get them? And why?"

"I don't remember actually." She remembered perfectly, but she wasn't going to tell him that. "It's been years." That at least was true.

"They were a present," he said, poking at the tissue paper, sifting through a pile of shamrock boxer shorts. "For you or from you?"

"From me," she said awkwardly. "I was going to give them to someone once, but things didn't turn out the way they were supposed to, so I never did. And I don't want to talk about it. If you want them, they're yours. But I refuse to discuss it."

The look in his smoky eyes was altogether too perceptive, as if he knew very well the circumstances of the shamrock boxer shorts. Which of course he did not, and she was not going to enlighten him.

"Take them," she said, shoving the box at him. "There's another bathroom downstairs. You can get dressed there, so I can finally have my room back. If that's all right with you.''

''Sure. Fine.''

Still casting curious looks at the shamrock boxers, Jack McKeegan bundled up his various items and finally left her to her bedroom.

Flannery breathed a sigh of relief. At least when she saw him again, he'd have clothes on, and that would be a substantial improvement.

All in all, things had to get better soon. Didn't they?

''JACK?'' Halfway down the kitchen stairs, Flannery caught herself. Clearing her throat, she started over. ''Mr. McKeegan? Mr. McKeegan, where are you?''

''In here,'' he called from inside the pub.

Mentally preparing herself, she took a deep breath and checked the back of her hair, to make sure her braid was tight, and then tried to enter the pub. But she had to shove to even budge the long unused door between the kitchen and the taproom. It creaked open mournfully, as if protesting the heavy-handed treatment.

Standing in the middle of the room, Jack was staring around at the pub like a lost soul. Still, he looked considerably less pale than he had a few hours ago, as if he were no longer feeling the effects of his hangover quite so strongly.

She noticed that Ken's jeans were too tight on Jack, but she wouldn't have changed them for the world. Jack in tight jeans was a fabulous sight.

And the blue sweater looked wonderful, too—much better than it did on her. She liked to wear her sweaters huge and baggy, and she had that particular style in ten different colors. As a matter of fact, she was wearing the dusty green version of it herself.

She wondered idly if Jack would notice that they were wearing the same sweater. Probably not. Men rarely noticed what she was wearing.

"Why is this door so hard to open if you're already in here?" she asked.

"I came in through the front, like I did last night," he explained vaguely. "Through the green door."

"What are you doing in here?"

"I don't understand it." Jack ran a hand through his hair as he turned around several times. "It's not at all the same."

"The same as what?"

"Last night," he returned impatiently. "Last night, when this place looked like a real bar. No spiderwebs, no dust. People were drinking and dancing, and there was a fiddler over there." He gestured to the far corner of the bar, where a floorboard was missing and several cases of grimy, empty beer bottles were stacked against the wall. "Everything is different," he said softly.

Flannery took a good look at the pub—something she hadn't done in years. It was the same as she remembered—dingy and neglected. Creaky wooden chairs and benches were still stacked on top of wobbly tables, and cobwebbed bottles of liquor were still shelved next to the murky, cracked mirror behind the bar.

"I don't understand," Jack muttered, as he traced a circle in the thick dust covering the bar. "I sat right here. The little man sat next to me. The brass rail—this one, right here—it was shiny last night, and the wood was polished. There was a party here."

But it was clear to anyone with eyes that no party had gone on in this pub last night, or last year. It was both a relief and a jolt when Flannery realized that. At least this way the likelihood of her family being involved was lessened. So what if Jack had come up with a gold coin like the ones her grandfather was always playing with? So what if he'd ended up in her bed?

There had to be some other explanation, and nobody would be carting her relatives off to the pokey.

"Jack," she said gently, "you know now there was no St. Patrick's Day celebration here. You know that, don't you?"

"How can this be?" He shook his head. "I know what I saw. I know what I did."

"But, Jack—"

"No," he said, taking her by the arms and gazing at her intently. "I was here, Flannery. I sat on a stool by the bar and I drank glasses of whiskey with a little man in a green suit who said he was a leprechaun."

"But, Jack—"

"Listen to me, Flannery. If there was no party here last night, then I'm losing my mind. Do I seem crazy to you?"

She pondered that one for a moment. "Well, sort of. I mean, I don't know."

"If nothing happened here last night, then where are my clothes?" His voice dropped and grew more emphatic as he got swept up in his own argument. "Where is my car? How did I get the gold coin? How did I know about Kathleen?"

"It could be a different Kathleen. It's a common name," she argued.

"But what about the rest of it?"

"I can't explain it, Jack. Really I can't."

"How did I know about..." he began, as the green door of the Inisheer Pub swung open, and a small man stepped merrily in.

Jack's face took on a triumphant, if savage, hue. "If I made this all up, then how did I know about him?"

"Granddad," Flannery said wearily. "Oh, dear."

Chapter Four

"All right, then," Jack said, in a low fierce voice, as he glared at her grandfather. "What did you do with my clothes?"

With his hands clenched into fists, he strode swiftly over to the doorway, where her grandfather was still standing. Flannery had to hurry to get there before he did, to wedge herself in between them.

"Hold on a minute!" she protested, doing her best to shield her grandfather. Unfortunately, that small gentleman seemed very curious about all the uproar, and he kept shifting around behind her for a better view.

"I've been holding on since last night," Jack snapped back. "Last night when he took all my stuff."

"And isn't this a muddle?" Granddad said cheerfully, finally managing to slip out from behind Flannery. "Perhaps I ought to be told what's behind this lad's troubles before we come to fisticuffs, eh?"

"Fisticuffs?" Flannery echoed in horror.

Jack was twice the size of her granddad and carrying around less than half the years. Surely he wouldn't fight with such a tiny, helpless old man?

She pulled angrily at his arm. "Mr. McKeegan, don't you even think of hitting my grandfather."

"I'd like to blast him one, I really would. After all he's put me through... Damn it, anyway." Shaking off her hand, he wheeled away, as if he couldn't trust himself not to start throwing punches.

"I can't say as I'm sure what it is that's happening here." The old man glanced between the two faces. "So, what's your name, then, lad? Perhaps we ought to begin with that."

"You know very well what my name is," Jack forced out between gritted teeth. "You were calling me 'young Jack' for several hours last night. And if you forgot at any point, all you had to do to jog your memory was glance at the contract you stole from me."

"Contract?" Flannery's grandfather looked very perplexed. "And that's the second time you've so much as accused me of stealing from you. Why, I've never stolen a thing in my life, and my own Mary Flannery will be setting you straight on that account. Isn't that right, darling?"

She hesitated. She wished she could back him up, really she did. But as for never stealing a thing in his life... Well, unfortunately, her granddad had been known to pocket things that appealed to him. Especially shiny, gold things, like the gold piece Jack had found in her bed.

She'd never actually seen him take anything, but she had found herself fending off angry neighbors who claimed their watches had been lifted. And then there was the owner of a secondhand store in town, whose coin collection had been pilfered. Several of these good people had suggested that Granddad was a bit of a kleptomaniac and that something really ought to be done. But who had the heart to punish a seventy-nine-year-old man?

Of course, this was the first time anything remotely like a contract had been brought up, so she could honestly say...

"I think her silence pretty much answers that one," Jack commented sardonically.

"No, it doesn't! He would never have stolen your contract, and I can say that emphatically." Trying to look supportive, she draped an arm around the little man. "Absolutely positively. Without a doubt in my mind. Unequivoca—"

"Okay, okay, I get the idea." Jack shook his dark head. "I don't know what game the two of you are playing, but I'm not sitting around waiting for the next installment in this master plan to drive me crazy."

"No one's trying to drive you crazy."

"Yeah, well, you're doing a fine job. But this is the end of it." With a murderous look in his eyes, he advanced on the two of them.

"What are you talking about?" Flannery asked bravely, retreating toward the green door and trying to pull her grandfather with her.

"Okay," Jack began, ignoring her as he concentrated on her granddad. "It's true that you're not dressed the same today." He cast a suspicious glance up and down the old man, as if surveying the worn wool trousers and waistcoat he was wearing, even taking the time to note the tweed cap perched on her grandfather's head. And then he pounced, using a stern, no-nonsense voice reminiscent of a prosecutor. "You do happen to own a green suit, don't you? And a green top hat, with a shamrock stuck in the hatband?"

"That I do." Her grandfather winked at Flannery. "Is that after being a crime now? The wearing of the green?"

"Ah ha!" Jack tossed her a winning look before he went back on the attack. "And isn't your name Sully?"

"That would not be my full and correct name, but there are those who call me Sully, yes."

Granddad's eyes were twinkling, and he was hopping slightly from foot to foot, a sure sign he was enjoying this. Flannery began to despair of ever getting out of this mess.

He's seventy-nine years old; I have to protect him, she told herself desperately. But what in the name of all that was holy had he gotten himself into?

"Sully, from Sullivan. And the rest of it... Let me think now...." Jack pressed two fingers against his forehead. "It was an old name, like Fergus or Finbar. No, that's not it. Turlough, that's it," he said triumphantly. "Are you not Turlough Sullivan?"

Flannery wondered if she could get away with something as obvious as wringing her hands. Jesus, Mary, and Joseph—he even knew her grandfather's name! Could things get any grimmer?

"Turlough Sullivan," Granddad agreed merrily. "That would be me. Same as my father before me."

"And do you contend that you are a leprechaun?"

Things had gotten grimmer. "Granddad," she tried to interrupt, before he said those horrifying words.

"But of course I'm a leprechaun," Turlough Sullivan announced proudly. "Same as my father before me."

"He doesn't mean it," Flannery insisted. "He's an old man, and he gets a kick out of pretending he's a leprechaun, but—"

"I know he's not a real leprechaun," Jack said in a very condescending tone. "What do you take me for?"

"Yes, and I am so a leprechaun," the little man in question interjected. "Mary Flannery, I'm that disappointed in you, I am. You know it as well as I do that Kathleen O'Shaughnessy of County Galway fell in love with a leprechaun back three hundred years ago if it's a day, and ever since, our family being straight descended from that very Kathleen O'Shaughnessy and the leprechaun, the blood of the Good People has been flowing in our veins." He made a little "hmmph" noise. "And now, here you are, Mary Flannery O'Shea, my own granddaughter, denying what's as plain as the nose on your face."

Flannery didn't know what to say in the face of that rapid onslaught of words. At least it seemed to have taken the wind out of Jack's sails that Granddad wasn't even trying to hide the fact; instead, he was positively brimming over with it.

"Okay, so you *do* admit you're a leprechaun, then?"

"Of course I do. And I will and I am!" Granddad shook his head in disgust. "Haven't you been listening, lad?"

"Then, please," Jack begged, with a definite note of desperation in his voice, "give me back my contract. Give me back my clothes. I'll get out of here and leave you alone, and I won't press charges—I'll never tell anyone—just *give me back my stuff.*"

"But I couldn't do that," the old man responded quickly.

"But, Granddad," Flannery said kindly, "if you took his things, you'd give them back, wouldn't you?"

"But I wouldn't. And I didn't!"

"Wouldn't? Didn't?"

"I wouldn't and I didn't take anything from young Jack."

"Oh, right." Now if she only knew whether to believe him. "I knew that. Of course you didn't."

His twinkly little eyes were the very picture of innocence. "Now why would I be thieving from the likes of young Jack, a fine Irish lad if ever I saw one?"

"That's the six-million-dollar question," Jack muttered, looking more frustrated and annoyed than ever.

Flannery took his arm and tugged him aside, over by the bar. After dusting two stools off with the sleeves of her sweater, she pulled him down onto one and took the other herself, so that their eyes were at roughly the same level. She'd felt at a distinct disadvantage gazing up at him.

"Why don't you let me talk to him alone?" she whispered. "I think he might be more open if it's just me."

Not for the first time, she wished she knew how to pull the seductive tricks her sister Kathleen was so good at. Maybe then he'd drop this ghastly inquisition long enough for her to sort things out. And maybe then he'd look at her with an expression other than hostility in those gorgeous blue eyes. Something in the general vicinity of lust might have been a nice change of pace.

But all she could do was peer hopefully at him from behind her tortoiseshell glasses, like the nearsighted botanist she was. "I think he may be afraid of you," she offered softly, only too aware the words fit her own frame of mind better than her granddads's. "He may be clamming up because you've frightened him."

"So you *do* think he's responsible? Even after your unequivocablies and absolutely positivelies?"

She clenched her jaw. "I didn't say that. Your story still sounds pretty farfetched to me, given the fact that no one's been in this pub for thirty years. Or have you forgotten that part of your Rip van Winkle fantasy?"

"No, I haven't forgotten," he returned. After a pause, he added, "Okay, you can talk to him alone. But you better get this cleared up, or I swear, I will go to the police. And little old Turlough may just find himself knee-deep in hot water."

"Okay, okay," she said anxiously.

Loudly he announced, "I'm going to go out now to see if I can find my car. Maybe whoever stole it ditched it somewhere close by."

And with a very distrustful parting glance, he swung open the green door and stalked out of Inisheer Pub.

"I like him," Granddad declared. "He may be in a bit of a temper just now, but I think deep down, he's a good lad." Grinning, he tweaked the bottom of Flannery's braid, the way he'd done when she was a little girl. "You've picked a live one, that you have, Mary Flannery."

"I haven't picked anything," she said firmly. "Now, come on, Granddad, tell the truth. Did you see him last night? Was there a party somewhere?"

"And I'm sure there were parties all over the map, darling child. It being St. Paddy's Day."

She sighed. Granddad was such a trial when he decided to play games. "Were you at a party? Did you meet Jack last night?"

"No, that I did not."

"Which?"

"Neither," he said grandly.

"What about Kathleen?"

Granddad glanced over at her. "That would be *our* Kathleen you're referring to?"

Since Flannery made a point of never mentioning her sister unless she was absolutely forced to, she understood her grandfather's surprise. But she persisted. "Yes, our Kathleen. Did you see her last night?"

"And where would I have seen Kathleen?"

"So you didn't?"

"Isn't that what I just said?"

She considered a moment. "You're sure? You only met Jack today, there was no party here last night and Kathleen wasn't here, either?"

"That's what I've been telling you, isn't it?"

"Yes, but..." At the mulish look on his face, she broke off. "Okay, okay, I believe you."

Before she could raise any more objections, he had scampered to the other side of the pub and was disappearing through the creaky door into the kitchen.

"Granddad," she called out. "You would tell me the truth, wouldn't you?"

But there was no answer. Turlough Sullivan, self-proclaimed leprechaun, had once more eluded the grasp of authority.

"YOU LET HIM LEAVE?"

If she'd thought Jack looked angry before, it was nothing compared to now. Against a backdrop of hazy gray sky, warning of an impending spring storm, Jack McKeegan looked like an avenging angel, just set down on Earth and not yet acclimated.

"You let him leave?" he demanded again, in an even more ominous tone.

Flannery backed up until she hit one of the two tall oak trees that marked the corner of the front yard. A low, gnarly branch tangled her hair, but she pushed it away, standing her ground. "What was I supposed to do?"

"You could've stopped him, held on to him, at least long enough to shake the truth out of him."

"No one is shaking anything out of my grandfather," she shot back, crossing her arms over her chest.

"But—"

"He swears he's telling the truth, that he doesn't know anything about any of this. And that's that," she asserted stubbornly. She started to edge out from under the oak tree to go around Jack and back into the pub.

"No," he returned, catching her arm, "that's not that."

She stopped. "It has to be."

"It can't be."

They just stood there, on the edge of the yard in front of the Inisheer Pub, glaring at each other.

"I gather you didn't find your car out here," she said finally, giving in first.

"No," he returned blackly. "I didn't. I walked down the road about half a mile in each direction, but there was no sign of it. So whoever took it didn't ditch it close to the pub, anyway."

"I hope you realize that the fact that your car was stolen positively lets my grandfather out, because he hasn't driven in years."

"That doesn't mean he couldn't."

"He didn't."

Jack shrugged. "So Kathleen stole the car. They're in it together."

"In *what?*"

"In whatever scheme they've concocted."

"You're insufferable," she muttered. "And you have no proof. No proof at all."

He smiled cynically and held up the gold coin.

"That plus two dollars," she returned smartly, "will get you a Big Mac in Metropolis."

"A Big Mac?"

Even from several feet away, she could hear his stomach rumble loudly. She closed her eyes against the sympathy she was feeling for Jack. It wasn't his fault he was a poor, hungry, half-hungover stranger in a strange land. "Okay, okay, I give up. How long has it been since you've eaten?"

"I can't remember. Sometime yesterday afternoon, I guess."

He stuffed his hands into the pockets of the too-small jeans, pulling them even tighter across the front, forcing her to look over his shoulder at the front door of the pub rather than directly at him.

Damn the man, anyway. His ability to get to her was becoming ridiculous.

"Come on, then," she muttered, brushing past him and making her way around the house to the back door. "I suppose the least I can do is feed you. I wouldn't want you fainting in my yard from lack of food."

Her own words from early that morning came back to haunt her. *I'm not making you coffee, I'm not feeding you breakfast... and I'm not doing anything else, either.*

"It's not breakfast," she argued under her breath. "What harm can a little lunch be?"

"What?" he asked, holding open the back door as she ducked inside.

"Nothing."

But there was no point in denying it. Jack McKeegan had already maneuvered her into several things she'd had no intention of doing. What would be the next casualty in this war of wills?

AFTER POLISHING OFF most of the groceries in the house, he very neatly washed his dishes and stacked them on the kitchen counter to dry.

It was an odd picture—handsome Jack McKeegan looking so pleased with himself for washing a dish. Flannery tried hard not to smile.

Turning from the sink, almost catching her smile, he asked, "Do you have a car?"

"Why do you ask?"

"Because I thought maybe you'd drive me into the nearest town—ten miles, wasn't it?—so that I can call my office and tell them where I am and why I'm not back yet."

"Fine." So far, it didn't sound too dangerous. "I'd be happy to."

He smiled. She didn't trust that smile. "And then I'm going to notify the authorities and let them handle the theft of all of my possessions. Maybe if they can find my contract fairly quickly, I can get out of this damn place."

"And I'm sure they'll believe your story, too." She knew she wasn't playing fair, and she didn't care. It stung when he called her home a "damn place." "Just how likely do you think it is that the police will believe a drunk stranger raving about an imaginary party in a pub they know good and well hasn't been used in thirty years? Not very likely, if you ask me."

"Nobody asked you."

"I'm willing to drive you into town so you can call your office." She paused. "And you can even call the sheriff, if you really want to. I suppose you really should, considering the fact that someone really did steal all of your things. But I have to tell you, as a kind and sympathetic sort of person, a Good Samaritan and all that, that it's to your own benefit to leave out the stuff about the pub and my grandfather."

"Yeah, right."

"Do you want them to think you're crazy? They won't buy any of your story if you leave in the preposterous part about the magically rejuvenated pub and the leprechaun."

Jack greeted her with no words, merely a distrustful stare.

"So I'm going to help you," she continued, filling the heavy silence, "and you won't involve my family in your mess. Right? Except for the fact that I found you here this morning, of course. You can tell them that."

He said nothing, just crossed his arms over *her* sweater.

"So do you still want me to drive you?"

"Yes," he said fiercely.

"I'll get the keys." Flannery spun on her heel and marched over to the back door, where the keys hung on a hook.

In the few seconds it took her to find the keys and dash outside, Jack had managed to discover the old ramshackle garage behind the house, and he'd heaved open the wooden door.

She did her best to ignore the incredulous look on his face when he caught sight of the monstrous old black Plymouth hiding in the garage.

"It runs just fine," she muttered, easing open the heavy driver's door.

Jack slowly folded himself into the passenger seat. "This isn't a hearse, is it?" he asked warily.

"It's a station wagon, sort of. And don't look at me like that. It's just . . . old, that's all."

"I'll say." He jumped when she started it with a noisy, uneven rumble. "Does it have a muffler?"

"Sort of."

"So it doesn't have a muffler."

"Well, part of a muffler." She shrugged. "It rides low to the ground, and the roads around here are murder on the tailpipe."

"Great." He cast a suspicious glance at the old-fashioned gearshift she was trying to crank into place. "This thing reminds me of a gangster movie."

"So?"

She happened to like the elephantine Plymouth. It had character.

"First you have no phone," he mused, as she backed the Plymouth carefully down the gravel driveway. "And then you have a car Winston Churchill wouldn't be caught dead in."

"Winston Churchill *is* dead."

"And he probably died in this car."

Pointing the long, round nose of the black monster out onto the road toward town, Flannery ignored Jack's insults.

"So am I in a time warp or what?"

"No." Flannery hitched herself up in the seat to see better over the steering wheel. "Well, sort of."

"You know, you say that a lot. I ask you a direct question, and all you can say is, 'Sort of.' It's really annoying."

"I don't think it's a bad trait to be able to see both sides of an issue," she told him loudly, practically shouting to be heard over the roar of the Plymouth. "So my answer means that there is some validity to what you're saying, even though I don't completely agree. And I don't give a flying fig whether that annoys you or not."

"Which is a hoity-toity way of saying that I was right in the first place."

"Wrong." She didn't take it kindly when her car, and for that matter, her entire way of life, were being disparaged. "This is not the big city, Mr. McKeegan, and we do things differently here."

"I've noticed."

"As to your question about a time warp, the answer is no, as you well know, you are not literally in a time warp." She gave him a superior smile. "But in Nowheresville, as I believe you called it, we don't believe in having a bunch of stuff we don't need, just to impress our neighbors."

"Now, Flannery, wait a minute. I never said—"

"Why have a phone," she continued, blithely ignoring his protestations, "if nobody calls? Why have a new car if you only drive a few times a month to get groceries? That may seem outdated or rustic to you, but that's the way we like it."

But instead of being put in his place by her little lecture, he just smiled at her, without a hint of contrition in those smoky blue eyes. "So if I offered to drop a fire engine-red Maserati in your driveway free of charge, you'd turn me down?"

She frowned. "What good would a fire engine-red Maserati do me?"

His eyes swept up and down her with a speculative gleam, and she told herself she had to look away or she'd crash the car.

"But with a Maserati, you could drive really fast on these back roads." His voice was barely a whisper as he leaned over closer. "Really fast."

It wasn't what he said; it was how he said it, in that husky, ticklish, dangerous voice. Like the wind through the trees on a stormy night.

Really fast, he'd whispered. Like a midnight ride in a too-fast car with a too-fast man.

Taking a deep breath, she concentrated on the road and the scenery around her, pretending that the lush overgrowth of trees she'd seen all her life was suddenly too interesting to ignore. A few scattered raindrops plopped on her windshield, but it did nothing to dispel the barometric pressure rising outside—or inside—the old Plymouth.

"You know, Flannery," he said softly, seductively. "I have a feeling you'd like going fast once you got the hang of it."

"You might be surprised," she returned tartly.

"No, sweetheart. *You'd* be the one surprised."

She wrenched the car into third gear, almost killing the vintage motor. It was safer than listening to Jack McKeegan.

We'll show him who knows how to go fast, she thought, whipping around a hairpin curve at twice the speed she normally would. The rain was coming down faster now, making the road a little slick, but Flannery didn't care. In fact, she was gratified to see him brace himself back into his seat, as if he were feeling a shade less than safe.

"Too fast for you?" she asked maliciously, stepping down on the accelerator, taking another curve like a maniacal race-car driver.

"Not as long as you know what you're doing." He paused, looking a little strained. "Where are we, anyway? If it's ten miles to town, shouldn't we be there by now?"

"I'm taking a different route." She peered into the rain, which seemed to be clearing into a heavy mist. "I thought we could cover more ground this way, keep an eye out for your car."

"Right," he said doubtfully.

"If someone ditched it after they dumped you in my bed—" she cleared her throat "—after they dumped you at my house, it should be around here somewhere. There aren't many roads around Inisheer."

"What is Inisheer, anyway? That's not this town we're going to, is it?"

"No, that's Crab Creek, where there's a store and stuff. Inisheer is just the pub." She glanced over at Jack, wondering how in the world she could describe Inisheer, which wasn't much of anything if she were going to be literal about it. "I guess it's weird for a pub to have a name like that, like it's a real place all by itself."

Jack nodded. His blue eyes were cloudy, and she could tell he was intrigued by the idea of Inisheer. It wasn't surprising; Inisheer had a way of doing that, of ensnaring people when they weren't looking.

She slowed the car as they neared a crossroads, but no other vehicles appeared through the gray day. "Inisheer was supposed to be a town," she told him, swinging the car onto the road to Rainbow Springs without thinking. "But it never got off the ground. My great-grandfather built the pub when they thought the railroad would go through here, but it went to Crab Creek instead, and Inisheer stayed the edge of the world—nothing but a pub in the middle of nowhere."

"And why Inisheer?"

For just a moment, she thought she could make out the vague outline of a rainbow over the next hill, where the springs were.

Wishful thinking, she told herself. *You want to see a rainbow there, so your imagination is providing one.*

"I don't understand the question," she said absently.

"The name. Where did the name come from?"

"Oh. It's an island—the real Inisheer, I mean. An island off the coast of Ireland."

She didn't know why she was reluctant to tell him, but if he made fun of the mystery that was Inisheer, she knew she'd feel like booting him out of her car.

"Go on," he encouraged.

She gazed straight ahead, still searching for the elusive rainbow that might or might not be there over the hill, letting the familiar words of the story of Inisheer spill off her tongue.

"My great-grandfather lived in Galway when he was a little boy. Even though it was a fine town, with churches and pubs and houses, and everything you'd want for civilization, off in the distance you could see the islands, all misty and mysterious, perched right there on the horizon. So my great-granddad decided that Inisheer, the last of the islands, must surely be the edge of the world. He said that beyond Inisheer was where you'd find sea serpents and mermaids and all manner of dangerous beasts. And if a fisherman was so unwise as to go past Inisheer, why, he might never come back."

Flannery caught herself just before she fell headlong into the old story. She managed a more modern-day smile, and finished up quickly. "So Inisheer was supposed to be this strange, wild, unearthly kind of place. And I guess the idea of it appealed to my great-granddad when he was twenty and dead-set on having his own town.''

"It's beautiful," Jack murmured, but he was looking at her, and she didn't know what to think.

She shrugged. "It's just an old story. My family's full of them."

But they had cleared the hill, and there was Rainbow Springs. And there was the rainbow, with misty, drizzled colors softly painting the gray-blue sky.

"Look, Jack!" The words were out before she could stop herself. "It's a good omen, really good, to see the rainbow here. Granddad says it means happiness and love and everything wonderful, right around the bend, if you see the rainbow at Rainbow Springs."

"Yeah, right," Jack grumbled. "My day has been so incredibly fabulous so far."

The spell broke, and she returned to reality, as the colors in the rainbow seemed to fade before her very eyes.

What was she doing, spouting nonsense about omens and rainbows, when the man had been through one of the worst days of his life, when he clearly couldn't care less about the magic she saw around her?

Flannery sat up straighter in the seat and steered a direct course for Crab Creek. She hadn't intended to drive to Rainbow Springs anyway, and she couldn't for the life of her figure out what she thought she was doing there.

"We'll be in town in a few minutes," she told him, as she pointed the old Plymouth away from the rainbow and into the dreary day.

As she glanced at her rearview mirror, she saw no hint of the rainbow. Not even one tiny splash of pink or violet brightened the gray sky.

Chapter Five

There weren't many businesses in the one-block district of Crab Creek, population 352. Flannery drove past the Gas & Grub, a combination convenience store/gas station where the town's few teenagers hung out, past the Coffee Cup, a decrepit little café where the old farmers hung out, and past the Dog & Dairy, the root-beer stand that would be shuttered and closed until May.

She didn't stop until she came to the last establishment on the street, a low-slung log structure that always made her feel like Abe Lincoln was right around the corner. The old general store had somehow managed to weather years of progress in the world outside without changing much inside. Now it sold ice cream and lottery tickets instead of sacks of feed or bolts of gingham, but the basic idea was the same.

The basic idea was down-home, no-frills, what-you-see-is-what-you-get, with everything from bread-and-butter pickles to chewing tobacco overflowing its plain wooden shelves. At the Crab Creek General Store, you could pick up your mail, find out the gossip, get your watch repaired and check out the latest in fishing tackles. It was also the only place in town with a pay phone.

As the bell on the front door tinkled to announce them, Flannery cautiously led Jack inside the log building, bypassing the front counter, where busybody Inez usually grilled anyone who ventured in the door. Today, thankfully, Inez was absent. Flannery could hear the dim sound of rumbling canned goods coming from behind the counter, so she supposed Inez was busy unloading supplies in the spare room.

"Back there," she told Jack, pointing out the pay phone tucked into an alcove at the back of the store.

It, too, was wooden, in the same rough-hewn style as the rest of the place, with an old-fashioned brass receiver dangling from a bracket on the side. Flannery happened to know it was a perfectly modern phone, ordered from the Sears catalog several years ago to preserve the rustic look of the general store, but she also knew it would seem archaic to Jack, just like everything else about life in the slow lane.

After glancing at the telephone box, Jack adopted an aggrieved tone. "A store and a phone right out of *Green Acres.* Why am I not surprised?"

Flannery pretended to be absorbed in collecting groceries in a basket as Jack gingerly picked up the receiver and started to make his call.

"Unfortunately," he said ruefully, "I've just realized that I find myself completely without funds. Can I borrow a quarter? I can call my office collect if you loan me a quarter."

"I'll put it on your tab," she returned sweetly. Under her breath, she ran down the ever-growing list. "Let's see, twenty dollars for the clothes, then there was lunch, and now phone calls..." She gave Jack a snide smile. "Your bill is really starting to add up, Mr. McKeegan."

"All the more reason to let me call the police to find my stuff, including my money and credit cards, so I can pay you back."

"Right." After a quick search of her purse revealed no change, Flannery wheeled and strode purposefully to the front counter. She didn't want to involve the gossipy store clerk, but she didn't have a choice if she was going to get Jack's quarter. "Inez? Are you back there?"

"Oh, my land, I've got a customer and here I am, letting the grass grow under my feet," Inez said loudly, wiping her hands on her apron as she emerged from the door behind the counter. "If you was a bear, you could've up and bit me, hon."

Inez was a big, raw-boned woman who always wore her steel-gray hair up in an untidy bun. As usual, she was dressed in a man's plaid shirt and jeans, with a heavy canvas apron that said Loretta on the pocket. As long as Flannery had been coming to the general store, the name Loretta had been on Inez's apron. Nobody had ever commented on it within Flannery's earshot, and she'd never felt brave enough to ask about it.

"Hi, Inez," she returned, in what she hoped was a casual voice.

The last thing she needed right now was Inez in a suspicious frame of mind. The woman was like a bull terrier with raw meat when she smelled hot gossip, and the news that a strange man had been sleeping in Flannery's bed would provide the whole county with dinner-table conversation for a good long time.

There was also the problem of what effect Inez's big mouth might have on Jack, especially if the town tattletale decided to start blabbing about Flannery's grandfather or her sister.

Hoping she could get Jack's change and let Inez get back to whatever she'd been doing with a minimum of fuss, Flannery set a dollar on the counter. "Can you give me some quarters for the phone?"

"Oh, you bet, hon. How're things out your way? Haven't seen you or that grandpa of yours in here in more than a week."

But as Inez cranked open the cash register, Jack chose to hang up the receiver, creating a soft clunk back by the phone. On red alert, Inez craned her neck and leaned out as far as she could go over the counter to see who was standing back there.

"A stranger," she decided, squinting at him from her awkward vantage point. "No, I surely have never laid eyes on that boy before. Good-looking critter, isn't he?"

Jack crossed his arms over his chest and waved cheerfully, oblivious to the fact that his timing with the receiver had just ruined Flannery's plans to keep a low profile.

"Now tell me, hon, who is that man?" Inez inquired with a sneaky smile. She gasped suddenly. "My land! Don't tell me you have a new beau, Flannery! After all these years you feeling frisky again?"

"Uh, no. He had, uh, car problems," she improvised. "Sort of an accident. Out near Inisheer. So I'm helping him call his office and, you know, get on his way."

"Oh, my land! Isn't that awful? The poor thing." Inez called out loudly, "You aren't hurt or anything, are you, hon?"

"He's fine—he's just fine," Flannery hurried to assure her. "But you know how these big city folks are. All he wants to do is get back home to the city as quickly as possible."

"He doesn't look in any hurry to me," Inez offered slyly. But she handed over the change, and then stood there watching as Flannery walked with it back to Jack.

"Keep your voice down," she whispered to him, "or everyone in town will know exactly what you're saying."

"So, Flannery, *hon,* are you feeling frisky again after all these years?"

His grin was devilish as he reached out and pinched her cheek. She batted his hand away, but the damage had already been done, and she felt her face flush with hot color.

"How many years has it been?" he teased. "And what exactly does she mean by *frisky?*"

"Will you please make your phone call so we can get out of here?"

"Sure thing, hon." Still smiling, he turned away and dropped a quarter into the slot.

Even though she told herself she had no right to listen in, Flannery was curious, and she busied herself looking over the various brands of canned corn that just happened to be the closest things to the phone. As she stared at the corn, Flannery heard Jack ask the operator for a collect call to Seaboard Development Corporation. She hadn't thought to ask him where he worked, but now it seemed he worked for a development company, whatever that was. Developing what, exactly, she wondered.

After a moment, Jack said, "Jennifer! Sweetheart, am I glad to hear your voice."

Flannery thought *his* voice sounded awfully warm and charming for a business associate. Sweetheart, huh?

Jack continued, "So, Jen, have you talked to the RuMex brass lately? Is everything on your end okay?"

RuMex? Flannery recognized the name from botany circles. RuMex was a big pharmaceutical company that manufactured everything from herb tea to the latest in prescription drugs, and they happened to hire a lot of botanists and chemists in their search for "natural" remedies. But what was Jack doing with RuMex? More to the point, what was RuMex doing in southern Illinois?

As Jack's side of the conversation lagged, she could pretty much guess what was happening on the other end. *Where are you?* that sweetheart Jennifer would be asking in her upscale, East Coast accent. *What happened to you?*

"You'd never believe it if I told you," Jack said grimly. "Suffice it to say I'm still in Nowheresville— somewhere in southern Illinois. And, no, I don't have the contract."

After a long pause, during which the lovely Jennifer no doubt expressed dismay and distress that there was no contract, Jack said, "Look, Jen, you can't say anything to anybody about this. Especially not Bucky. If he or anyone else asks where I am, tell them I've been delayed a few more days because of a small hitch, but everything's going fine otherwise. No, I had the contract, all signed, all squared away. I was on my way home."

Another hesitation. "Let's just say I was mugged. The contract, along with everything else I had on me, was stolen.

"No, no reason to panic. I'll just redo everything as quickly as I can. I need you to fax me..." He turned to Flannery, who made a pretense of being torn away from her search for the perfect corn. "Is there a fax machine in this town?"

"I really doubt it."

Impatiently, he directed his attention back to Jennifer. "Forget the fax. Express me new copies of the contract ASAP, and I'll take it from there. I'll also need money and clothes." He spared a glance down at the sneakers Flannery had provided. "And shoes, too. Yeah, use your own judgment—at least a couple changes of clothes. And just draw the money from my travel account. Great. Thanks, Jen, I really appreciate it."

So the lovely Jennifer had access to his money and his clothes? This grew more and more interesting.

"Anything else I should know about?" Jack asked. "Yeah, the deal went down really sweet, even better than the terms we discussed last time I talked to you.

"I don't see any reason they should balk—they were happy enough to sign on the dotted line last time, and nothing's changed. Right—two hundred acres—and exactly what RuMex wanted as far as soil and weather conditions go. It's a little farther from a major airport than what they put on the wish list, but well within the specs. And since they'll be building an airstrip of their own right off the bat, I don't think that should be a problem."

The part about the airstrip caught Flannery's attention. So RuMex, a huge, multinational corporation, was building something in her own backyard that was big enough to include an airport. This was getting more and more ominous by the minute. Clearly, Jack's all-valuable contract involved some kind of big development project for RuMex, like a smoke-belching plant or a high-profile research facility—exactly what remote, mysterious, magical Inisheer didn't need.

As she mulled over the idea, things began to fall into place. If her grandfather had stolen Jack's contract—and she still refused to admit that he had—the operative question was, what would Granddad want with a passel of papers?

But if that contract was the drawing card for bulldozers and airplanes and all the signs of the twentieth century her grandfather despised, well... Granddad's St. Patrick's Day conspiracy began to make a lot more sense.

"What's your address?" Jack asked, and it took a second before she realized he was talking to her.

"Oh. Well, it's just Inisheer. Why?"

"Express mail," he explained. "They'll need an address."

"Better send it here, hon," Inez chimed in from clear across the store. "This is the nearest post office." And she quickly reeled off the address of the general store.

Great. The town busybody now knew as much as Flannery did. As Flannery grabbed groceries off the shelves with a scattershot approach, she wondered if she'd hit on the answer to this mess. But Granddad had sworn he didn't take the contract. And with him denying any involvement, how was she going to get it back? Or should she leave it lost, since she wasn't any more fond of the idea of progress than her grandfather was? It didn't matter much, if Jack was going to replicate the contract anyway, with some speedy assistance from his pal Jennifer back in the home office.

"So," Inez announced, breaking Flannery's reverie, "are you keeping that boy out at your place for a while? Not many like that passing through these parts, if you ask me."

Nobody asked you. "He's very anxious to leave."

"Big business goings-on, hmm? Sounds like a real wheeler-dealer, if you ask me. Big city boy, down here for a little business, looking for a little fun on the side.

Might as well take your fun where you can get it, right, hon?"

"I don't know. I mean, I just gave him a ride into town to use the phone."

"Mmm-hmm," Inez murmured, as if to say, *Make up another story for me, Flannery. Maybe I'll believe this one.*

Jack was still gabbing away to his pal Jennifer, so Flannery dumped her groceries in a pile on the counter and fished around in her purse for her checkbook. She hoped that would give Inez the hint to start adding things up.

"So how's that sweet old grandpa of yours, Flannery, honey? Haven't seen him in a while."

"He's fine." They were verging on dangerous conversational ground here. She sent a glance back at Jack, but he was still occupied.

"That grandpa of yours gets into more trouble than any ten men half his age." Inez went rolling on before Flannery could stop her or at least deflect her. "I heard about Harley's coin collection. Whew, he was mad when your grandpa took all the gold ones."

"Uh, hold on," Flannery tried, but Inez refused to be detoured.

"Now I know you paid him for them coins, but Harley's still fit to be tied. And Mavis Mueller—she moved over by Eddyville, did you know that?—anyway, Mavis says your grandpa filched her Civil War brass button collection, and then he stole her laundry right off the clothes line. I said, 'Mavis, that's what you get for hanging out your laundry in March.' Why, it's too darn cold for that. But Mavis says she likes that air-dry smell."

Flannery closed her eyes. All she needed was for Jack to hear Inez's incessant chatter about Granddad supposedly stealing things.

"And Mavis told me she was thinking of calling in the sheriff to get her laundry back."

"But I'm sure my grandfather didn't take Mrs. Mueller's laundry."

"Oh, don't you worry, hon. Mavis won't call the sheriff." Inez laughed and stuck a pin back in her drooping hairdo. "You didn't hear, I guess, but Mavis and the sheriff had a falling-out about a year back after Mavis's no-account son Virgil tried to poison Karla Kytch after Karla . . ."

Inez swept on into new streams of gossip while Flannery let her mind wander. As long as they didn't concern her family, these small-town scandals didn't bother her in the least.

"And then Virgil wrote his name with weed killer in everybody's grass up and down the whole block. Do you believe it? Why, that boy is a menace, much worse than that sweet old granddad of yours."

As Inez took a breath, reaching under the counter for a paper bag, Jack came up quietly behind Flannery. He tapped her on the shoulder and she jumped, startled.

"Are you all set?" she asked heartily, to cover her nerves.

"I guess." He retrieved his hand and ran it hastily through his hair. "At least the ball is rolling to get me out of here, and that's a big step in the right direction."

All she wanted was to clear this mess up, and Jack's departure was part and parcel of that, but Flannery felt curiously bereft at his words. "Right," she said absently, as Inez poked her big, square face out from under the counter.

"Well, hon, one good thing. Having this good-looking boy around ought to take your mind off Kathleen and all those old troubles." As Flannery felt herself stiffen, Inez went blithely on, stacking cans in a brown paper sack as she spoke. "How is Kathleen, anyway? I heard they're coming home. Now, they haven't moved back yet, have they?"

"I didn't know they were coming back," Flannery whispered.

"Your own sister, and you didn't know?" Inez demanded. "I guess you two are still feuding then, right, hon? Why, I'd have thought you would've cleared that up years ago, being your only sister and all. Now, me and my sister, we fight like cats, but we're family, and family means everything, hon." She clucked her tongue sharply. "You got to mend your fences, hon. Bury the hatchet, patch it up, forgive and forget."

"Last night," Jack said softly. "I was right—it was Kathleen."

"What was that, hon? Last night? You and Kathleen?" Inez's broad face lit up with the possibilities. "You and Kathleen . . . well, if that don't take the cake. Now, don't get me wrong, I hadn't heard a word that there was trouble between that pair of lovebirds, but you never can tell, can you, hon? Even though I'm real cut up to hear about it, of course. But Flannery's probably turning cartwheels, right, hon?"

"Excuse me," she mumbled, running from the store without her groceries. And without Jack.

She huddled in the driver's seat of the Plymouth, waiting for him, dreading what Inez might be filling his ears with, but unable to go back in to get him herself. She hated the idea that he would hear anything about what had happened so long ago. Couldn't he just leave and go back to Boston without all that ugliness seeping out?

"It was eight years ago," she whispered to herself. "Why does it still have to keep coming back to haunt me?"

It was only a few minutes before Jack joined her in the car, balancing the sacks of groceries as he maneuvered the heavy door open. "I would've been happy to do the right thing and pay for your groceries after you left me, shall we say, holding the bag," he said lightly. "But as we both know, I haven't got a dime. So Inez said to tell you she put it on your account."

He paused, watching her intently, as she remained silent. She was so humiliated that she wanted to sink into the cushions of the immense Plymouth and never come out. But there she sat, her hands on the steering wheel, as Jack continued to watch her with sympathy in his beautiful blue eyes.

Even though she didn't ask, he reassured her, "She didn't say anything more than what you heard. I, uh, set her straight about the fact that I don't know Kathleen, and that was about it."

She nodded, but she didn't offer any words, and she didn't move to start the car.

"Flannery, are you okay?" he asked finally.

She nodded, biting her lip. Damn him. Now he was being nice to her, and she couldn't stand it.

"I don't know what that was all about, but I can't help noticing you don't respond real well when your sister is mentioned," he said gently. "Do you want to tell me what's going on?"

Her voice was soft, but emphatic. "No."

"Could it have anything to do with what happened to me last night?"

She shook her head.

"Okay, then I guess it's none of my business, is it?"

"No," she said again. "It happened a long time ago, and it's nobody's business." Of all the people in the world, the last one she wanted to know this tawdry story was Jack. She added, a little more harshly than she intended, "And it's certainly none of *your* business."

"Sure," he murmured. "No problem. Look, why don't I drive?" He leaned over her and pushed open her door. "Switch with me, okay?"

"Why do you want to drive?"

"No reason. I just want to."

"But why? You don't even know the way."

"Sure I do. I watched while you drove." His narrow lips curved into a small smile. "I thought maybe we'd go past the place where you saw the rainbow and look for another one. Seems to me we could both use a little good luck."

He was being nice again. Damn the man. He was awfully attractive when he was trying to be charming. Grudgingly, she asked, "You want to go to Rainbow Springs?"

"Yeah. I just realized it's a bad idea to ignore good omens."

"You're humoring me," she grumbled, even as she got in on the passenger side and let him take the wheel. "I don't like being humored."

"Everybody needs to be humored once in a while." His smile widened, and a spark lit his blue eyes. "Even hard cases like you."

"But it stopped raining. There won't be another rainbow."

"There's always another rainbow." And with that, he popped the clutch and started the car, and then, with a horrible gnashing and grinding of gears, pulled the Plymouth away from the general store.

She winced, feeling the injury to her beloved car as they stuttered along. "Are you sure about this?"

"Sure I'm sure. I haven't driven a stick shift in a while, that's all, and I've never driven anything as old as this monster. But I'll get the hang of it." He grinned suddenly. "And my terrible driving keeps your mind off whatever it was that made you so cranky, doesn't it?"

Unable to disagree, she smiled, too.

"So be quiet and watch the scenery or something, will you?"

"Yeah, okay." As if she hadn't seen these same rolling hills every day of her life.

They were nearing Rainbow Springs, and as she'd suspected, there was no sign of the misty spectrum of colors she'd spotted earlier. *I knew it,* she thought sadly. *You don't get good omens twice.*

But as they rounded the last curve, Jack suddenly growled, "What the hell?"

As he screeched the car to a stop, Flannery sat up straighter in the passenger seat. "What?" she demanded, looking around frantically. "The rainbow?"

Without answering, he wrenched open his door and took off across the rain-soft field, and Flannery had no choice but to follow.

"Jack, what is it?" she asked, running to keep up on the slippery grass.

But then she saw it. Jack had already leapt inside, and he was digging around under the seats while she faltered in the background several feet away.

It was a small red convertible, with the top down, parked under a weeping willow near the springs. Jack's car, clearly. It would have been hard to spot from the road—just a splash of red mostly obscured by the long, sweeping branches of the willow tree—but she really thought she would've noticed when they passed the springs before.

The sound of rushing water from the spring obliterated whatever swear words Jack was throwing at the car as he pulled an assortment of items up onto the front seat in a careless pile.

She moved closer, in time to hear him say, "Well, my clothes are here." He held up a wrinkled white shirt and a dark suit jacket. "Even the things I wore last night." His jaw tightening into a hard line, he tossed the clothes into the back seat and climbed out of the car. "But no contract."

"No contract," she echoed. "I'm sorry, Jack."

"I did come across one other item of interest, however," he announced grimly. He advanced on her. "I found it on the dashboard. Sort of like a gauntlet being thrown down, don't you think?"

He extended his hand until it was right under her nose, and then opened it, revealing what he held in his palm.

Another cold coin.

"Oh, dear," she whispered.

Chapter Six

She was feeding him again. Dinner, this time. And she'd found herself pulling out all the stops, with chicken-and-ham pie in a potato crust—something her grandmother had invariably made when Flannery was having a bad day. That and a decent cup of tea had been Grandma's recipe for fixing everything except major illness, which called for the really big gun—beef broth.

As she mashed the potatoes for the crust, she realized she hadn't meant to get started as hostess *extraordinaire,* with complicated dishes and flowers on the table. But she liked to cook, and she'd had daffodils begging to be picked, so it wasn't that big a deal.

Besides, it was a rotten day all around. She'd had Kathleen thrown up in her face, Jack was on the verge of a nervous breakdown and it would do them both good to eat a proper meal.

Jack sat at the heavy, weathered wooden table in the middle of the big kitchen, staring at his two gold coins. He'd placed them side by side in front of him, and now he just sat there, staring. Every once in a while, he'd pick one up and examine it more closely, rolling it this way and that, feeling the heft of it.

He was obsessed with the gold coins. And she was getting worried about him.

Abruptly, he shoved himself away from the table and strode over to the sink, right next to her. "It couldn't have been there long," he declared.

"What?"

"The car," he explained impatiently. "The car! The top was down when we found it."

"You found it." She mashed her potatoes more violently. "Not *we*. You."

He gave her an odd look. "Right. Anyway, it was raining when we first drove by Rainbow Springs. If the car had already been dumped there, with the top down, the inside would have been wet. It wasn't. So it had to have been left there after the rain stopped—*while we were in Crab Creek*. Do you get it?"

"Yes." She paused. "Is that important?"

"I don't know. But then, I don't know much of anything anymore."

"Come on, Jack," she coaxed, but he was too involved in whatever it was that was driving him crazy to pay attention.

"Did you notice," he began, leaning back against the counter and crossing his arms, "when I drove the car out from under the tree, the ground was soft, and the tires left big ruts all the way to the road?"

"Okay." She shrugged and kept mashing. "That makes sense. After so much rain, I mean."

"Exactly." As he gave her a level, measuring gaze, Jack paused.

"What is it?"

He said slowly, "There were no tire tracks there when I found the car."

"So?"

"There were no ruts, no smashed grass—not one thing to indicate that somebody drove it across the field. So how did it get there?"

She definitely didn't care for the direction he was taking. After setting down the potato masher, she said clearly, "Well, it had to get there somehow."

"But how?"

"I don't know." Throwing up her hands, she suggested, "The person drove it across the field before it rained, when the ground was still hard."

"But the inside of the car was dry, remember?"

"So this mystery person ditched the car before the rain, and then came back and put the top down after."

"Yeah, sure," he returned cynically. "Car thieves always return to the scene of the crime to put the top down."

"So what are you suggesting? Maybe that a giant hand came swinging down from heaven just to drop off your car?"

"Exactly."

"A giant hand?" she asked incredulously.

"No, of course not." Gazing at her intently, he took her hands inside his, and she felt herself go very still. "Think about it, Flannery. How did it get there?"

"I don't know," she whispered. At the moment, she didn't know anything except that he was holding her hands too tightly, and she couldn't think, couldn't breathe.

"You can construct rational, sensible theories all you want about the timing and the rain, but it just doesn't wash," he went on. "Before the rain or after the rain, a car on grass would make some kind of marks. But it didn't. Which can only mean that it wasn't driven under that tree."

"But, Jack—"

"And what does that leave?" he asked roughly, jiggling her hands, making her crazy. "How about Turlough Sullivan, up to his tricks again?"

"Now, wait a minute," she broke in, pulling away from him. She put a hand to her forehead in disbelief. "This is unreal. Are you actually going to suggest that my grandfather the leprechaun wiggled his nose or something to miraculously *fly* your car to Rainbow Springs?"

Jack clenched his jaw. "I don't know what to believe."

"This is a bit off-the-wall, even for you," she muttered. "First, magic pubs, and now, flying cars. Have you listened to yourself lately?"

"I know what I must sound like." He let out a long breath. "And no, I don't believe it, either."

"Well, thank goodness for that." She turned back to the pieces of their dinner, shaking her head as she started to fill the baking dish. "Magic? Jack, you can't go around spouting stories like that."

"It's just this place. I don't know what it does to me. You've lived here your whole life, and you don't believe in magic?"

"No." Her voice was indistinct, muffled. "I—I can't."

He just looked at her for a long moment. "I have to have some explanation."

Jack began to pace back and forth in the kitchen, his footfalls pounding the tiled floor so heavily that china and crockery started to shake on the wooden shelves of the big old country cupboard.

"Why don't you forget about all this?" she inquired, in what she hoped was a calm, soothing tone. "You know, look on the bright side. You've got your rental car back, and your own clothes.''

She spared a moment to watch Jack's beautiful body go through its paces. One look at him, and she wanted to go along with whatever he said no matter how preposterous. Now if only his mind were half as convincing as his body was.

Much as she'd liked watching him in Ken's too-small jeans, she appreciated him even more in his own soft corduroys, worn enough to mold to his body, to slide slightly over his thighs or cup the contours of his bottom as he moved around the room. For whatever reasons, he'd chosen to leave on her sweater, and the dusty blue of the yarn blended very nicely with his pale gray cords.

She alternated between being pleased that he'd liked her sweater enough to keep wearing it, and annoyed enough to want to rip it off his body. Of course, there were other reasons for that, too....

But he spoiled the view by sitting down at the table and once again staring a hole in the gold coins. ''I hope you don't mind about the sweater. That I kept it, I mean. It's been chilly, and this is warmer than anything I brought.''

''Oh, no, I don't mind,'' she said quickly. ''I order all my clothes from catalogs, so when I find something I like, like that sweater, I just order ten or twelve of them.'' She had no idea why she was telling him this. It must make her sound like an idiot. ''Anyway, one less hardly matters.''

''Uh-huh.'' He gave her a strange look, but then shook his head. ''Well, I'm glad the car and the clothes showed up, anyway, but I still need that contract.''

"I thought Jennifer was going to send you new copies to get signed all over again."

As soon as it left her mouth, she realized that this statement revealed she'd been eavesdropping on his call. Luckily, Jack was too absorbed in his own foul mood to notice.

"Yeah, if I have to. But it makes me look like an idiot to tell the sellers that I *lost* the contract." He sighed. "Plus I'm afraid they may hold me up for more money this time. But if I could just get my hands on the originals, I'd be golden."

"Okay." Flannery set plates and silverware neatly on the table. "And why do you think gawking at a couple of gold coins will help find it?"

"There's a message here—I'm sure of it. Or a clue. Something."

As he rose and began to pace again, rattling the cupboard, Flannery tried to soothe him enough to safeguard her dishes. "Jack, you're getting obsessed. Maybe you should give it a rest, have some dinner, get some sleep. In the morning, you can get a fresh perspective."

Jack lifted an eyebrow. "Does your grandfather usually eat dinner here?"

"Well, I wouldn't say *usually,* but he shows up when he feels like it."

"Let's hope tonight he comes in like a homing pigeon," Jack said under his breath. "I've got a few questions for Mr. Leprechaun."

Flannery was keeping her fingers firmly crossed that tonight would be a night Granddad *didn't* feel like it. She could only handle so much discord and disharmony in her own home before she blew a gasket.

All through dinner, she tried to make pleasant conversation to distract Jack, but it did little good.

He'd placed the gold coins neatly in the middle of the table, right next to the vase of daffodils, and he was still glancing back at them every thirty seconds or so, as if he thought they'd rise up and speak to him, giving him his answers.

When he wasn't peering at the coins, he was keeping an eye on the back door, as if he expected her grandfather to pop in at any minute.

"I keep telling you, if he isn't here by now, he isn't coming."

"Then where is he?" he demanded. "Where can one old man go?"

"I've been trying to figure that out for years."

Jack rose, dropping his napkin next to his plate. "Look, dinner was really nice, and thank you. I mean, seriously, thank you. But I—I can't sit here like this anymore." He sent one more hopeful look at the back door, as if willing it to open. "So when will he be back for the night?"

"He doesn't sleep here all that often," she said softly, regretfully. "I'm sorry. I know this is upsetting and I wish I could help, but—"

"Let me get this straight. Your grandfather is what, seventy years old?"

"Seventy-nine."

"Seventy-nine." Jack went on the prowl again, and Flannery winced. This back-and-forth stuff was giving her a headache. "He's almost eighty, and he eats and sleeps somewhere else, somewhere you don't know where? What kind of a granddaughter are you? Shouldn't you be looking out for him, taking care of him?"

"I would if I could." She shrugged, helpless. "He's always been like this, or at least since my grandma died.

I ask him where he goes and what he does, but he gives me some nonsense about meeting with the Little People or going to the Fairy Kingdom. You've met him—you saw what he was like. Good grief—you were even starting to believe him.''

"You could have him committed," Jack said darkly.

It was Flannery's turn to rise from the table. "He's a little inconvenient, so I should put him away, right? For your information, I love my grandfather, and most of the time he's really a wonderful person. Besides," she whispered, unable to keep the catch out of her voice, "he's all I have."

And then she brushed past Jack and started for the stairs.

"There's a spare room down the hall," she said in a rush. "Linens and everything are already there. I'll see you tomorrow."

"Flannery, wait," he called. "I'm sorry. I didn't mean—"

But she wasn't listening. She was thinking about climbing the stairs and wrenching the sheets off the bed, remaking the bed with fresh, new, clean linens, linens that had never been near Jack McKeegan's long, lean body. And then she could crawl into bed—alone.

It should have been a comforting prospect. So why did it sound so awful?

SHE'D BEEN KEEPING out of his way, and she really didn't know what he'd been doing to occupy himself. But she knew he was there—in her house. She could feel it.

It was as if the house had a pulse, a heartbeat, when he was inside it. And she knew the minute he came in.

After dithering in the kitchen for several minutes, curiosity got the better of her, and she went looking for him. There he was, in the bar, staring at those blasted coins again.

But why? The new copies of the contract had arrived days ago, and Inez had been so excited to get express mail that she'd taken it upon herself to pop out to Inisheer personally to deliver the package to Jack.

Flannery had mixed feelings about the arrival of the contract, especially since she'd taken the opportunity to sneak a peek when Inez brought them over. Why not? She was sure that Inez had scrutinized it within an inch of its little paper life, and pretty soon everyone within a hundred miles would know what it was all about. Why shouldn't Flannery know, when she was harboring the party-of-the-first-part at her own house?

After a quick perusal of the contracts, it wasn't hard to decide how she felt about it. She hoped their arrival would cheer up Jack, but she hated to see its ugly little terms anywhere near Inisheer.

"Jack," she said softly, as she shoved the door into the pub open all the way, letting a little fresh air into that dusty place. "Shouldn't you be out running around, getting new signatures?"

"I'm two for three," he returned absently. "My other seller had a heart attack and happens to be in intensive care, which screws up everything."

"Oh, I'm sorry."

"Yeah, me, too." Jack pushed at the gold pieces. "If he dies, I'll have to renegotiate with his heirs, and who knows how long that will take? On the other hand, if he recovers, I can go ahead and try to get him to sign again. Right now, they won't let me see him until he's out of intensive care."

"Well, I'm not surprised!" She gave him a look of extreme displeasure, the best chastising glare she could come up with. "Aren't you being pretty cold-blooded about this? The poor man may die, and you're just worried about your lousy contract."

"It's not a lousy contract," he mumbled.

"It certainly is."

But he didn't hear; he was off in never-never land with the gold pieces again. "If I could figure out what these things are supposed to mean, I could find the original contract, and then it wouldn't matter if the guy is in a coma."

She stalked over to him, sweeping the gold pieces off the bar and into her pocket. "You're obsessed. And it *is* a lousy contract. As a matter of fact, it's a stinky, ugly contract that would practically make the whole southern half of the county an amusement park for RuMex. Thank God it's not a factory, but this is almost as bad."

"It's a think tank," he protested. "And it's completely sound ecologically. Low-impact, and all that."

"You call an airport, a four-story building and a private hotel for RuMex bigwigs low-impact?"

At least her heated comments were enough to get him to turn away from the bar and look at her. "I had no idea you felt this way."

"Well, now you do."

"Flannery," he ventured, with a speculative look on his gorgeous face, "you wouldn't by any chance be working with your grandfather to keep this deal from coming off?"

"Now you're getting paranoid as well as hallucinating." She crossed her arms. "Lovely."

"I know you're helping him. He hasn't shown hide nor hair around here for days." His gaze measured her, and he managed a faint smile. "You warned him off, didn't you?"

"You're nuts."

"You're driving me crazy."

"You already were crazy."

Jack's smile grew even more threadbare. "Not this crazy."

"Look, Jack," she tried, swinging herself up onto the stool next to him. "I'm starting to like you, when you're not acting loony-tunes. So as a sort of friend, let me give you some advice. You can't sit around staring at a couple of coins all the time. Inez has already brought out two or three messages from your office, and they sound sort of anxious to hear from you. Shouldn't you be doing something about that?"

"No." He clenched his jaw and stared straight ahead, so that Flannery was watching him in profile. "They want me to find an alternate parcel of land in case the guy dies or backs out. But, damn it, I had the deal sewn up. It was perfect! I would've had a vice presidency for sure. I don't want to have to kill this deal and find whole new parcels."

"I know what's really bothering you," she decided after a moment. "Whatever happened on St. Patrick's Day, somebody messed up your deal. They beat you. Leprechaun 1, Jack McKeegan 0. And you can't stand it. You want that contract back as a way of showing up whoever stole it."

"You're awfully good at amateur psychology, aren't you? Amateur being the operative word."

Restless, he left his stool and strolled around the tavern, with his hands stuck firmly in his pockets. First he kicked at an overturned chair, and then he sauntered behind the bar, gazing deep into the old cracked mirror hanging there.

He was wearing an odd, intent expression, and Flannery didn't like that look at all.

"What are you thinking?" she asked warily, watching him in the mirror. He looked like the Phantom of the Opera, with half of his face reflected normally, and the other half distorted and misshapen by the long crack running through the old, wavy glass.

"The pub," he said softly.

"What about the pub?"

He spun around to confront her, returning both sides of his face to their former glory. There were sparks of enthusiasm in his blue eyes when he announced, "Maybe it isn't the coins at all. Maybe the pub is the answer."

"You've lost me. What kind of answer?"

"The pub is the first mystery, right? How did the pub get cleaned up like new for one night, and then put back to the original condition, complete with dust and cobwebs?"

"The obvious answer is that you were very drunk, too drunk to realize that you weren't here that night, but at some other bar," she countered. "If you weren't so stubborn, you'd admit that."

"Baloney. I was here. And this bar was in tip-top shape." A sardonic smile flitted across his lips. "Walt Disney can do that kind of trick—so can any studio in Hollywood. So add Granddad to the list."

She tried not to laugh. But the idea of her eccentric little grandfather as a special-effects wizard was just too silly. "Jack, you're nuts. But you do make me laugh."

True to form, Jack wasn't listening. He was gently tapping the walls and feeling for cracks, as if he expected to find secret passages.

"Look, Jack, I still say you're bananas, but go ahead and search the pub all you want." Under her breath, she added, "At least that ought to keep you occupied."

"Yeah, okay," he said vaguely.

"As a matter of fact, I have work of my own to do. I've been neglecting my plants terribly since I've been back, so I really ought to spend some time in the greenhouse. Jack, are you listening?" He nodded, and she went on, telling him, "It's behind the house, about a hundred feet back, if you need anything."

"Sure, sure."

As she eased through the awkward door back into the kitchen, Jack called out, "Flannery, if you see your grandfather, hold on to him this time, okay?"

She ducked her head. "I'll see you later."

IT FELT GOOD to be elbow-deep in dirt. Flannery tied her hair back securely in a ribbon, and got down to work repotting and fertilizing. For the first time since she'd been back from the conference, her world felt sane and organized and *safe*.

Ever since she was a little girl, she'd liked grubbing in the dirt. It was best when it was thick, rich, black dirt, rife with minerals. Her dirt smelled like life to Flannery, like spring, and the never-ending cycles of growth and decay and rebirth.

When she was small, she'd begged for seed packets instead of dolls or pretty dresses, and photos of little Flannery invariably showed streaks of dirt across her nose, fresh from the garden.

When she was a teenager, she'd gotten her granddad to build the greenhouse, way at the back of the cultivated part of the lawn. It was all glass, the size of a long shed, with long benches crowded with clay pots, and lots and lots of dirt—Flannery's version of heaven in the backyard.

"Who cares about Jack McKeegan?" she asked the flats of white clover she was watering. "He's a crank, a crazy person, a menace to my peace of mind."

She hummed a little song to her pots as she checked their progress against the clipboard hanging from the wooden bench.

"You guys are doing better than the hybrid," she told the pots of white clover. "Have to cut down their nitrogen, I guess."

As a botanist, she had chosen not to go into academia, which would have required living in a college town, side by side with platoons of other plant scientists. And somehow she had managed to scratch by as a sort of free-lancer. She sold vegetable and flower seeds to a few catalogs, and she had a good business with organic vegetables for health-food types.

But her real love was research. She'd been lucky enough, or smart enough, to get a grant from a large livestock feed company, to create a vitamin-rich strain of red clover. As a sort of side project, she was also working on creating a new strain of white clover. There was no real potential for income with her little experiment, but it was fun to fool around with.

Trifolium flannerius? Or would she call it *Trifolium O'Shea?* She smiled to herself, enjoying the idea that someday her name might be in the botany textbooks.

But first she'd have to get it to grow faster. So far, *Trifolium O'Shea* was a weak sister to regular old white clover. She picked up one of the hybrid pots and poked around in the dirt, gauging how the roots were doing.

"Maybe if I tried sandier soil," she mused.

"Hello, darling child."

She whirled, clapping the pot of clover to her pounding heart. "Granddad?"

There he was, in the flesh, all five-foot-four of him, dressed as usual in sturdy wool trousers and a tweed waistcoat, with a plaid cap tipped over his forehead. His small, wrinkled face was alight with pure pleasure as he gazed at Flannery.

"God," she said with a sigh. "You scared the living daylights out of me. I didn't hear you come in."

"Now, of course you didn't hear me," he said cheerfully. "And what kind of leprechaun would I be if I were waking the dead with the sound of my footsteps?"

She squinted up toward the house, but she didn't see any sign of Jack. Thank goodness.

"Where have you been?" she demanded. "I haven't seen you for days."

His eyes twinkled as the little man bent up to pat Flannery on the top of the head. "Sweet Mary Flannery, don't be bothering about my whereabouts. You know I always turn up, right as rain."

"But you're usually not gone this long." With a firm hand, she set the clover pot back on its bench, in the proper place, and checked the right boxes on its progress report. "And we usually don't have a visitor like Jack McKeegan spitting nails all the time you're gone."

He tipped his head to one side. "You are being kind to the boy, aren't you now, Mary Flannery? Treating him proper, I should hope."

"Treating him proper? Of course I am!"

"And it's that glad I am to hear it." Shaking his finger in her direction, he sent her a doubtful glance. "Because, darling child, you have a way of being a bit severe now and again, and I wouldn't want to think you'd chased young Jack away. He's a grand lad, and you ought to be doing your best to encourage him, not dressing him down, if you catch my meaning."

Flannery's mouth dropped open. "I'm not going to encourage him, whatever you think you mean by that."

"Now, Mary Flannery, I know what's best."

"And does that include spiriting away his contract to keep him from developing the area? The deal will go through sooner or later, anyway." She bit her lip. "There's no stopping progress."

"Don't you worry about it, darling. Your granddad has it all in hand."

"Does that mean you did take it? You did, didn't you? Oh, Granddad, this time you're in real trouble."

"I did not take it, and I've told you as much several times now." He shook his head in disgust. "Are you listening to me, child?"

"Yes, but..." She saw him turning to leave, and she caught his sleeve. "Are you coming home tonight?"

His gaze shifted past her without lighting anywhere in particular. "I really couldn't say just yet."

"Granddad—" she began, in a warning tone.

"Don't be pulling your long face at me, young lady." He tugged his sleeve away and set his face in a wounded expression. "If I were to find young Jack's prized contract—notice my word *find,* not *return,* since I've said from the very start I wasn't the thieving sort—well, if I were to do young Jack the good deed of finding his contract for him, wouldn't that be a fine turn of events? Inisheer would be run over with all kinds of trouble—airports and stores and fancy houses."

He sneered. "Hmph. And isn't that a distressing idea. And on top of that catastrophe, this grand young man would be departing quicker than an Irishman can down a shot of whiskey. Where would that leave you, darling girl?"

"Don't tell me you did all this..." She closed her eyes against the inevitable conclusion. "Matchmaking?" she asked weakly. "You did this for matchmaking?"

"I didn't do a thing," Granddad contended. "Wouldn't I be after taking credit, if it were my handiwork?"

She tried to rein in her temper, to remain patient with her grandfather. He didn't respond well to shouting. "If it isn't your handiwork, then whose is it?"

"Well, now that's an interesting question, isn't it?" Granddad scratched his grizzled chin. "I don't rightly know. But I'm thinking my own father may be at the back of this."

"Your father?" Flannery swallowed, wondering how much worse things could get. "Granddad, your father has been dead since 1963."

"Well, I know that's when his mortal body left this earth, but leprechauns are immortal, Mary Flannery." Smiling kindly, he patted her head, as if she were a young child. "You know that, now don't you, darling?"

"Of course," she murmured. "Leprechauns are immortal."

As her grandfather launched into one of his many stories about the Good People and the various forms they took, philosophizing on how exactly the human-leprechaun combination worked with respect to their family, Flannery caught a flash of movement out of the corner of her eye.

"Jack," she said quickly. "Granddad, you have to leave. Jack is coming."

"Oh, I see what's happening here." He beamed at her. "You young folk are wanting to be alone, is it?"

She tried to protest, but he just smiled, pinched her cheek, pressed something into her hand and skipped out the back of the greenhouse.

"What...?" Just what she needed. A gold coin. "What am I going to do with this?"

As Jack loomed ever closer, she searched around for someplace to hide the stupid thing, reaching for a pot of clover just as he cleared the door. Hastily she stuck the coin down into the dirt and then hurried to rinse her hands off under a hose. Flapping her hands to dry them, she wheeled to face him, plastering a big phony grin on her face.

"Hello!" she called out gaily.

Before she had a chance to get any other words out, Jack danced across the greenhouse, sweeping her up into his arms and hooting, "You'll never believe what I found!"

"What?" she asked, dazed, trying to brace herself on his shoulders as he swung her around, trying to keep her hair out of her face as it threatened to spill around her shoulders.

His blue eyes were ablaze with triumph as he tightened his hold, pulling her down level with his face. "It's wonderful," he whispered hotly. "This whole damn place is wonderful."

He let her down slowly, drawing her closer, settling her up against the full length of his hard, strong body. As he gazed into her eyes, he paused for one split second.

And then he kissed her.

Chapter Seven

The whole idea of it caught her by surprise.

At first she just stood there, too shocked to move. But then, almost without realizing it, she began to kiss him back. Her arms crept up around his neck, and she found herself pressing closer, meeting the warm, inviting pressure of his lips with a wild abandon that was new to her.

It was a crazy kiss, a shower of sparks, a blaze of chemistry. Flannery felt sixteen again, sixteen and never-been-kissed, as if the very idea of it were new and exotic, something to be tested and tasted and explored.

He slipped his hands into the heavy hair at the nape of her neck, sliding off the ribbon she'd tied it back with, pushing his fingers through the long waves. Murmuring hungry words, he moved his hands to cradle her face, slanting his hot, moist mouth across hers, deepening the kiss.

Waves of pleasure seeped through her veins, but it was pleasure mixed with hot passion and a skyrocketing heartbeat. From the reverberations of this one kiss, she wanted to strip off her clothes, sink to the floor of the greenhouse and make love with Jack till the cows came home.

"We don't have any cows," she whispered against his lips.

"What?"

"Nothing."

Greedily, she leaned up and into him, starting it all over again. She'd never, ever been kissed like this, not even when she was married, a newlywed, once upon a time a million years ago.

She loved the feel of his lips and the taste of his mouth. *He wants me,* she realized, and the very thought was intoxicating, euphoric, setting off little signal flares in the pit of her stomach.

"Flannery," he murmured, tracing the slope of her neck with soft kisses.

"Y-yes?"

"Flannery," he said again as he nibbled her earlobe.

She had never heard anything as tantalizing as the sound of her name on his lips. She loved it. In fact, she loved everything about this amazing, mesmerizing experience. She loved it so much that she was drowning in it, and she didn't care.

He backed her up against an almost empty table, bending her back with the force of his embrace. In the periphery of her consciousness, as she slid down onto the table, she caught a whiff of fresh earth and moist leaves, and she suddenly realized where she was and what she was doing.

In the greenhouse, getting altogether too intimate with *Jack McKeegan.* What in the name of all that was holy was she thinking of, acting like a love-starved teenager at her first drive-in movie?

"Jack, stop," she choked out, shooting upright. She put one hand against his chest and the other to her own flaming cheek. "I can't believe what's happening here."

He stood back, just gazing at her, not saying anything, as if allowing himself a moment to regroup his faculties. Lord knew she needed the time, whether he did or not.

"It's okay," he said finally. His lips brushed her forehead in one last, chaste caress, and then he turned away.

She knew instinctively that he hadn't planned to kiss her, and he certainly hadn't expected to trigger this staggering range of emotions. Who could've known?

But if she were honest with herself, she had to admit she'd suspected. She'd seen him lying in her bed, practically naked, and she'd had a very good suspicion that it would be like this. And that was why she was trying so hard to run in the other direction.

"Well . . ." Trying to cover her jumpy nerves, she pretended to look around for her hair ribbon. Of course she didn't find it. She could barely see! Anxious to fill the silence, she said the first thing that came into her head. "That was . . . different."

She winced. *That* was stupid.

"Different? I'll say."

"I'm, uh, sorry that I, you know, stopped it."

"I'm sorry, too."

His narrow lips tilted into a mocking smile, and she wanted to take the tip of one finger and sketch the curve of that smile. At the same time, she had the urge to use her fist to forcibly smash the smile off his face. She wondered idly if it were possible to kiss a man and kill him simultaneously.

"But we had to stop," she said quickly.

"Did we?"

"Oh, yes. It couldn't go on. Not for another minute. Not even for a second."

"Why not?"

The hot spark in his eyes and the wry angle of his mouth still looked very dangerous to her well-being, and she backed off, bumping her hip into a different table, this one full of clay pots. She rattled the pots and scared herself silly. But at least steadying her plants and pretending to rearrange the table gave her something to do, anything to look at other than Jack McKeegan's maddening face.

"Why did you come out to the greenhouse?" she inquired, in her best matter-of-fact, everyday-occurrence voice. "Didn't you say you found something?"

"Yeah, that's right. A box. I found a box." He shook his head, hard, as if to get himself back on a reality track. "A box full of old papers and photographs, among other things. I think you'll find it interesting."

"Well, I hope so." She offered a shaky little laugh. "The way you came barreling down here, it's got to be some box."

"You'll see."

"It's still up at the house?"

"It was too heavy to carry," he explained.

"You left it . . . Oh, dear."

Anything important had a way of disappearing around Jack. And she knew her light-fingered grandfather was on the loose and in the vicinity, even if Jack didn't.

"Come on," she told him, catching his hand and towing him out the greenhouse door and over the yard. "We'd better make sure your find stays found."

Jack dug in his heels. "You've seen him, haven't you?"

In the face of a direct question, she could hardly lie. "Well, yes. But he still says he doesn't know where your things went to because he's not the one who took them."

"Of course that's what he says." He gave her a nasty look. "You promised to hold on to him."

"You told me to hold on to him, but I didn't promise anything." When she saw dark clouds begin to gather on Jack's brow, she added, "If I could figure out how to hold on to my granddad, believe me, I would've done it long before this. He's very good at being slippery."

"I'll 'slippery' him," Jack muttered as he marched up to the house.

She trailed along after, trying unsuccessfully to keep up with his long strides, and she got to the kitchen just as Jack cursed and shoved open the heavy door into the pub.

"Voilà," he said dryly.

She saw the mystery box immediately. Thank goodness it was still there. She allowed herself a small sigh of relief, sending up a prayer of thanks that this one item had managed not to get itself lost or into the hands of her granddad.

The box sat in the middle of the barroom floor, surrounded by small piles of papers and pictures no doubt left there by Jack. It was a big old thing, more like a small trunk than a box, made of dark wood with rosewood inlays. It was actually very pretty, and she had a vague recollection of having seen it before. But not in the pub—in the attic, with the other family mementos. What was it doing in the pub?

Some ten feet away, she hesitated. "Where did you find it?"

"Under the bar, stuck behind a case of beer glasses and a big carton of old rat poison."

She shot him a quick glance. "That's jolly. I hope the bartenders kept the rat poison out of the beer glasses and vice versa."

"It's your family's bar, not mine," Jack countered. "My family would never keep rat poison in the pub, I can assure you."

"Your family has a pub?" she asked in surprise.

"*Had* a pub, in South Boston. It was called Callahan's Daughter, and my grandfather ran it. He was Callahan and my mother was the daughter." He smiled cynically. "The McKeegans, on the other hand, were and are all lawyers—back to the dawn of man, I think. My dad and my brothers are lawyers, too. No menial jobs like tending bar for those guys."

"You have brothers? I never really thought about you having a family back in Boston."

"Yeah. The older brothers—both at my dad's firm. McKeegan and O'Loughlin. It's a great law firm, or so they tell me. And my little sister, Maureen, is a media specialist in D.C., the kind of person who makes nasty commercials for political campaigns. So she's really strayed from the flock of lawyers."

Curious all of a sudden, Flannery gazed at Jack. "And what does that make you, at your development company?"

He shrugged. "An overachiever? I don't know. I didn't want to be one more lawyer in the family, I'll tell you that." A shy smile flitted across his lips. "When I was a kid, I swore that I'd run Callahan's Daughter for my mom as soon as I got big enough. She kept telling me she didn't really want the bar reopened, but that was all I wanted to do when I grew up."

"It's kind of funny that you'd have a pub in your family." She edged a little closer, wishing she knew him well enough to take his hand or offer a hug. He looked so open and vulnerable with the past shining in his eyes. "Just like me. I mean, it's kind of a coincidence."

"Oh, I don't know. I think half the Irish in Boston have a claim to a pub somewhere back in the family history." He grinned. "If not, they wish they did."

"I guess that's why my great-grandfather built Inisheer." Sharing his smile, she leaned in closer to the old box. "Did you find anything about that in there? About the early days of the pub?"

"Better," he said mysteriously.

"What."

"Look and see for yourself."

"Oh, we're being coy, are we?"

When he didn't answer, she sat cross-legged on the floor of the pub and picked up the nearest pile of papers. A quick perusal showed absolutely nothing of interest, unless one were interested in how many barrels of beer the Inisheer Pub used on a weekly basis between 1929 and 1931.

"Prohibition didn't come to Inisheer," she announced. "Big deal."

"Keep looking."

This game was getting old fast. "Jack," she said sweetly, getting to her feet, "I'm not in the mood for playtime. If you don't tell me what this is all about within the next thirty seconds, I'll get out the rat poison and feed it to you personally."

"Okay, okay." With a flourish, he pulled a wrinkled sheet of yellowed parchment out from behind his back.

"Oh, so you were hiding it. I should've figured you'd cheat." She grabbed for the paper and glanced at it quickly. Baffled, she raised her gaze to Jack's face. "But what is it?"

He just grinned and crossed his arms over his sweater.

Skeptical, she turned it on its side, but it still didn't look like anything, so she gave it another quarter-turn.

In a disappointed tone, she asked, "This is the big mystery? One old, ugly piece of paper with some chicken scratches on it? Don't tell me—it's an early Picasso sketch and my grandfather and I are now worth millions."

"It's not a Picasso sketch," he returned testily. Gingerly, he tugged the thing from her fingers and rotated it back around to the way she'd had it at first, then carefully handed it to her his way. "Can't you see? It's a treasure map."

"A treasure map?" She didn't know whether to laugh or cry. With Jack in the room, either was entirely possible. "A treasure map?"

"Of course," he said impatiently.

He bent over her shoulder and pointed at the bottom corner of the paper, but all she noticed was the warmth of his breath against her cheek and the soft wool of his sweater-clad arm rubbing hers. Flannery closed her eyes, and willed herself to ignore it.

He's not that close, and he's not breathing, she told herself. *He doesn't have an arm, he didn't kiss you fifteen minutes ago, and you don't remember what it felt like.*

Oh, yes, you do.

"No, I don't," she whispered vehemently.

"No, you don't, what? Look at the map, will you?" He rustled the paper. "There are initials in the corner— TS, for Turlough Sullivan—and 1923, which must be the year he drew it. This thing here—the little barrel—that's Inisheer."

"That's not a barrel! It's just a scribble."

"It's a barrel," he repeated, "and it stands for Inisheer. Behind it there's a wiggly line—there's a creek back there, right?—and over here are two Y-shaped things—the oak trees out front, see?"

"Well, that would make sense," she said grudgingly. "Those oaks are the reason my great-grandfather, the original Turlough Sullivan, built the pub here. Twin oaks are supposed to be a fairy gate." At Jack's mystified expression, she added, "A pathway to the other side, so the Little People can go back and forth. At certain times—I don't know exactly how it works—fairies can come through the gates into our world, and it's only in the space between twin oaks that they can get back."

He narrowed his eyes slightly, as if he thought she might be putting him on. After a moment, he asked, "So you agree that the barrel is the pub and the Ys are the oaks?"

"Well, maybe, but that doesn't mean it's a treasure map." She hated to rain on his parade, but... "Why can't it just be a map? Maybe old Turlough drew himself a map to remember how to get home after a night on the town, or maybe to show his in-laws how to get to the pub for a visit?"

"Because there's a pot of gold," Jack said triumphantly.

Leprechauns and pots of gold. She should have expected this. After stifling a sigh, Flannery scrutinized Jack's treasure map. "Excuse me, but I don't see anything that remotely resembles a pot of gold."

"The round thing—over there—with the little round things in it."

"That could just as easily be a hamburger with pickles on it."

"They didn't have hamburgers in 1923," he scoffed.

"So it's a bowl of vegetable soup. How on earth did you decide it was a pot of gold?"

"It's under a rainbow," he explained in a condescending tone, as if she were no better than a small child.

"Two half circles are a rainbow? There are half circles all over this thing."

"I think the other ones are caves."

"Oh, so all the other ones are caves, but the one over the hamburger is a rainbow. How convenient."

"It's not a hamburger," he growled.

"So what's the puffy cloud thing, and the sloppy-looking *M?* Is that maybe the McDonald's arches?"

With dignity, he announced, "No, it is not the McDonald's arches. I don't know what it is. I haven't figured that out yet."

"He hasn't figured that out yet," she said under her breath. "Saints be praised, something exists that Jack McKeegan hasn't figured out."

Neatly, he removed the parchment from her grasp, folded it and stuck it into his back pocket. "I thought the map was enough of a discovery to come and get you, but I didn't have time to consider all the angles. Who knows? There may be something else in this stuff that explains the map."

"Like a handy decoder ring?"

"You know, Flannery," he said darkly, "you can really be a pain when your mouth gets rolling. This snippy side of you isn't very attractive."

She could feel her cheeks color, and she drew her shoulders back, holding herself rigid. "Do you think I care what you do or do not find attractive?"

"Yes."

"Well, you're wrong."

"No, I'm not."

"Yes, you are!"

"Flannery," he began, in a low, dangerous, tricky sort of voice, "don't get started with me." And he took a few steps in her direction.

She raised a hand to forestall him. Why did it seem like she was spending half her life backing away from Jack McKeegan? "Don't touch me," she said nervously.

But he kept coming. "Are you going to pretend I didn't kiss you, and you didn't kiss me back? Are you going to pretend you don't care that I find you extremely attractive?"

"You do not," she tried, edging up against the hard wood of the bar as she retreated.

"Yes, I do." He braced his arms on the bar, one on each side, encircling her, trapping her. "If I weren't such a sensitive, liberated guy, I'd call this more than an attraction. I'd say I was hot for you."

The light in his eyes reflected that heat, and she began to believe him. She began to need a fan to cool her flaming face. Or maybe a few ice cubes.

"It's a fire, Flannery. A raging inferno."

And then, just when she thought he'd bend forward those few extra centimeters and cover her mouth with his, and she could respond with enough return fire to scorch him down to his Top-Siders, he leaned back on his heels and turned away.

Gruffly he said, "Let's get back to the box."

She was still trembling, but she tossed back, "Right. We need to get cracking if we're going to find that secret decoder ring."

"A map legend is more what I had in mind."

He began sifting through the piles of old photos and papers around the box, ignoring her completely.

"I knew he wasn't attracted to me," she said under her breath. "He was just toying with me, trying to prove a point."

"What are you muttering about?"

"Nothing."

She plunked herself down on the floor and grabbed a pile of remnants from Inisheer's past. At least her family history might prove entertaining, which was more than she could say for Jack.

Restlessly shuffling papers, Jack was silent for several minutes, and Flannery found herself caught up in the contents of a small keepsake box.

"Look," she said sentimentally, "my grandmother's four-leaf-clover necklace. And a lock of her hair! She was the real Mary Flannery—the one I'm named after." She pulled a strand of her own hair over her shoulder and compared it to the little ribboned curl. "Almost exactly the same color. Isn't that wild?"

"Hmph," Jack responded, digging around in the bottom of the big chest that had started all this. His voice was muffled when he mumbled, "What's this?"

"What's what? No more treasure maps, I hope."

Still fussing with her grandmother's trinkets, she waited until Jack brought his new prize over to her, and then she peered at it. It was a black-and-white picture, about eight by ten, framed in tarnished silver, showing the bar in the full swing of a party. People in old-fashioned costumes were dancing around the tables, and banners and bunting were hung over the mirror behind the bar.

"There used to be lots of pictures like this on the walls," she told him fondly. "Even back from the earliest days of the pub, they took pictures of the important parties and anniversaries. They put them up over the booths and behind the bar, I think.''

"But look at it, Flannery. More closely," Jack urged.

"It's a party." She shrugged. "So what?"

"You don't understand." He tapped the dusty glass with one finger. "This is exactly what this place looked like the night I was here, for the St. Patrick's Day party. The people are dressed the same, there's the fiddler in the corner, and even the bartender looks like the same guy. The writing across his chest says Malachy, and I'm pretty sure that was his name. Plus," he declared with conviction, "your grandfather and Kathleen are there, right in the front. Ol' Turlough's even wearing his leprechaun outfit, down to the shamrock hat. Now what do you have to say to that?"

Raising dazed eyes to his, Flannery felt the first stirrings of real doubt about the events of that fateful night. "But, Jack…" she started, trailing off before she could think of how to tell him.

"What?"

She swallowed. "This isn't my grandfather *or* my sister."

"Oh, come on. Of course it is. I know you're always trying to protect them by lying to me, but I've got you dead to rights this time. Here they are, at exactly the kind of party I stumbled into the middle of. Underneath them, somebody wrote, 'Turlough and Kathleen enjoying themselves.'" He smiled with relief. "So they've done this before, and they pulled it again for St. Patrick's Day, and this is the proof."

"But, Jack…"

"What?" he demanded.

"That man isn't my grandfather. Oh, I know he looks like him, and he even has the same name, but that's the *first* Turlough, the one who founded the bar. And that's Kathleen all right, but Kathleen my *mother,* not my sister."

He glanced again at the photograph and then at Flannery. "I don't get it."

"I know what this picture is, Jack," she said slowly, trying not to panic. "Look at the banner above the mirror—it's fuzzy, but you can just make out, 'Farewell, Sully. We'll miss ye.' This is my great-grandfather's retirement party, Jack. In 1962, the seventieth anniversary of the bar. A year before I was born."

"It can't be," he muttered, snatching back the picture.

"It is." She tried to manage a laugh, but all that came out was a desperate little whimper. "If you were at a party with these people, you had a one-night stand in 1962."

"But, Flannery..."

"Now, hold on a second." She exhaled a long breath. "There has to be a logical explanation for this."

"Oh, God, I fell into a wrinkle in time. I was in 1962. I almost slept with your mother!" He shot her a horrified look. "What if I did and I don't remember? What if I'm your father?"

Flannery choked in midbreath. "My father?" she cried. "You're not my father. I had a perfectly normal father named Tom O'Shea, who was a fireman in Chicago. He and my mother died in a car accident in 1968."

"Oh. I'm sorry."

"Well, I'm not sorry you're not my father, but I *am* sorry you've chosen this moment to lose what's left of your mind."

"I can't think about this," he muttered, dropping the picture back into the box like a hot potato, and then pacing back and forth. "I'll just take the map, find the pot of gold, get my stuff back and then I will leave this crazy place before I belong in a straitjacket. Yeah, that's it," he said, picking up volume and assurance at the same time. "I'll follow the map and find the pot of gold."

He made for the green door under a full head of steam, obviously thrilled to be set on a course of action.

"Just one question, Jack," she called out, catching him before he got to the door. "Why do you think the map will lead to your missing things? The pot of gold is ridiculous enough, but even you can't argue that your contract is on that map."

In a superior tone, he told her, "Your grandfather thinks he's a leprechaun. Where does a leprechaun hide his valuables? With his pot of gold, of course."

"Of course."

He paused, and then said quietly, "You know, you can come with me if you want to."

But she shook her head. Purposely not looking at him, she said, "I have work to do in the greenhouse. Lots of work. But you go ahead, have fun."

As she watched him dash out the door, Flannery tried not to worry about him. He was a grown man, and if he decided to believe in fairies and hobgoblins and pots of gold, it wasn't her problem. If he decided to go traipsing all over the countryside, following a preposterous excuse for a treasure map, who was she to stop him?

"But maybe I should've told him where he was going," she mused out loud. "I mean, it was obviously a map of Rainbow Springs. I suppose I could've told him that much.''

She chewed her lip. "Nah. I have work to do, and at least this way, he'll be out of my hair."

But before she could let herself retreat to the greenhouse to get some work done, she'd really have to straighten up the mess on the barroom floor. She could hardly leave papers and photographs strewn around like that.

Briskly, she made a stack of old files and prepared to set them inside the old wooden trunk, but as she leaned over it, she caught sight of the framed photo Jack had found. She dropped the files back onto the floor, just standing there for a few seconds, willing herself not to pick up that picture, but knowing she was going to do it, anyway.

"Might as well get it over with," she muttered, and she took it out and let her eyes roam over it. Longingly, she fingered the glassed-over image of her mother.

"Turlough and Kathleen enjoying themselves...."

"But they're both dead," she whispered. "And they couldn't have come back for St. Patrick's Day, or any other day."

It was better this way, she told herself, with her mother and her great-granddad, still dancing and laughing, at a never-ending party. Her mother, ever young, ever beautiful and vivacious and carefree, just the way she was in the picture.

She hadn't thought about her mother in a long time. "I still miss you, Mama," she said out loud. "And I wish I hadn't let you go away so long ago. That never changes, does it?"

Against her better judgment, she let her gaze slide over to the green door leading out from Inisheer into the rest of the world.

"I suppose I'm going to have to go after him. Someone's got to watch out for the poor, deluded thing."

And she slipped out the front door of the Inisheer Pub before she had a chance to think better of it.

Chapter Eight

Jack pulled out the map and studied it. He'd been positive he could follow its obscure trail when he left the pub, but now he wasn't so sure.

For one thing, the creek didn't flow at the same angle it looked like it should, if those wiggly lines were really the creek. And the map indicated a bridge, or at least a small arch over the wiggly lines, right where he thought he was, but there was no bridge here.

So now what?

Intent on the map, he sat down on a big, flat rock, but found himself caught instead by the trill of a bird overhead, and the soft murmur of water from the creek at his feet. There was a smell of new leaves and budding trees in the air, as if the last few days of rain had started things growing and taking root all around him. Winter had still been the order of the day when he left Boston, yet here, near magical Inisheer, the signs of spring were already in full force.

Peace descended upon him as he just rested there on the rock, listening to the bird call to its friends, and the babbling brook talk to no one in particular. He rubbed his arms through Flannery's sweater, warding off the slight nip in the air, as he leaned back farther on the rock, gazing up into a sky the color of a robin's egg. It didn't seem to matter that he wasn't moving or achieving anything at the moment.

When was the last time he'd felt this peaceful, this in tune with his surroundings?

It shocked him to realize that he absolutely couldn't recall when. He hadn't taken a vacation recently, but even last year, when he'd flown to Aruba, he'd had files and reports along for the ride.

He felt good and exhausted after a tough game of tennis or racquetball, but that hardly counted as peaceful. In fact, if ever he didn't play well, if he lost a game or a match, his leisure-time activities began to feel more like added pressure than relief.

He frowned, musing over this paradox. How odd, how distressing, to come to the conclusion that John Patrick McKeegan, Seaboard Development's hottest hotshot, did not know how to relax. When had he lost the knack?

"I was a fun kid," he told the birds. "I flirted with all the cutest girls, I played hooky when I felt like it, I knew how to play—just play—for no reason. Stickball, football, soccer, hockey—all of it—because it was fun. I had a life!"

So when had that all changed?

He hadn't a clue.

As he gazed into the sky, pondering this puzzling turn of events, soft color began to suffuse the horizon. A band of palest purple was followed by a splash of watery blue, and then ribbons of delicate green and yellow.

"A rainbow," he said out loud. "But it's sunny. How can there be a rainbow?"

The bird above him sang out more loudly, as if providing the answer. Now if Jack only spoke Sparrow...

"A rainbow," he mused. "And where there's a rainbow, there's a pot of gold."

Jumping to his feet, he followed along the path of the creek, keeping the rainbow in sight as he looked for a way to get across the water. There were shallow places and a few handy stones, but nothing that seemed all that promising. Finally, he came to a bend in the creek where a dead tree had fallen completely across, providing a natural bridge of sorts.

Eyeing it, Jack weighed his chances of getting over without falling in. Oh, he wouldn't kill himself even if he did take a tumble; the water wasn't high enough to drown a toy poodle. But he would get wet, and he would embarrass himself, and that was bad enough.

"Oh, why the hell not?" he grumbled. "You never do anything just for fun, do you, Jack? Maybe now's the time to start. So what if you get a little soggy? Maybe it'll be fun to take a swim in March."

With determination, he set one foot after the other on the wobbly, rotting log, stepping nimbly and carefully until he had made it safely to the other side.

"Yes!" he cried. Crossing one small creek had suddenly become much more exhilarating than ten service aces at tennis.

With the creek at his back, he took off through the trees in the general direction of the thing on the map that Flannery had called a hamburger.

"Hamburger, hah. I know it's the pot of gold, and so does she."

The rainbow was straight ahead of him, and he was sure that was a good omen. Wasn't there a rainbow on the map? Maybe this rainbow and that rainbow were one and the same.

He could almost hear Flannery's voice mocking him for once again putting forward implausible theories.

The map was drawn in 1923, and rainbows don't stick around for over sixty years, Jack. And they don't pop up just to lead you in the right direction, either.

And he'd be forced to admit that she had a point.

Sanity, reason, good common sense—they all agreed with Flannery. But she and her common sense were back at Inisheer, toiling over pots of dirt, while he was out hiking and having a great time on a beautiful spring day. So who was the crazy one?

Jack smiled broadly, enjoying his outing even if it came to nothing. With the sun shining, he began to feel too warm, and he stripped off the sweater, exposing the plain white T-shirt underneath. Without missing a step, he tied the sweater around his waist and kept right on walking.

Whistling seemed the thing to do at a moment like this, but he hadn't whistled in years. Did he remember how?

"Sure," he said, giving himself a pep talk. "You just put your lips together and blow."

Something from an old musical, about the corn being as high as an elephant or something, came to mind, and he experimented with the tune, managing a few notes that sounded right. As if in answer, a bird warbled back from somewhere not too far away. Jack stopped, enchanted. A bird had answered his whistle. And it even sounded like the same tune! Was that possible?

After racking his brain, he came up with more of the song, and he whistled the little ditty out loud and clear.

And there was the bird, singing back at him. He was starting to feel pretty good about this outdoors thing, as if he and nature were on the same wavelength.

So he and the friendly bird went on that way, dueling musicians, as Jack followed the rainbow and marched toward his pot of gold.

FLANNERY GOT THERE before he did, but then she knew where she was going. It also helped that she wasn't following that silly old map he'd found, because so many things had changed since it was drawn. And once the map was out of the picture, modern roads became a possibility, which meant taking the car and going on the highway, for a much faster and smoother trip all around.

So she wasn't in the least surprised not to find Jack at the springs when she arrived. After parking the monster Plymouth just off the road, she cooled her heels near the water for a while. With one hand shielding her eyes from the sun, she directed her gaze into the trees, scanning the direction she thought he would come from. But there was no Jack.

Finally, she got bored watching for him, and she hiked around to the far side of the springs, the rocky side, where small caves and other openings dimpled the limestone. If Jack had been right, and the half circles on the map really were caves, then his "treasure" should be hidden here.

She didn't believe a word of the treasure nonsense, but it actually wouldn't be all that weird to find *something* in the caves. These little recesses weren't really substantial enough to be called caves, or to hide anything of any importance. But they were the perfect size for generations of children to play Jesse James the outlaw or Huck Finn on the lam from Aunt Polly. Flannery and Kathleen had scared themselves silly in those caves, hiding each other's dolls when they were fighting, and then retrieving them when they made up.

She hadn't gotten very far, not even into the opening round of caves, when she heard Jack's voice, clear as a bell, say, "Just put your lips together and blow."

"What?" She spun around, almost knocking her head on the top layer of rock, but Jack wasn't there. "Oh, I forgot," she murmured, feeling foolish. "He must be near a hole in the ground."

He didn't have to be all that close for his voice to come through loud and clear. It was one of the tricks of these caves, since they were linked to the underground stream that fed the springs. Wherever there were fissures in the layers of rock, voices could carry, working on the same principle as paper cups on string. Anywhere in between the springs and the creek, you could hear the sounds, as if they suddenly came out of nowhere. It was spooky and inexplicable when you were a kid but the greatest of fun.

"At least I know he's still okay. He didn't fall into the creek or anything if he's quoting lines from old movies."

Immediately she clapped a hand over her mouth. If Jack's words could filter through the tunnels in the rock and get to her, then her words would run right back to him.

Intrigued, she continued to listen for sounds from Jack. He was whistling, and the notes came tripping through the cave's telephone system as clear as day. But what was that tune?

"It's from *Oklahoma,*" she decided. And she pursed her lips and got right up next to the biggest crack in the wall, feeding him the next part just to be ornery. Unlike her, he wouldn't have a clue where the sound was coming from. "He'll think God is whistling to him," she said, giggling to herself.

·As Jack's tune began to sound closer, Flannery left the cave and carried her part of the duet to higher ground. She still couldn't tell exactly where he was, but he ought to be arriving at the springs very shortly.

"See you soon," she whispered mischievously.

ALMOST BEFORE HE REALIZED how much ground he'd covered, the landscape began to look familiar. It was still low, green hills, with a scattering of trees and rocks, even an occasional flower—not very different from where he'd been, and not different enough to figure out why it rang a bell.

But now he heard the sound of rushing water again. He shouldn't be anywhere near the creek, and there was nothing on the map except what Flannery had called the "puffy cloud."

As he came into a clearing, it all added up, and he smiled to himself. So far, his reading of the map had been right on target.

There was the springs ahead of him, Rainbow Springs, bubbling in its pond and accounting for the sound of water. Since the pond had an irregular shape, he decided that the "puffy cloud" was really the springs in a two-dimensional form. He'd have to see it from the air to be sure, but it sure seemed likely at the moment.

And the low-hanging willow where he'd found his car, now directly across the water from him, was what Flannery had described as a sloppy *M*. Its long, droopy branches curved down to the water, creating the vague outline of an *M*.

"McDonald's arches," he grumbled, beginning to get a very strong hunch. "She knew what it was. She's lived here her whole life, and she had to recognize all of these places on that map."

So was she just being contrary, as usual, or was she hiding something on purpose? Or perhaps she simply found it amusing to send him on a convoluted cross-country hike to get to a place that would take five minutes by car?

"When I see her again, I'll kill her," he said clearly. "I will strip her naked, tie her to a tree, pour honey all over her body and bring on the red fire ants."

But the mental image of Flannery stripped naked took his thoughts in an entirely different direction.

"Yeah…" he whispered, letting his mind's eye run up and down the length of her body, completely and irrevocably bared to his eyes.

Her skin would be a pale, creamy white, from stem to stern, with maybe a few scattered freckles to make things interesting. The slope of her neck, the round rise of her hip—perfect. All that marred his view was a sweep of auburn hair, tipping over her shoulder and slipping down the curve of one small, beautiful breast.

In his fantasy, she was smiling, beckoning him closer, with a naughty look in her eyes. And enough heat to melt steel.

"Oh, yeah. I can use the honey," he said roughly. "But forget the ants."

The vision was so real, he could feel the warmth of Flannery's skin, and he almost tripped, thinking he could reach her. As he righted himself, he suddenly caught a flash of green between the branches of the willow across the way. The delightful pictures evaporated into thin air.

"Sully?" he called out. "Is that you?"

There was no answer, but Jack peered across the springs, trying to get a better picture of who or what was over there. Yes, it definitely looked like the outline of a small man, just visible behind the protective covering of tree branches.

"Turlough Sullivan, don't you move," he thundered, clambering down over the rocks to get to the other, grassier side.

It took several minutes to negotiate the springs, to come racing around and up to the willow. By the time Jack crashed through its low-bent branches, there was no sign of his nemesis.

"Sullivan, show your face!" he ordered, but there was no answer.

He almost thought he heard a mocking little laugh, but as he whirled in its direction, there was nothing there. He shook his head, wondering if it had been his imagination. Had Turlough ever been there, under the tree? Or was that, too, a trick of wind and light?

Jack backed out from under the willow, slowly, silently edging down closer to the springs, pondering on the state of his mind. If he couldn't depend on his own senses anymore, what could he trust? Staring at the willow, trying to be ready in case Sully reappeared, he wasn't paying attention to what was behind him.

"Ooof," she said, as they bumped into each other, bottom to bottom.

Jack spun around just as Flannery lost her balance and began to totter on the edge of the water. As he reached for her, she took another step backward, flailing her arms. Something gold and shiny flew from her hand in a pretty arc, flashing in the sunlight as it splashed into the spring.

"Stop wiggling," he commanded, catching her solidly and hauling her up into his arms.

She wasn't all that heavy, but she sure was slippery, and the most secure way to hold her seemed to be to toss her over one shoulder, in the old fireman's carry. He didn't have time to think of anything better, or they'd both be swimming. So, with a strong push, he flung her up and over his shoulder, even though the wiggling only got worse.

"Jack," she protested, "put me down!"

Her voice wobbled as she bounced against his back, and Jack smiled wickedly, knowing she couldn't see how amused he was. He kept walking, paying no attention to her pleas.

"Jack," she said again, in a nastier tone. "I'm warning you...."

"Aw, be quiet."

Safely up on the grass, he bent down and loosened his hold, planning to set her neatly on the ground without further ado. But she wouldn't seem to disentangle from his arms.

She was still hanging on to him, he still was holding her and her hair was still wound around his neck. He made a halfhearted effort to free her, but he realized, with a fierce ache in his gut, that he didn't want to let her go.

"Oh, God, Flannery," was all he could manage to say, in this sappy, pathetic voice that he didn't even recognize as his own. Whatever it was that happened every time he touched her, it was happening again.

As he lifted a hand to trace the curve of her cheek, he felt her tremble under his fingers. "Sweetheart," he murmured, feeling flattered and awed that his touch affected her that way. And he bent his head down to meet her lips.

Until he heard a sneeze. A definite sneeze. It didn't come from Flannery, and it didn't come from him.

He lifted his head. "Did you hear that?"

"What?" she asked breathlessly.

"Nothing." But without moving away from her, he cast a wary eye over her head to see if old Turlough was lurking anywhere near.

"Jack?" Flannery put a weak hand to her forehead. "Jack, I—I don't know how to deal with this. I've never felt like this before, like I'm going to die if you touch me, or faint if you don't." She gazed up at him hopefully. "Have you?"

Her green eyes were wide and troubled, and her small, pretty features were clearly in distress. Jack felt terrible for upsetting her. On the other hand, he also felt like pulling her down under the nearest tree and tearing her clothes off with his teeth. He dropped his hands away from her, before things got any more out of control.

"Oh, no," he whispered roughly. "It's new for me, too."

"So you do feel it, too?"

"Oh, yes." He sighed deeply. "Oh, yes."

Her cheeks flamed with color. She was adorable, and he only kept his hands off her by clenching them into fists and stuffing them into his pockets.

She said primly, "We can't keeping doing this, getting ourselves in the situation where we have to back off before we—you know."

"Why not?"

"You know as well as I do."

Flannery was being sensible again, and he hated it. "Do I?"

She nodded slowly. "It's like you're a traveling salesman, and I'm the farmer's daughter. Pretty grim, isn't it?"

"That's flattering."

"But it's true." Head down, Flannery twisted away. "I'm sorry, Jack, but I'm not the kind of person who has flings with whoever walks in the door."

"I never said you were."

She gave no indication that she'd heard him. "I might as well admit it," she said, in a low, unhappy voice. "If you want to know the truth, I'm not the kind of person who has flings at all—with anybody."

He knew he was risking her anger, but he figured it would be healthier than her current mood. Smiling cynically, he asked, "And what about ol' Ken?"

"Ken? Are you crazy? You know I wouldn't do anything with Ken," she returned hotly. "Jack, you *know* that."

"Yeah, I do." His smile widened. "But I wanted to hear it from you."

"That you would think, for even a minute, that I would...you know, with *Ken,* well, it's disgusting."

"I believe you, I believe you," he said hastily, catching her hand and pulling her back into his arms. She stiffened and tried to pull away but he tightened his hold. "Who said this was supposed to be a fling? I didn't. If you want to know the truth, I don't go in for quickie affairs, either. And I would never start something with you with the idea that it would only last for a few days."

"But what else—"

"Shh," he told her, clasping her hand in both of his and tugging it up between them. "Flannery, I can't believe how stubborn and unimaginative you can be. You

live here, with all this magic, and yet you refuse to believe in it.''

"We've been through this before." She shook her
head. "There is no magic here, Jack. You've had a few
strange days, but I'm sure there's a reasonable ex-
plana—"

"No," he interrupted firmly, "there isn't. Do you
know how I got to the springs? You think I followed the
map, right? Well, I followed a rainbow. I saw a rainbow
in the sky, on a perfectly sunny day, and it led me right
here, exactly where I was supposed to be."

"Jack, there couldn't have been a—"

"Yes, there was." He took her by the shoulders and
forced her to look him right in the eye. "There was a
rainbow, Flannery. I swear to God there was one. And
not only that, but a bird sang to me, a tune from *Oklahoma*. It was the darndest thing."

"Well, that I can ex—"

"No, I don't want to hear it. I'm tired of denying these
things. They're everywhere—the pub that came to life
again for one night, the coins, the magic disappearing
car—all of it. I don't know how it happened, and I don't
care anymore. Maybe your grandfather *is* a leprechaun."

"But, Jack—"

"I know. It sounds crazy. It is crazy." He turned away
from her, running a hasty hand through his hair. "I
don't care if I'm certifiable." He opened his mouth to
say more, closed it and then opened it again, determined to have his say. "Here's the most bizarre part—I
like it this way. I really do. I realized that today. It may
be nutty, but it's fun."

"But I still don't understand what this has to do with you and me, and whether or not we want to..." Flannery bit her lip, clearly not willing to fill in the blanks.

"We're part of the magic," he said quietly. "The best part. Whatever is happening between you and me is just as outrageous as the rest of it, and we don't have a choice. We have to go for it, see where it leads."

"We do have a choice, Jack, and I choose to keep my sane, regular old life, thank you very much." She moved back over to the water and stared resolutely down into its depths. "I do *not* believe that the things that happened to you were magic, and there will be an explanation, if we look for it."

"Fine."

"And I do not want any kind of relationship—fleeting or otherwise—with someone who came here to bring progress and all the unholy terror that goes with it to a place I love." She raised her chin. "You're not my sort of person, Jack. I want someone who cares about the same things I do, and wants the same life I do. If that were you, you wouldn't be in on this RuMex deal."

He shrugged. "Well, I'm rethinking that, too."

"You're not!"

"I am."

Jack slid up next to her, near the water's edge. When he leaned over, he could see another of the coins winking at him from below the surface of the pond. A vague memory suddenly wafted to the forefront of his brain, the memory of something gold flying out of Flannery's hand when she'd started to fall. A coin. She'd found another coin.

"Where did you find it?" he inquired casually. "And when?"

"Here, just before you got here," she answered. And then, "Oh, well, I was going to tell you. I never got a chance."

"You weren't going to tell me."

"No," she admitted. "No, I wasn't. I thought it would upset you, you know, and you'd go around obsessing on it like the others."

"Nope." He turned his head to one side to peer down at it. "It's another sign, don't you see? I'm doing the right thing." He nodded, sure of his direction for the first time in a week. "It's all part of the magic. God, I love this place."

"Don't get too carried away here. The gold coins..." She looked anxious, but she continued in the same tentative sort of voice. "The gold coins are from my grandfather. I can't explain the other things, but the gold coins, well, my granddad likes to play with them. He's been known to steal them, and then he leaves them for people he likes." She exhaled a quick breath. "Of course, he's also been known to steal them back again."

"It doesn't make any difference."

Jack was bound and determined not to let her talk sense into him this time. Every time they'd discussed these matters before, she'd rained on his parade, leaving him more confused than before they started. But he was crystal clear in his mind now, and he didn't care if Flannery brought in her best ammo.

"Jack, did you say you'd changed your mind about RuMex? Were you kidding me?"

"No." His gaze wandered over the pretty little spring, with its clear blue water and tall border of trees. "I'm really starting to think that this place is magic—Rainbow Springs and the pub at Inisheer and all of it. But RuMex and the airstrip and the golf course... If I put through the RuMex contract, what chance does the magic have?''

"Oh, Jack, it's so true. It would all be ruined!" Flannery had become as bubbly as the springs. "I mean, not that there's real magic, not the kind you mean, but it is a special place, and it's *my* place, and I would hate to see that change."

"I couldn't agree more."

She gazed up at him with real affection in her eyes, and Jack liked the look of it. "I'm a little surprised," she said. "You've been so hell-bent on this search of yours, and I thought it was for the contract. What are you going to do now?"

"Look for the pot of gold, of course."

"But you can't. Not in the rain." She glanced up at the sky, which had turned a threatening shade of gray. "The caves—they fill up with water when it rains."

He shrugged. "I can wait for better weather."

"But Jack, even if the weather is wonderful, you won't find a pot of gold. I know I've kept things from you, about my grandfather and the coins and all." Her features were set in a very sincere expression. "But I'm sure there's no pot of gold. You're wasting your time."

"Now, Flannery," he said fondly, draping an arm around her. "How can any Irishman worth his salt pass up a chance to best a leprechaun and find the pot of gold?"

Flannery gave him a dubious smile. "You are kidding, right?"

"Sort of." He grinned down at her. It was such fun ruffling Flannery's feathers. "Actually, I'm having a great time and I don't care what I do. I feel like I'm on the vacation of a lifetime. Maybe everyone should come to Inisheer and fall off the edge of the earth."

FROM BEHIND A NEARBY BUSH, the man who thought he was a leprechaun tried not to chuckle too loudly.

"And isn't it grand?" he whispered. "Mary Flannery and young Jack getting cozier every day, and now there are to be no bulldozers near Inisheer. Ah, Turlough Sullivan," he said, congratulating himself, "you've done a fine job, to be sure. And getting finer!"

He pressed his tiny hand over his mouth, giggling to himself. Life as a leprechaun was a good bit of fun, now wasn't it?

Chapter Nine

Flannery woke up in a cold sweat.

She felt like she'd had a total of three minutes' sleep all night, and here it was morning already.

"It's your own fault," she grumbled, grabbing a handful of sheet and pulling it up over her head to block out the gray streaks of morning light.

No wonder she'd slept poorly. What did she expect, tangled in the sheets Jack had used? Sweet dreams, maybe? Not a chance. So what if she'd washed them twice since he'd been near them? They still reminded her of Jack and nothing else.

As she fingered the embroidery along the hem, all she could think about was him wrapped in this sheet, him waltzing around her room wearing nothing but this sheet, him sitting in this very bed with her initials sliding precariously across his naked lap.

It was enough to give a girl nightmares of a very warm variety.

"They were my favorite sheets before he came along," she muttered. "And they'll still be my favorite sheets long after he's gone."

Fat chance.

She knew she should get up and face another rainy day, brush away the cobwebs from last night's tossing and turning and get on with her life. But still she huddled under the covers, wishing she had *Jack* and the Irish linen to share her bed with.

"You could go find him," she told herself, as she finally inched out of bed in her demure white cotton nightgown. "He's probably not even awake, and you could sneak into his room and slip under the covers with him before he even knows you're there."

Soon enough, he'd know she was there. She could wake him up and make love to him, and then, dammit, he'd know she was there.

But she knew as well as she knew her own name that she would never in a million years pull a stunt like that. Kathleen would, of course, and that's why Kathleen ended up with all the marbles and all the boys. But not Flannery.

Looking out on the morning drizzle, she contemplated the sorry state of her love life. "You're a chicken, Flannery. You can't say yes, and you can't say no. So now both of you are stuck in limbo, waiting for you to make up your feeble mind."

After Jack's philosophical awakening, when he'd decided he didn't want to wreck Inisheer any more than she did, it had become harder and harder to keep him at bay. She wished she could just give in and shout to the rooftops, "Yes, yes, yes! I want to make mad, passionate love with Jack McKeegan."

But she couldn't. It wasn't that she didn't want to, it was just that she *couldn't*. The fearful, cowardly part deep inside her kept refusing to let her go. Given the kind of person Jack was and the place he came from, and the fact that they had absolutely nothing in common—except her sheets, of course—it seemed awfully likely that he would hurt her, forget her and scar her for life. How could she say yes and risk all that?

So if she couldn't say yes, how about no? How about saying no, once and for all, and meaning it?

A heavy pounding on the back door penetrated through the soft downpour of spring rain, ending for the moment any speculation on her future with Jack. Flannery quickly tossed on her robe and trekked down the kitchen stairs to the back door, wondering who in the world would come knocking at this hour.

She pulled open the screen door, and there was Inez from the general store, pushing her nosy way in.

"Morning, Flannery," she offered, untying her plastic rain bonnet and shaking it out in the middle of the kitchen with a shower of water droplets. A steady trickle dripped off Inez's black rain poncho, puddling on the hardwood kitchen floor.

"Inez? What are you doing out so early?"

"Oh, I am sorry, hon." As she eyed Flannery with obvious curiosity, Inez patted down a few of the wiry hairs that had escaped her untidy bun. "I didn't interrupt anything, did I?"

"What could you interrupt at six o'clock in the morning?" Flannery asked sleepily.

"Well, you know, hon," Inez said with an exaggerated wink and a broad swipe from one wet, ponchoed elbow, "you and that cute boyfriend of yours from New York City getting frisky in the a.m."

"He's from Boston, and he's not my boyfriend."

"That isn't what I hear," Inez cackled. "Mavis Mueller said that MarLynn Sterba told her that Karla Kytch said—before Virgil Mueller tried to poison her again, of course—"

Flannery jumped in before she had to hear what who-knows-who said about who-knows-what. "Inez? Did you drive all the way out here in the rain for a reason? Or just to catch me up on the latest gossip?"

"Well, I can take a hint, hon. You're keeping it under wraps, I guess. I don't blame you, not a bit."

"Inez? The reason you're here?"

"Uh-huh." Inez hiked up her rain poncho, spraying water around her in a three-foot arc, and extracted an envelope overflowing with small sheets of paper. "I have to say this, hon, no harm intended now, but you folks are gonna have to get yourselves a phone one of these days, because I can't be leaving the store to be running all the way out here to Inisheer to deliver your messages."

"I'm sure Jack appreciates your effort, Inez."

"Well, he better."

"He does. But right now I think he's still sleeping. So why don't you give me the messages and then you can get back to the store?"

"Oh, I couldn't do that," Inez hurried to put in. "No, sir. That wouldn't be right. I'll have to personally deliver these to Mr. McKeegan himself, so I know they went to the right person, y'see."

For about two seconds, Flannery almost bought Inez's hopeless story about having a sense of duty. But then her common sense returned. She knew very well why Inez was insisting on hand-delivering the notes; the old busybody wanted to check up on the sleeping arrangements at Inisheer. If she forced Flannery to go rouse Jack to personally accept his messages, then the old bat could see where he'd been roused *from*.

"Right this way," Flannery said pleasantly. "He's down the hall, on the first floor, in the *guest room.*"

Nothing like hitting Inez over the head with the fact that they weren't even sleeping on the same floor, let alone in the same bed. "Not that it's any of her nosy business," she mumbled under her breath.

"What was that, hon? I didn't catch what you said."

"Nothing. Nothing at all."

Flannery tripped down the hall, with Inez trailing behind, until she reached his door. After knocking softly, she called out, "Jack? It's Flannery." And then louder, "Jack? Are you awake?"

The door was wrenched open. "I am now."

His short, black hair was disheveled and spiky on top, and his face was almost as rumpled as his hair. He looked adorable. His smoky blue eyes were sleepy and unfocused as he opened the door a little wider to talk to her.

All he was wearing was a pair of shamrock boxer shorts.

Flannery gazed down at his pants, open-mouthed. Behind her, she heard Inez let out something like, "Whooeeee."

"What do you want?" he asked in a grumpy voice.

"Uh, Inez has messages for you."

Speechless for once, the older woman awkwardly shoved the sheets of paper at him and then retreated back into the narrow hallway.

He peered down into his hand. "Did you have to wake me up before the sun's even out for more lousy phone messages?"

"The sun's not coming out today. Rain again," Flannery returned automatically.

"I'll look at these later. Like in a few hours." Without giving them so much as a glance, he dumped the whole stack of memo sheets in Flannery's hands and turned to close his door. But he hesitated in the doorway. "Aw, hell. All right. Give them back."

Flannery obliged, managing to transfer the slips without touching so much as one millimeter of his skin. "I think I will...uh, go make coffee," she said with sudden inspiration. "Come to the kitchen if you want some, Jack." For Inez's benefit, she added, "After you get dressed."

"Right," he mumbled, shutting his door forcefully.

Flannery led the unwanted messenger back down the hall to the kitchen. Pointedly, she picked Inez's rain bonnet up off the floor and offered it back to her. "Wouldn't want to keep you."

"Uh-huh," Inez said slowly, jamming down her hat and tying it securely under her chin. "Nice setup you got here, Flannery. That's one fine-looking boy. Wouldn't waste him if I were you." Again, she jabbed a wet elbow in Flannery's ribs. "When you start getting up there in the age department, like me and you, hon, you don't get that many chances with fellers at all, and ones like that boy are rarer than fleas on a weasel. Grab what you can grab, if you ask me."

Nobody asked you. She didn't know whether to be more mortified that Inez was lumping them both into the "old maid" category or that Inez thought she was pathetic enough to need that kind of advice. *Rarer than fleas on a weasel, indeed.* With a resounding smack, she slammed the door shut behind Inez's broad behind.

Jack coughed gently to let her know he had entered the kitchen. He raised an eyebrow. "What'd she do, mention Kathleen again?"

"Very funny."

She busied herself with the coffeepot, ignoring the fact that he was up and dressed and looking extremely attractive. Wearing a white button-down shirt with the sleeves rolled up and casual black pants with little pleats at the waist, and with his hair still wet from the shower, he looked better than anyone had a right to this early in the morning.

If *she* threw herself together and arrived at the breakfast table under five minutes, she'd look like the Wicked Witch of the West. Like she probably did right this minute. But not Jack. No, he came in like a dead ringer for Prince Charming. The swine.

"So," she said brusquely, "what was in the messages that was so important? Or did Inez drive out here on a fact-finding mission? Or maybe just to insult me?"

"Ah, so that's it. She insulted you." Yawning, he folded his long body onto one of the kitchen chairs. "Don't tell me, she accused you of being hot for my body."

"I wouldn't consider that an insult," she murmured, before she had a chance to think better of it.

"Neither would I," he returned lazily.

His smile warmed her from all the way across the kitchen, bringing home to her exactly how much she liked Jack. He could be so sweet when he wanted to. But this was no time for such sweet temptation, when the morning air was still soft and languid around them, when Jack's hair was still slightly tousled from his bed.

"So what did Inez say that upset you?"

"If you really want to know," Flannery said breezily, as if it didn't matter in the least, "dear, sweet Inez said that I'm getting up there age-wise, and I ought to grab you while I have a chance, because Lord knows, old, dried-up spinsters like me don't get many chances."

"Well, I do think calling you dried-up is a bit premature, but I'm not going to argue with the grabbing part." Tipping back his chair, he raised his arms away from his body. "Grab away."

"No thanks."

"Too bad."

"So," she prompted, setting a cup of coffee down in front of him, acting very cheery. "The phone messages? Were they important?"

"Not really."

She narrowed her gaze. "So what were they all about?"

"Nothing."

"Nothing, huh?" Evasive, wasn't he? "Jack, Inez already knows what they said, because she's the one who took them. And if she knows, the whole county will know before noon. You might as well tell me."

"Okay, okay. No big deal." He let out a short breath. "They were from my office, as I'm sure you've guessed. Who else would be sending urgent messages to me here?" Fiddling with the saucer under his cup, Jack frowned. "They want me back in Boston for a progress report."

"Now?"

"Now."

She felt a slight chill descend around her. She'd expected him to leave—that was the whole problem, after all—but not quite yet. Not until she had more time to prepare herself.

A panicky little voice inside her began to whisper, *You can't go yet, Jack. Not until I understand what this all means and what I want.* But she already knew what she wanted. She wanted him. She just couldn't have him.

"So, are you going?" she asked, in a very small voice.

"No."

She tried not to sag at the knees with relief. "Oh," she said instead. "I see. But how can you not go? Isn't this a command performance?"

"I don't want to go." Forcing a cheeky grin, he told her, "Come on, Flannery. You can't kick me out now. Not when I haven't found the pot of gold."

"Can you really do this?"

"I'm doing it, aren't I?"

"Oh, yeah," Flannery said softly, dropping into the chair next to him. "You're doing it, all right."

SHE WAS LEARNING that Jack was very good at ignoring the obvious. He didn't want to go back to Boston, so therefore his company's demand that he return did not exist. Poof! Gone, just like that.

So when she heard the sound of sawing coming from the pub, she knew who it had to be. Jack, playing avoidance games.

"Hi," she said as she bulldozed her way in through the sticky door. "I thought you were supposed to be looking for clues to the pot of gold, or solving the RuMex problem, not fixing up the pub."

"Have you seen these pictures?" He cast a careless hand in the direction of a row of photos he'd laid out on the top of the bar, before going back to the two-by-four he was working on. "This place was gorgeous in its heyday. I think it would be a real shame to leave it in a state of disrepair. I mean, this bar has potential—great moldings, a stamped-tin ceiling—the carvings behind the bar are worth a small fortune all by themselves. Flannery, with a little TLC, it could be fabulous here. And besides," he added with a shrug, "as long as the rain keeps up, I'm stuck inside. I figured I might as well enjoy myself."

"This is enjoying yourself?" she inquired doubtfully. She wasn't all that fond of sawdust and drills and pounding nails, as a rule. Gingerly, she picked up one of the boards he'd already cut, and then set it back down next to its neighbors. "Jack, this looks like a long-term project here. You can't just start this and leave it half-finished when you light out for Boston."

Jack kept on sawing. "Who says I'm going back?"

"You mean, not going back, as in, *forever?*" she asked, shocked.

Still he didn't look up. "Would that be so bad?"

She wouldn't tell him the truth. "You can't be serious."

He paused, then lifted his gaze to her. Softly he asked, "Does that mean you don't like the idea?"

"Jack!" she exclaimed, horrified. "You can't make *me* decide something like that."

"Flannery, Flannery, you take everything so seriously." Dropping his saw with a clatter, he swept an arm around her waist and pulled her over to the pictures on the bar. "Now, tell me the truth. Wasn't this place something when it was hopping? Admit that it was a palace."

"It was a palace," she echoed dutifully.

"You can do better than that." Jack tugged her closer, spinning her around and backing her into the bar, pinning her there with the length of his body. He leaned into her, his lips poised only centimeters from her ear. Nipping her earlobe, he murmured, "A little enthusiasm, please."

She tried not to smile. It wasn't funny; it was awful of him, wretched, mean-spirited, to capture her like this. He was being idiotic, really he was. If only he weren't so cute about it. "What if it was a palace?" she demanded, batting him away from her ear.

"Then it deserves to be restored." He bent down to nuzzle her neck at the same time he reached in and tickled her ribs without warning.

"Yeah?" Breathless from trying not to laugh, she made a move to catch his hands, but it was a futile struggle. All she accomplished was to plaster herself up against him and his clever, wicked hands even closer. "Stop, stop," she begged, wheezing with giggles, going limp in his arms. "I'm very ticklish. Please, please, stop."

"No," he whispered. "You deserve it."

"Oh, my land!" someone said loudly, banging open the green door. "Why, I couldn't pry one thin dime between the two of you!"

"Inez," Flannery managed, recognizing those strident tones even before she extricated herself out from behind Jack. "It isn't what you think."

"Took my advice, didn't you?" Inez asked with a sneaky smile. "I thought so."

Jack's features were very grim, and he set a protective arm around Flannery's shoulders. "What are you doing here? Have you ever heard of knocking?"

"Oh, pshaw, hon. Nobody knocks around here." Inez bustled right over and held out a new stack of messages. "You better start talking to those folks back home, hon. They seem to be getting real riled at you."

"If those are from Boston, you can throw them away."

"Well, now, they are from Boston, all but one, but you don't mean that, do you?" She waved the sheath of messages in his face.

"Oh, all right." He ticked through them quickly. "Bucky, Jen, Andrews from RuMex, my mother, my sister, Calabresa from RuMex, even one from old J.B." He gave Flannery a bleak smile. "My boss. The big boss."

"Sorry."

"Don't be." He held one last sheet out. "There's one for you, too."

"For me? Someone called for me?"

"I told you you ought to get a phone of your own, I did. Hon, I'm no switchboard. And this service I been giving you, out of the goodness of my heart, well, it can't go on. I got work to do," announced Inez.

Meanwhile, Flannery had had a chance to glance down at the contents of her message. *It was from Kathleen.*

"Terry and I will be coming home soon to see you," it said. "Let me know when would be best."

Flannery crumpled the paper into a tiny ball and pitched it across the room into the farthest corner where the worst dust and dirt held sway.

She felt like she needed some air.

"I'm sure you do have things that need to be done, Inez," she said sharply. "And that's why you're leaving right now, aren't you?"

She put her hands behind Inez's back and physically pushed her out the front door before the big, rawboned old battle-ax could pitch a fit.

Jack arched a dark brow. "So, what was that all about?" he asked casually.

"Nothing."

"Seems like I've heard that before," he mused. "And then you said, 'Inez already knows what they said, because she's the one who took them. And if she knows, the whole county will know before noon. You might as well tell me.' I think that's the gist of it."

"I'm impressed. What, do you have a photographic memory?"

"Quit dodging the issue. Flannery, you look like you're going to cry any minute, and you threw that thing across the room like it bit your finger." He leaned back onto a bar stool, watching her carefully. "So what bad news did you get?"

"Will you let it go if I tell you I'd really rather not talk about it?"

"Maybe."

He seemed to be considering, and she figured she'd better go on the offensive before he realized she'd escaped. "You know, Jack, you don't look so hot yourself. Are things getting more serious at Seaboard?"

"Serious enough."

"Meaning?"

"You don't want to hear this."

She stuck her hands into the pockets of her jeans as she edged closer. "Try me."

"What it means is that my rival for the vice presidency—that's Bucky—is hot for the RuMex project, and they just may give it to him if I don't get back with answers." He threw up his hands. "Only I don't have any answers."

Surely he must have expected that they'd replace him, if he were off in never-never land and not responding to their repeated phone calls. "So what happens if they give it to this Bucky guy?"

"It's very simple," he answered roughly. "I get called back to Boston with my tail between my legs, and Bucky Boy starts haunting these parts, scaring up a new deal for RuMex. Bucky not being a sentimental kind of guy, the

RuMex headquarters and all its accompanying airports and hotels and strip malls will be rammed down your throats so fast you won't know what hit you."

"So you have to go back," she said slowly. "You have to explain to them that things have changed and that RuMex can't build here anymore."

"And how do you propose I do that?"

Flannery inched closer, so that she was standing right next to him. "You changed your mind, Jack. Maybe they will, too, if you explain to them why this place is special."

"I can't bring them all here and show them." Running a hand through his hair, Jack rotated on the bar stool. "It would never work."

"You could try," she said quietly.

Her hand hovered in the air behind him. She wanted desperately to touch him, to soothe the knotted cords at the nape of his neck. But it was too intimate a gesture.

Nonetheless, as if by their own volition, her fingers slipped to his neck, rubbing gently against his warm, vibrant skin. Her eyes fluttered closed for only a moment. She loved the feel of him and the motion of her fingers against him.

She whispered, "You can't know unless you try."

After a moment, he asked, "Will you come with me?"

It felt like a bomb had dropped at her feet. Her? Go to Boston? Her hand fell away from his neck. "I—I couldn't."

"Why not?"

Because the whole idea scares me witless!

"I can't," was all she could say.

"But, Flannery," he whispered in a provocative, persuasive tone. "You're so much a part of what's special here. I think they might understand it better if you were with me.''

"No, Jack, I really don't think so.''

But Jack wasn't taking no for an answer. "I want you to come with me,'' he urged. "Then it won't be so much like leaving you.''

"Leaving me?''

He wasn't playing fair. But maybe he was telling the truth. Maybe he really didn't want to leave her, in the same way that she didn't want him to go. And if it wasn't true, if he were only faking it, how had he known exactly what she wanted to hear?

"You don't want to leave... because of me?'' she asked, incredulous.

He shook his head with more than a hint of irritation. "I don't understand this, Flannery. I've never in my life had more trouble getting it across to a woman that I like her, that I'm interested in her. Do I come off to you like that much of a lightweight, or some kind of Casanova? Why do you find this so hard to believe?''

"It's not you,'' she said heatedly. "It's *me*. I mean, I'm not exactly a femme fatale, for you to run into in the middle of nowhere and get hopelessly entangled with. I wish I were a siren or a temptress, but I'm not. Look at me, Jack. Take a good look at me.'' She turned away, staring down at the rough, uneven plank floor of the Inisheer pub. It wasn't smooth or polished or pretty, and neither was she. "I'm a nearsighted, smart girl with a green thumb, and that's about the best you can say.''

"It's not the best I can say.''

"No?''

"No.'' Laying a firm hand on her sleeve, he forced her around to face him. "I see a woman, not a girl, someone with character and integrity and a lot of moxie.'' He smiled. "I see a beautiful woman who was brave enough to threaten me with a perfume bottle when I invaded her turf, who stuck herself in front of her grandfather when she thought I might hurt him. I like what I see, Mary Flannery O'Shea, and I'd like to see more."

"I want to believe you...."

"Then *do*." His narrow lips curved in a more sardonic smile. "What do you think I'm doing, hanging around Inisheer? Rainbows and leprechauns are nice, but there's more to it than that. I thought you knew that."

I could go, she thought, as if the idea had only just occurred to her. *I could go to Boston with Jack, and maybe it would be great fun.*

And if she went to Boston, maybe Kathleen would come to Inisheer, find no one home and be gone before Flannery got back. It was a very inviting prospect. No brawl, no battle, no Kathleen...because Flannery wouldn't be there to fight with.

"Okay," she said in a rush. "I'll do it. I'll go."

Jack laughed and rose from his stool, catching her in his arms. He hoisted her up in the air, easily twirling her above his head, as her hair fell forward and obscured both their vision.

"You'll love it!" he said enthusiastically. "You can meet my mom and see Callahan's Daughter—or what used to be Callahan's Daughter, anyway—last time I saw it, they were selling gelati there."

"Jack, this sounds like such fun. I really think we'll have fun, don't you?"

But once more the green door of Inisheer opened upon an ill-timed interruption.

"So," her granddad said cheerfully, "what's all the excitement about?"

Slowly, deliberately, Jack lowered her to a standing position, letting her slide down his body and linger there. With a hint of regret in his eyes, he set her away from him.

"We're taking a trip," he announced. "Flannery and I are going to Boston."

"Well then, you'll need a chaperon, won't you?" The little man thrust his chin out stubbornly. "If you're carrying my Mary Flannery off to parts unknown, then I'll be coming along for the ride."

Flannery bit off a particularly pungent curse she would've liked to throw at her grandfather. Great. He did his vanishing act when she wanted him around, and then he chose to pop up and play protector when she would gladly have done without him.

"Granddad, you can't—" she began kindly.

"Oh, yes, I can," he returned, with the signs of a fit of temper about to break on his wrinkled little face.

Behind her, Jack said wryly, "Why shouldn't he come, too? I doubt they've ever had a real-live leprechaun show up at Seaboard Development."

If it was okay with Jack, she could hardly complain. "Okay," Flannery allowed. "If you say so."

After all, her grandfather could use an out-of-town holiday as much as the next man. And it might defuse the tension between her and Jack to have a third party along.

So why did she have such a bad feeling about this?

Chapter Ten

"You look very nice. Have I told you that yet today?"

Flannery smiled wanly. "Yes. Only six or seven times."

He could tell she'd been nervous ever since they got in the taxi—hell, ever since the plane took off from whatever podunk airport they'd started out from—and he was trying to be helpful, to soothe her jangled nerves. But if he couldn't think of anything better to say, maybe he'd better stop trying.

"I can't remember ever seeing you in anything but blue jeans and baggy sweaters." He smiled. "Except for your robe, of course. It's nice to see something different for a change."

She'd told him once that she bought all her clothes from catalogs, and he'd recognized a certain outdoorsy theme to the things she chose. But this outfit was more Rebecca of Sunnybrook Farm than L.L. Bean. Or maybe Rebecca of Sunnybrook Farm by way of San Francisco.

She had on a simple white cotton blouse, with a touch of Irish lace at the collar and cuffs, and a long, full skirt in a soft blue-gray color that reminded him of cloudy days. Under the skirt, he could just see the edge of a lacy cotton petticoat. Under all that, she wore white tights and little black lace-up boots.

It was all pretty enough, if rather sedate, but there were touches that surprised him, like the funny embroidered belt she wore, ablaze with butterflies and flowers, or the short velvet jacket, with brightly painted porcelain cats for buttons. She'd left her hair long and loose, and its dark red waves were the perfect complement to her distinctive attire.

A little fussy, a little prim, but very smart—the outfit was Flannery. All in all, he thought she looked urban and stylish, like she'd fit in perfectly wherever he took her. So why did she seem so petrified?

"Are you okay?" he asked, finally, taking her hand.

"Sure. I'm great."

But her gritted teeth and glazed eyes didn't look fine to him. Maybe she just didn't like to travel. Or maybe she was worried about her grandfather, who was chatting happily with the cabdriver, gabbing along about Larry Bird and the Boston Celtics, of all things. He'd never have figured the old man for a basketball fan, but then he supposed even leprechauns needed hobbies.

So what was Flannery's problem?

Jack pointed out landmarks and scenery along the way, directing the cabbie on a rather meandering route just so he could point out Boston Common, Beacon Hill and the State House, and then into the Back Bay to see Trinity Church reflected in the Hancock Tower. It was very touristy stuff, the kind of thing Jack showed visiting clients on their first trip to his city.

Flannery looked where he told her to look, and commented politely, but she wasn't showing much enthusiasm. She didn't seem to be the same feisty person he knew from Inisheer.

"Okay," he announced, leaning back into the taxi seat. "You don't seem to be that excited by sight-seeing. What would you like to do?"

"It's a beautiful city, Jack. Really. And you're being ever so nice to point things out." Ruefully, she admitted, "But I'm afraid it's mostly just a blur of glass and bricks to me. Everything is so *tall,* and there are so many people. I suppose I sound like a real hick, don't I?"

He shrugged. "You're just not used to it."

"I've been to big cities before. I guess I always feel a little uncomfortable, sort of hemmed in. Does that make sense?" Shivering, she added hopefully, "Would it be possible to go home now?"

He was about to be outraged. "To Inisheer?"

"No, of course not." For the first time that day, he'd coaxed a real smile out of Flannery. "To your house, or apartment, or wherever you live. We are staying at your place aren't we, Jack?"

Relieved that she wasn't planning on bolting back to Illinois, he nodded.

"I appreciate the tour and all, but I'd really like to just relax, if that's okay." She laughed self-consciously. "Maybe take a bath?"

Ah, yes. He remembered now about Flannery and her bathing habits. Hadn't she told him that traveling wore her out, and all she wanted to do was take a bubble bath when she got home? "I have a wonderful tub, as a matter of fact. It's a whirlpool." After making sure that her grandfather was occupied and unlikely to notice, he leaned over and whispered, "Plenty big enough for two."

As Flannery blushed and stammered something unintelligible, he did the gentlemanly thing and changed the subject. "I added the whirlpool when I fixed up my bathroom about a year ago."

"You don't seem like the kind of person who'd fix his own bathroom," she said in surprise. "Somehow, I can't imagine you snaking out a drain."

"Fix up, not fix." He grinned. "Whole different animal. And fixing up, not fixing, is what I'd like to do to your pub. I got interested in rehabbing after I bought an old house that needed lots of work. It's a great house in the South End."

"Oh," she said with a spark of interest. "Isn't that where you said your grandfather's pub was?"

"No, that's South Boston. This is the South End. South Boston is east and north of the South End."

"Oh."

He could tell she was about as confused as he'd been when he was floundering at Inisheer, with no telephone and a car from the Dark Ages. "Don't worry about it," he told her. "Anyway, I think you'll like my house. It's a restored row house, brick instead of brownstone."

She gazed at him as if she hadn't a clue what he was talking about. That wasn't surprising; she probably didn't.

"It's a beautiful place," he went on. "I did a lot of the work myself—not just the bathrooms, but the plaster, wallpaper, new wiring. All that stuff. After my house, your pub should be a snap."

Flannery just smiled, that exhausted smile that didn't quite reach her eyes. Even old Turlough seemed to have run out of Boston Celtics talk; in the front seat, he, too, was quiet.

As JACK LET THEM IN the front door of his house, he felt
sure things would start looking up. His house was beautiful, a real showplace. What could go wrong?

Still holding her slouchy canvas valise, Flannery hesitated inside the door as if she were afraid of stepping on
the carpets. For the first time, Jack saw his "showplace" through someone else's eyes. The ceilings were
high, the wood dark, the furnishings posh and impos-
ing. Every brass candlestick was polished, every piece of
Waterford crystal dusted, and each potted palm trimmed
twice a week. No muss, no clutter, just a gallery of expensive objects arranged like a museum.

Staring at the finery, Flannery looked stunned.

But Sully wasn't as shy as his granddaughter. Immediately, he scampered into the living room, peeking
around the specially made lace curtains to look out the
bowfront window. And then he took a long look at
Jack's shining hardwood floors, covered only partially
by expensive Persian rugs, at the carefully selected art
prints and the subdued leather furniture.

"Mighty grand," he declared, leaning forward to peer
at the convoluted blobs of an original acrylic painting by
an up-and-coming artist. "It's a grand place, Jack, and
that's for certain. A regular castle, fit for the high kings
of Tara themselves."

Sully's eyes were lit with mischief, and Jack hoped he
was being complimented, not insulted. "Thank you," he
said dryly. "I think."

"Well, Flannery, and isn't our Jack the high and
mighty one, living in digs as fine as this?"

"Oh, yes," she murmured. "You were right, Jack. It's
a beautiful place."

As he felt the magic of Inisheer begin to waver, as
hard, cold reality stared him in the face, Jack studied

Flannery's subdued expression. Since the first day he'd met her, he'd been able to read her like a book. Right now, her green eyes showed a hint of fear, a tinge of panic, and her soft, wide lower lip trembled, displaying vulnerability and maybe a trace of insecurity.

I don't fit in here, her face told him. *It's too big and too grand for the likes of me.*

It didn't make him like her any less, to see so clearly that she was daunted by the luxury of his house, but it made him wonder what he'd expected of her. Set back on her heels this way, what kind of impression would she make at Seaboard?

Yes, indeed, the magic of Inisheer was fading fast. It had seemed like such a lark at the time, to bring Flannery onto his turf, to play big man in the big city, to wow the execs at Seaboard with his story of the magical land that time forgot, the land that RuMex should forget about, too. But now... now it didn't seem like such a lark.

What the hell had he thought he was doing?

"WILL THIS MEETING ever end?" Jennifer had scrawled on the piece of Seaboard notepaper she'd passed over to him.

"Never," he mouthed back. Trying not to draw attention, he fidgeted with his tie. During his vacation at Inisheer, he'd gotten out of the habit of breathing around tight neckwear, and now he found it almost impossible not to wrench the thing off and throw it out the window.

"Jack? Did you perhaps wish to add something to the discussion?" J. B. Seton inquired, in his best pseudo-Boston Brahmin voice.

J.B. wasn't really that high on the social ladder, but he had a very nice pedigree nonetheless, and he really did come from one of those mythical "old Back Bay" families. Seaboard Development, under the helm of a previous generation of Setons, had been around since the days the Back Bay was still under water, and J.B. never let anyone forget that fact.

Conservative and cautious, J. B. Seton was about as close to Boston Brahmin as anybody could find these days. Nonetheless, Jack respected the old man. He'd never gotten anything but a fair shake from J.B.

"Jack?" J.B. prompted. "What have you to say for yourself?"

After being read the riot act for the better part of an hour, Jack was ready to talk about anything other than the RuMex deal, which was what had landed him in this hot water.

Nonetheless, he ventured, "Well, sir, I'd like a chance to discuss this whole thing, if I could. You're absolutely right that I am behind RuMex's proposed timetable, but there have been some developments on site that have changed the picture a bit. After I lay that out for you, I think you'll see that we really ought to consider relocating RuMex's headquarters to someplace a little less..." Even knowing it sounded idiotic, he couldn't think of anything better to say. "Less special, sir."

Bucky chuckled from his place at J.B.'s right hand, raising one of his sandy eyebrows. "Special, McKeegan? If it weren't special, it wouldn't be right for RuMex, isn't that right, sir?"

"Right," J.B. agreed. "Absolutely. What's special about the acreage in question is that RuMex wants it. If price is the impediment to closing the deal, you have some leeway there, Jack. Your initial figures were well below what RuMex indicated they were willing to pay."

"Price isn't the issue," he tried.

Before he could go on, Turlough Sullivan poked his tiny head between the big mahogany doors to the conference room, and asked impatiently, "Are you ready for us, then? Mary Flannery and I are champing at the bit out here. Surely it wouldn't be too much trouble to hear us out and send us on our way?"

"Who," J.B. inquired in a deadly voice, "is that?"

"Turlough Sullivan, your honor, and pleased to know you." Sully grinned from ear to ear as he skipped all the way down to J.B.'s end of the table, offering a small hand to shake.

J.B. looked down over his half spectacles at Jack and then back at the creature who wanted to shake his hand. "Jack? What is this all about?"

"I had planned to bring Mr. Sullivan into the meeting in a few minutes, as a witness of sorts, to speak of the unique character of the area, and the reasons we ought to rethink our position on RuMex. Mr. Sullivan lives at Inisheer, sir, near Rainbow Springs."

"That's right, I do," Sully agreed helpfully. "Young Jack is square on the money regarding that."

"Sully, if I could..." He motioned for Turlough to keep quiet.

"Oh, sure and my mouth is running away with me, isn't it? I'll have a seat, then." He perched in the empty leather executive chair next to Bucky, who favored his new companion with a scandalized expression.

"I, uh, believe," Jack continued, trying to make the best of things, "that RuMex's proposed headquarters would severely impinge on the underground water supply that feeds the springs. Not only would we be stuck with environmental consequences we did not originally anticipate, but we would be responsible for destroying something very... special."

"But we've already got the EPA okay, don't we?" Bucky asked sourly. "So what if one rural spring dries up? One kaput pond is not worth blowing a project like RuMex."

"Jack?" J.B. inquired. "What about the EPA?"

"We do, in fact, have an okay from the Illinois Environmental Protection Agency. But as you know, sir, that can be rescinded if new information becomes available." He was bluffing like crazy, but he'd always been a hell of a poker player, so he forged right ahead with his impromptu argument. "I wouldn't want to get any further into the project before we addressed this potential problem."

"You're doing a fine job, Jack," Sully called out approvingly. He began to rock in his tall chair. "Just grand, lad."

"And what information does Mr. Sullivan propose to add to the discussion?" J.B. asked coolly.

"That's what I'd like to know." Bucky sent another nasty glare over at the little man. "This guy isn't Seaboard's usual clientele."

"I'm here," Sully confided in a stage whisper, "because I'm a leprechaun."

A hush of silence greeted the outlandish statement. Jack clenched his jaw and stared straight ahead, unable now to stop the disaster unfolding in front of his eyes.

Holding center stage, Turlough Sullivan went blithely on. "Oh, yes, I am a leprechaun, same as my father before me. And if you and your RuMex start moving around the good black earth of Pope County, overturning my pot of gold, what am I to do then?" He shook his tiny index finger at Bucky, and then pointed it at J.B. "It'll be the very worst idea you ever had in those small minds of yours to fool with the likes of a leprechaun."

"That person threatened me!" J.B. choked.

"A leprechaun, Jack?" Bucky howled, as the room went up for grabs. "This is a joke, right?"

"Not exactly."

Several members of the company apparently found the situation humorous; they were guffawing, much to J.B.'s dismay. He didn't like being interrupted, and he really didn't like losing control of his meetings.

"Maybe we can get back to the issues here," Jack tried, but there was too much talking and laughing going on to make much of an impression.

"Granddad?" Flannery called, as she, too, stuck her head around the mahogany doors. "You didn't..."

"He did."

"I tried to keep an eye on him. I was only gone for a minute." After one look at Jack's murderous expression, she added, "Remember, this was your idea."

"So the leprechaun has relatives," Bucky crowed. "Does that make you one, too, doll? Or a fairy, maybe? Where's your magic wand?"

"What is the meaning of this?" J.B. thundered. "Jack, I am astonished, simply astonished, that you've brought these people here. Why would you do such a thing?"

He had no idea. He wondered how much mileage he could get out of *I thought it was a good idea at the time.* Not much, judging from the look on J.B.'s apoplectic face.

"They can be very interesting, sir, under the right circumstances, and I thought you might begin to under-

stand some of the charm of the place if I showed
you—''

"Please remove them and their *charm* back to Kentucky or Tennessee or wherever they came from—''

"Illinois, sir. Southern Illinois.''

"Fine,'' J.B. roared. "Illinois, then. But take them
away this instant! Do you understand, Jack? Are we
clear on this point, Jack?''

"Yes, sir.''

"Good.'' Pressing his thin lips together, J. B. Seton,
stalked from the room, with Bucky not far behind.

"Great idea, Jacko,'' he tossed back. "Real entertaining.''

"But they didn't listen at all!'' Flannery protested.
"They didn't even know what state we were in, let alone
how unique and wonderful it is at Inisheer.''

"I should have realized this wouldn't work.''

"Yes, you should,'' she shot back.

"I'm afraid I don't understand a bit of it,'' Sully told
his granddaughter. "They seem like a flighty bunch, if
you're asking my view on the matter.''

"No one,'' Jack said tightly, "is asking.''

"Well, begging your pardon, young Jack, but I don't
see as how that's any way to be treating the only man in
the room on your side of things.''

"Yeah!'' Flannery tossed in. "Exactly.''

As the rest of the Seaboard associates filed past on
their way out of this pitiful excuse for a meeting, Jack
ordered, "Sit down here and wait for me—both of you.
I have to salvage something out of this mess if I still want
my job.''

"You were ready enough to forget your job when you
were back at Inisheer,'' she pointed out.

Her eyes were flashing all kinds of messages at him, but the one he saw most clearly was a feeling of utter betrayal.

"Wait a minute," he commanded, but Flannery shook her head.

"Now you've decided your job is more important than any of the things you saw back there. Haven't you, Jack?"

"I don't know yet what I've decided."

"I do," Flannery declared, as he walked past her, slamming through the mahogany doors. "It's written all over your face."

What he didn't need right now was Mary Flannery O'Shea and her self-righteous put-downs. What he didn't need right now was Mary Flannery O'Shea reading his face.

Jennifer was waiting for him in the hall, sending waves of concern and curiosity his way. "Thought you might need these," she said, holding up his RuMex files.

"Thanks, Jen. I appreciate your help." He sighed. "And if I haven't said it before, I appreciate your not saying anything about...you know."

"About you getting mugged and losing the contract?" Tall, slim Jennifer arched a beautifully shaped eyebrow. "Don't get me wrong—I'm dying to know what happened to you down there in Hicktown, U.S.A. But, jeez, Jack, get it together, will you? I don't want to have to work with Bucky if you screw this up. He's a real cretin, you know?"

He strode ahead of her down the plushly carpeted hallway, toward J.B.'s sumptuous corner office. "You may be the in-house liaison for that cretin very soon, Jen. I can see the handwriting on the wall after that fiasco we called a meeting."

"Yeah, you didn't do too well, did you?" Jennifer looked him up and down cautiously. "You know, Jack, I have to say this. I mean, she's cute and everything, but I don't think she's worth throwing away your career, do you?"

He halted abruptly. "Who says this is about her? I happen to have found an extremely nice, idyllic spot that I don't want to see wrecked. Flannery helped me to understand that, as a moral and responsible person, I should not go ahead with the plans for RuMex, but otherwise, this is completely my idea, not hers."

"And since when are you a moral and responsible person when an important deal is on the line?"

There was a long pause. "Good point," Jack admitted.

Jennifer handed over his files. "Here, take these, and get going after J.B. He likes you or he never would've given you this project in the first place, so I know you can talk him into letting you keep it." She gave him a friendly punch on the shoulder. "Good luck, pal."

"Thanks." He squared his jaw. "But J.B. isn't going to yank me yet. I know him. Not yet."

"Hope you're right."

He proceeded down the hall feeling like a kindergartner on the way to the principal's office. When he finally reached J.B.'s office, Bucky was lounging in the hall. Exactly what he didn't need.

"He's in there waiting for you, McKeegan. I hope you've got something good prepared to get yourself out of this jam."

"Save it, Bucky."

"It was bad enough you didn't swing the deal on time, but bringing in those hillbillies really clinched it."

Jack had his hands on Bucky's tie before he knew how angry he was. Yanking up, pulling Bucky like a puppet on a string, he was gratified to see the other man's face go purple.

"First of all," he said savagely, "they are not hillbillies. Second, I don't care what you think. RuMex is my deal, and it's staying my deal. No matter how much you kiss up, J.B. knows you haven't got the guts to go to the mat when it counts."

Grinding the tie one last time, Jack released his hold, shoving Bucky across the hall.

Bucky loosened the constriction at his neck, and then pretended to laugh. "What's happened to you, McKeegan? You used to be such a stand-up guy. Now you blow a deal completely, and over a pretty face. Jack, Jack, I'm surprised at you."

"Stay out of my way," he warned.

"Yeah, Jacko," Bucky taunted, from safely out of range. "You thought you'd impress the girl and save her house from big, bad RuMex. Or is it her farm, huh? Can't let those cows and chickens get stomped on. But this story you came up with... Well, you went a little too far, Jacko. Did you see the look on J.B.'s face when that little dude said he was a leprechaun?" Bucky laughed harshly. "Priceless, McKeegan. Priceless."

Tuning it out with a supreme exertion of self-control, Jack said nothing, just pushed open the door to J.B.'s outer office. He already knew what his boss would say. He already knew that Bucky wasn't going to get RuMex yet, no matter how much he provoked Jack.

And, as it turned out, he was right.

"Now, Jack, you and I go back," J.B. said, around a good deal of huffing and puffing. "I brought you up myself, through the ranks, and I don't extend that kind of helping hand to very many of my employees."

Jack knew his part. They'd been through this before. All he had to do was sit and murmur the right responses, and J.B. would do the rest.

"No, sir, you don't," he responded. "And I am appreciative."

"I know you are, Jack. And you've done an exemplary job for Seaboard through the years. I don't think either of us has a quarrel with that notion. I had you in mind for the vice presidency, Jack. I'm sure that's no surprise to you, either."

"Thank you, sir. I'd be very pleased to step into the vice presidency."

"Of course you would." J.B. frowned. "But you've dropped the ball on this one, Jack, and I am very disappointed."

"Sorry, sir."

"Indeed you should be." Rising from behind his huge desk, J.B. sent Jack a stern glance. "I can understand needing a little extra time. It happens. But this thing with these leprechaun people—"

"Sir, I can explain."

J.B. waved his hands wildly. "No, no, don't bother. There's simply no excuse. I prefer simply to forget the whole debacle."

"All right. If you say so."

"It is only because of the history between us that I'm offering you another chance on this one, Jack. I want you to go back to Kentucky or Tennessee or wherever it was you were, and I want you to sew up the RuMex expansion plans, and I want you back here on the double."

Only now did J.B. manage a smile, a hearty, fatherly one, as he came out from behind the desk and ushered Jack out of his office.

"I trust we understand each other," he said ponderously.

"Absolutely, J.B." With relief, Jack cracked open the door into the hall, the gateway to freedom. "Perfectly."

"Excellent," J.B. boomed behind him. "And I will expect the RuMex contract on my desk in forty-eight hours."

Jack had no idea how he was going to accomplish that, or even if he was going to try, but he said, "Fine."

As he swung open the door the rest of the way, preparing to leave J. B. Seton's office far behind, Jack saw Flannery hovering in the hall. And from the fire in her eyes, he knew that she'd heard J.B.'s words.

At least she had the grace to wait until the boss was safely out of hearing range before she started her tirade.

"The contract on his desk in two days?" She was fuming. "Delightful. When were you planning to tell me? Or were you planning to tell me at all?"

"Flannery," he began, but she cut him off.

"I don't want to talk about it. I just want to go home, and I don't care if you're coming or not." She said flatly, "*My* home this time. Not yours."

"Oh, I'm coming." He stuffed his hands into the pockets of his Brooks Brothers suit and strode down the hall, wanting nothing more than to be far, far away from Seaboard Development. Bitterly, he added, "I've got a contract I have to get signed."

Chapter Eleven

Flannery had never been so happy to see the green door of Inisheer.

There had been turbulence on the flight from Boston to Chicago, turbulence on the flight from Chicago to Carbondale and even worse turbulence between her and Jack, as they'd fussed and feuded the entire trip. By the time they got to the airport in Carbondale and picked up the old Plymouth for the drive home, they were barely speaking to each other.

It didn't help matters that the Plymouth seemed to have lost another piece of its muffler along the way, giving it a roar as well as a rumble. Jack didn't say anything; he just stared at her accusingly, as if even the car's exhaust problems were her fault.

Meanwhile, poor, exhausted Granddad had snoozed on the flights and then again during the car ride home to Inisheer. He hadn't seemed to notice either the lack of sound coming from Flannery and Jack, or the excess sound coming from the noisy car.

Yes, she could definitely say she'd never been more thrilled to see her own front door. Until the front door opened, and her younger sister walked out.

"It's our darling Kathleen," Granddad declared, and he danced up onto the front porch to give her a hug and a kiss.

Flannery stood stock-still where she was, with one hand still hanging from the door handle of the Plymouth. Kathleen was even prettier than Flannery remembered, with that dramatic blaze of curly red hair against creamy white skin. Wearing a short, peachy dress that showed off her long legs and lushly curved body, Kathleen looked sensational.

"I wondered where you guys were!" she said gaily. She shook a finger, its nail painted hot orange, at Flannery. "You can run but you can't hide!"

"I can try, can't I?" Flannery muttered under her breath.

As her granddad mumbled something about cause for a celebration and headed into the pub, she slammed the car door and took a few steps away from the protective cover of the Plymouth.

Jack fixed her with an odd look. For her ears only, he noted, "That was the message you got before we left, wasn't it? That Kathleen was coming home. So that was the reason you agreed to go with me—just to avoid seeing Kathleen."

"Didn't work, did it?"

"Flannery," Kathleen said nervously, "are you going to say hello to me or not?"

"Of course. Hi, Sis." Sliding her hands into the wrinkled pockets of her long pastel skirt, she raised her chin and met her sister's vapid green gaze head-on. "How are you?"

"Fine, just fine." Kathleen chewed on a polished fingernail. "How about you, Flan? Are you okay down here?"

That never concerned you before, did it? But she said, "Oh, sure. I'm fine."

"This is the scintillating conversation you couldn't face?"

She ignored Jack. "So, is Terry with you?"

A sullen pout crossed Kathleen's features, turning her from alluring to merely so-so. "You'd like to hear he's not, wouldn't you? Well, he is, Flannery. He's with me, and he's staying with me, and I'm sorry if you don't like it."

"*This* is more of what I expected," Jack put in cynically.

"Shut up," Flannery ordered. "Will you please be quiet?" To her sister, she directed an abrupt, unvarnished question. "What are you doing here, Kathleen?"

Kathleen colored slightly. "Well, I... I mean..." Awkwardly, she tapped one toe against the worn wood of the porch.

"Why on earth did you have to come back here?"

"Well, I—" she started again, just as Granddad came waltzing back out the green door.

"Look who's here," he proclaimed. "She's brought Terry with her." He reached behind the door, pulling out Kathleen's husband like a rabbit out of a hat. "Isn't it grand? The whole family back together."

"Grand," Flannery echoed grimly.

Strangely enough, Terry wasn't as good-looking as she remembered. While Kathleen seemed to have blossomed, Terry had sort of faded. She remembered him as a golden boy, with a thick shock of wheat-blond hair that ruffled in the breeze when he ran around the bases on a home run. She remembered him as strong and slim and impossibly handsome, with a little-boy grin that would melt her heart. But now, he was too soft around the waist, too florid in the face and his hair was beginning to recede in the front. And the boyish grin seemed to have been painted on.

He looks like a used car salesman, she realized. How odd. That's exactly what he was.

She couldn't do anything but stand there, rooted to the spot, like a tree stump, and stare at him. It was almost scary to realize that she didn't know anything about him anymore.

He was the same boy she'd wrestled with in the back seat of too many cars to keep track of, the same boy she'd kissed and held and made love with on hot summer afternoons. She'd known every angle of his body, and thought she knew every thought in his head. But she didn't know him at all anymore.

The others were shuffling their feet, watching Terry and watching her, as if they expected one or the other to burst into flame at any moment.

Determined to stand her ground without flinching, Flannery reined in her wayward thoughts. "How are you, Terry?" she asked clearly.

"Fine." He dipped his head self-consciously, inclining it in her direction. "And you?"

"I'm fine."

"This again," Jack grumbled. Flannery almost hit him.

"Flannery?" Kathleen ventured, moistening her lips. She wound her fingers through Terry's and pulled him closer. "We have an announcement to make, Flan. I hope you'll be happy for us."

"I already heard. You're moving back here."

Her voice sounded braver than she felt. *But I don't want her back here,* her heart cried. *Or him, either. Why can't they stay away from me?*

Without thinking, without giving herself a chance to rehash the Boston trip or carry a grudge, Flannery edged closer to Jack, seeking a little emotional shelter from the storms of the past in the arms of her present. She felt Jack settle in behind her, and she leaned into him, only an inch or two, shamelessly stealing comfort from the warmth of his body.

"You knew?" her sister demanded.

"Inez said there was a rumor to that effect."

"Well, moving back is only part of it." Kathleen glanced anxiously at her husband. "Terry's going back to work for his dad, taking over the car dealership down in Dixon Springs."

"Wasn't doing so well in Indy," Terry said gruffly. "You know, I always did want to work for my dad."

"Oh, yeah, I remember that well enough."

Jack's gaze narrowed on her, as if he were trying to figure out the significance of every chance remark. Clever, perceptive Jack—he was plenty sharp enough to have a pretty good idea of what exactly had transpired here eight years ago. She should've told him before this, but she'd never been able to bring herself to it, somehow. She'd kept holding on to the hope that he wouldn't have to know, wouldn't ever have to meet Terry or Kathleen, wouldn't ever have to see for himself how pitiful her past was.

"And with the baby coming and all," Terry added lamely. "Well, you know . . ."

Kathleen smacked him. "Terry! Is that any way to announce it? It was supposed to be this big deal, and you just let it drop out like it's nothing!"

"Sorry," he said sheepishly, but Flannery knew he wasn't.

She could see it on his used car salesman's face. He was glad it was out, pleased she knew, strutting with the pride of imminent fatherhood. Terry didn't want to wait for a big announcement; he just wanted Flannery to hear about it as quickly as possible. Maybe even to twist the knife a little.

"A baby," she said dully.

"A baby?" her granddad cried, clapping Terry on the back. "And isn't it splendid news? Perhaps you'll be blessed with a son to carry on the leprechaun tradition. Won't it be grand?"

"We're thrilled, Granddad," Kathleen bubbled. "Aren't we, Terry? And Terry's mom and dad are so excited, too! They're throwing us a big party, tomorrow night, in Crab Creek, and they've invited practically the whole town. And I'm so glad you got home, because of course you all have to be there, too."

"Of course," Flannery mumbled.

And then she hotfooted it out of there before she belted someone.

"Isn't anyone going after her?"

Jack's gaze skipped from face to face, but they all stared back at him blankly.

"She'll be all right," Kathleen said carelessly, waving a slender hand. "She pitches these hissy fits, but she's always okay after a while."

"How would you know what she is? As I understand it, you haven't seen her in eight years."

"Now wait a minute," she stormed, hands on hips. "She threw *us* out. We tried to do things as nice as possible, you know, to not hurt Flannery's feelings, but she told us to leave and never come back. So why should I always be running after her trying to fix things, when *she's* the one flying off the handle?''

Jack decided he didn't like Kathleen much. Her eyes were too close together and her voice was decidedly shrill. He didn't know why it bothered Flannery so much that her sister was having a baby, but he knew she'd have her reasons. Flannery always had her reasons. And between this bosomy number in the too-tight dress and honest, sensible Flannery, he'd take Flannery every time.

Coolly, he posed a rather barbed question. ''So why did you come back? Obviously, she doesn't want you here.''

''I thought maybe my sister would be happy for me,'' Kathleen spat out. ''Like once in her life, she might think of *me* first.''

''Kathy,'' Terry started, in a calming tone, but she smacked him again.

''Shut up, Terry! I'm having a baby, damn it, and I want my sister to be happy for me!''

Turlough Sullivan patted her gently on the cheek. ''Now calm down, Kathleen, darling. Sure as St. Patrick drove the snakes from Ireland, Mary Flannery will come around. She needs a little time, but then she'll be right as rain.''

''How would you know?'' Jack demanded. ''You're as bad as they are. You're never around when she needs you, because you're too busy gallivanting around who knows where, pretending to be a leprechaun.''

''Now you hold your horses, lad! Mary Flannery is blood of my blood, daughter of my daughter—''

''Stop it, all of you!'' Kathleen broke in. ''I'm really sick to death of everybody blabbing about Flannery. *I'm* the one who has big news, and I want people to talk about *me* for a while."

Jack was in no mood to listen to that kind of drivel from a grown woman. "Give it a rest," he growled.

"Who cares what you think?" Kathleen shouted. "Who are you, anyway?"

"He's Jack," Turlough offered helpfully. "Jack McKeegan. Jack and Mary Flannery and I have just this moment returned from a trip to Boston, and quite a trip it was, let me tell you."

"Granddad..." Kathleen heaved a big, self-pitying sigh. "Do we have to talk about this now?"

"Yeah, Sully, didn't you hear? Mother Theresa here doesn't like to talk about anything but herself."

"Terry!" she shrieked. "Did you hear him insult me? Are you going to let him say that?"

"Well, yeah, Kathy," her husband muttered. "What can I do about it?"

"While you fight this out, I'm going after Flannery," Jack said fiercely. Without another word, he took off in the same direction she'd headed. He'd had more than enough of her relatives for one day.

AT FIRST HE THOUGHT she might be taking a bath. They had just arrived home from a trip, after all, and she did like her bubble baths on that sort of occasion. But Flannery's tub was empty.

"Damn it."

He wheeled around in her room, noting that the sheets on the bed were the same ones he'd slept in, that the perfume atomizer was lying on its side, forgotten, on Flannery's dresser. One of her omnipresent sweaters was tossed on the bed, and he picked it up, rubbing the soft wool between his fingers. It was the green one. She must like the green one. She wore that one a lot.

"Damn it, Flannery, what the hell is going on?" Aggravated, he threw her sweater back on the bed. "And where are you?"

If she'd headed for the woods, to sit by the creek or listen to the birds, she could be anywhere. There were trees all around Inisheer for miles in every direction.

Maybe Rainbow Springs? Maybe she'd go throw pennies in the pond or hide out in one of the caves.

But then it hit him. The greenhouse. If she was upset and she wanted to work it out, she'd go to the greenhouse.

Once he'd figured that out, it only took a few moments to get there. And the door was open. Quietly he slipped inside Flannery's sanctuary. She was at the other end with her back to him. Since she didn't turn away from what she was doing when he walked up behind her, he could only assume she hadn't heard him come in.

Watching her for a long moment, he smiled to himself. He'd never seen filthier hands. She hadn't bothered to change her clothes from the trip, so there she stood, in a pretty pastel skirt and delicate white sweater, playing with dirt.

While transferring a plant from a small pot to a larger one, apparently she had spilled out a whole pile of soil. Now Flannery was grubbing around in it, rubbing her hands in it, smashing it in big fistfuls.

"What the hell are you doing?"

"Repotting some clover," she said briskly. "Why?"

"Why do you think? I was worried about you."

"I'm fine."

"Why did you run away like that?"

"Like what?"

"Come on, Flannery, no more games." He caught her and pulled her closer, ignoring the proximity of her grubby hands to his white shirtfront. "I don't understand what the problem is between you and your sister, and I don't understand why this bothers you so much. You're upset, and I want to help. But you're going to have to level with me."

"Kathleen and I have a history, that's all." Looking down at her shoes, she avoided his eyes.

"I guessed that much," he said quietly. "But so what? You said yourself it's been eight years. Don't you think that's long enough to get over the fact that your sister stole your high school boyfriend?"

Her eyes flashed up to meet his. "You're pretty good at this, Jack. I didn't know if you'd put it together."

"I'm sorry. It seemed pretty obvious, from the way you all treat each other."

Shrugging off his hands, she sent him a chilly smile. "Give yourself a gold star. You're right. Terry was my high school boyfriend. Practically the only boy I knew. I still don't know why he chose me when he could've had any girl in the county, but there you have it." And then she raised her chin, looking Jack right in the eye. "But he wasn't just my boyfriend. He was also my husband."

Jack felt like someone had just delivered a hard blow to his solar plexus.

"You were married?" He couldn't imagine Flannery married at all, but especially not to Terry, the wimp in the front yard. Jack fought back the urge to go throttle Flannery's ex-husband, as well as her idiotic sister.

Flannery had been married....

Well, at least this explains the men's sneakers in the box at the back of the closet and... "The shamrock boxer shorts," he mused aloud.

"Right." Crossing to a small sink, she began to clean the soil off her hands, meticulously washing away every last trace of black dirt. Over the sound of running water, she said blithely, "Those stupid boxer shorts. I should've thrown them away a long time ago. They were supposed to be his Christmas present. But when I brought them home for him, I found him with Kathleen." Her voice developed a very caustic edge. "Merry Christmas, Flannery."

"You found them together?"

She lifted a hand. "Not the way you think—not in bed or anything. Just *together*. I came home from college for Christmas break. Terry lived with his parents then, so he could work at his father's car lot while I was away at school."

Jack wished that she would get mad, yell and scream, anything but this paralyzing monotone. Anything but washing her hands again and again. "So you were married, but living apart?"

"He didn't want to go to school, but I did. Everybody in town thought I was crazy to go away and leave him, but I wanted school so badly." She shrugged. "It seemed like a perfect plan to me at the time. You see, we were going to get married and be in love and spend every minute of every vacation together. Only things got screwy right away. Terry was lonely, Kathleen was available.... You can guess the rest."

"How long—" he hesitated "—how long were you married before he started seeing Kathleen?"

"I don't know. I never wanted to know."

Finally she switched off the faucet, drying her hands on a paper towel. When she turned back around, Jack saw dark humor in the ironic curve of her lips, and the suppressed memory of old heartache deep in her eyes.

But he saw something else, something he hadn't expected. Shame. Flannery was ashamed of her past.

He couldn't stop his next question. Softly he asked, "But how could he want Kathleen, when he could have had you?"

"Oh, Jack." She pressed a clean, pale hand tightly over her mouth, and her eyes brimmed with sudden tears. "Look at her. Look at me. How can you ask that?"

"I don't want to look at her. She's not very interesting, is she?"

"She's beautiful. She's always been gorgeous. You don't have to be interesting if you're beautiful." After a quick, deep breath, Flannery dabbed at her eyes. "Everybody always wanted her. Why wouldn't Terry?"

"So you hate her, you hate his guts, you tell them never to darken your door again and you get over it." Jack bridged the distance between them, unable to go another minute without holding her. "Come here," he said gruffly, pulling her into his arms. "It's over, sweetheart. A long time ago. Unless you're still in love with him?"

A real live, honest-to-goodness laugh broke free from Flannery's lips. "Are you kidding? With that fool?"

"Glad to hear it."

"But I don't hate him," she said plainly, pulling back slightly. "Or her. I never did. I mean, I really did understand, even from the beginning."

"It's okay to get mad, Flannery. You have the right to be furious after what they did."

"But I'm not," she protested. "I mean, after it happened, and people blamed me, I knew they were right. I had been stubborn and willful, going away to school and leaving my husband behind, and in a way, I deserved what happened.''

''The hell you did!''

''Jack, it's okay.''

''No, it's not okay.'' He felt like shaking her. ''And this 'I blame myself' crap is probably the reason you've never really gotten this out of your system. It still hurts, doesn't it? And you're still hiding yourself away, on the edge of civilization, in penance for something that wasn't your fault in the first place.''

''I am not!'' She backed farther away, and a blaze of anger lit her dark green eyes. ''I live here because I like it, because it's where I always wanted to be, to raise my plants and raise my family. Always. That's why I made them go away, and I stayed here. It was my choice!''

''Right.'' Jack's mouth curved derisively as he jammed his hands into his pockets. ''What a great choice. So you get to live out here all alone, poking at roots and berries, with that Ken guy the best you can muster for a date.''

''You make me sound like some dried-up old shrew,'' she cried. ''Like that woman in the Dickens book, crumbling away in her wedding dress a hundred years after she got jilted. I have a life, you know. I am not sitting around brooding about Terry and Kathleen and poor little me!''

''Then why did their baby announcement get to you? If you don't care, why does their baby matter?''

Silence hung between them.

''I don't know,'' Flannery said finally, sounding frustrated. ''It just does.''

''It matters because you're angry with them, you're mad as hell, and you've never been able to admit it.'' Jack pounded a fist on a nearby table, making flats of plants jump. "Let it out, Flannery. Say, 'I hate them. They're a couple of prize jerks who made my life miserable and I don't want them to be happy. I'd rather see them boiled in oil.' It may not be pretty, but it's perfectly normal. And you can't keep swallowing it when you're really, truly, righteously mad."

She clenched her jaw so tightly, he wondered how her teeth could stand it. In a very controlled voice, she vowed, "I am not angry. I understand that they didn't mean to fall in love or to hurt me, but they did. And that's the end of it."

"It will never be the end of it until you stop punishing yourself instead of them, until you blow off the steam you've been holding inside for all these years."

She said nothing.

"So," he ventured, "are you going to their party?"

"At Terry's parents? What, are you crazy?" Flannery laughed weakly. "Scratch that. I know you're crazy. But not in a million years would I subject myself to the torture of going to that awful party. Everyone in town knows what happened between Terry and me. His parents were my in-laws! I called those people Mom and Dad, for goodness' sake. How could I go to their party?"

"You can show them and everyone else in town that your life didn't end when your marriage did."

"I don't have anything to prove," she shot back.

He took her cool, small hands inside his. "Let me take you to the party. We could dance together, get a little tipsy together, have some fun. Flannery, you won't even know they're in the room."

"I'm sorry, but I won't go to their party."

He had more to say, more stinging words to shock her out of her self-imposed exile, but he didn't get a chance to use them. As he opened his mouth, the greenhouse door opened, and Ken, of all people, walked in.

"Swell," Jack muttered. "That's all we need."

"Ken?" Flannery put on a good show of recovering her equanimity. "We were just talking about you. What a surprise."

"Talking about me? Only good things to say, I hope."

"Well, uh, sure. Of course. But what are you doing here?"

"I hadn't heard from you in *days,*" Ken explained warily, giving Jack the once-over. "I wanted to make sure you were all right, alone with this person."

Jack wasn't sure he appreciated being called "this person," when he had a perfectly good name. "The name is McKeegan. Jack McKeegan."

"Right." Ken pursed his lips. "Him."

"But Ken, you've never stopped in here before, without being invited."

"Flan," he whispered loudly, leaning past Jack, "I thought you might need some help, out here all alone in this place."

"I'm not alone—I live with my grandfather."

"Besides," Jack put in nicely, "I've been here to protect her."

"But it's you I need protecting *from.*"

"I thought so," Ken concluded with obvious satisfaction. "What happened? Who is he, anyway, and what is he doing here? Why didn't he have any clothes?"

"None of that is any of your business," she told Ken, and Jack silently saluted her.

"But Flan—"

"Ken, this is nothing to do with you. As a matter of fact, I've been meaning to tell you that I don't think we should, um, see each other again."

"Glad to hear it," Jack muttered.

Flannery shot him a dark look, and he shut up. He figured discretion was the smartest tactic at this point, since she'd been already pushed far enough for one day. No telling what violence she might do now that Ken, her would-be suitor, had entered the fray.

Ken ignored the interchange; he was busy poking into the pots on various tables. "These don't look so good," he announced, casting a suspicious eye at her clipboards. "Flan, your *Trifolium pratense* will never make the grade. You've been neglecting your work, haven't you? Tsk, tsk. Not enough nitrogen."

"The nitrogen is fine," Flannery snapped.

"Ooh, these are worse." After stooping over to peer into a different set of pots, Ken picked one up to study it more closely. "Not very sturdy, are they? What are they, Flan? Looks like *Trifolium repens,* but not quite. An extra leaf." His high forehead crinkled as he pondered the plant. "What is this? It can hardly be *Trifolium* with four leaves. I guess that makes it *Quatrefolium,* huh?"

As Ken snickered over his own in-joke, Jack took a good look at what was in the pot. "Flannery, that's clover. You work with plain old clover?"

"Well, yes. It's not plain, though." Acting a little self-consciously, she revealed, "I have a grant for the red clover, the taller stuff with the skinnier leaves, over there. I'm boosting the nutrients for possible use as cattle feed. If it works. So far, it's okay, but not good enough."

"I'll say," Ken blurted.

Jack advanced on Flannery. "And do you have a grant for the four-leaf ones, too?"

"Well, no. That's a project of my own. I'm sort of creating a new strain."

"Sort of? It's not 'sort of' at all." After another look at the pot full of spindly four-leaf clovers, Jack rubbed his forehead in disbelief. "The rational, reasonable, sensible Flannery O'Shea is out here in her potting shed growing four-leaf clovers."

"It's a greenhouse, not a potting shed."

"Flannery! You're making four-leaf clovers!"

"I know that."

"But why?"

Finally catching the idea that an argument was brewing, Ken lifted his head from the clover he was inspecting and interjected, "It's a perfectly accepted method of scientific discourse to create new strains of plant life."

"I don't care," Jack said with intensity. "Flannery, I want to know why you choose to spend your time with four-leaf clovers."

"Because I like them."

He inched closer, bracing himself with one hand on the table behind her. Breathing down her neck, he persisted, "Flannery, don't fool with me. You like them because they're lucky, isn't that it? They're magic, and you know it."

As always, when they got this close, her pupils widened and her breathing became irregular. "No, of course not," she whispered.

Lord. All he wanted to do was kiss her, when he ought to be thrashing her. Determined not to let it happen again, he removed his hand and backed up to the other side of the plant table, so that a minifield of clover was between them.

"I don't get it, Flannery. Why couldn't you believe in the pot of gold and the rainbow when you're growing four-leaf clovers as a career? It's no more logical, no more reasonable.''

"But these are real, Jack. Not magic."

He shook his head. "It's the same old argument, isn't it? I want you to believe in the magic that's staring you in the face, and you can't do it. All you can do is come up with objections."

"You didn't do so great yourself when push came to shove," she said hotly. "Where was your magic in Boston? You let it all go down the tubes easily enough."

That stung his pride more painfully than he wanted to admit. "I didn't want to. But you wouldn't help me out. You were too busy acting like a stick, like you hated Boston, like you hated my house."

"I did hate Boston! I did hate your house!"

"I knew it." Savagely, he spun on his heel and headed for the door. "Look, I'm tired of this. I'm tired of hitting my head against a brick wall."

"Yeah, well, I'm tired of feeling like your charity project."

Where in the hell did that come from? If he'd ever thought he understood Flannery, that idea evaporated into thin air. "I never once suggested anything like that."

She rubbed her arms and avoided his eyes. "It's how I feel."

He couldn't leave without giving it one last shot. "If you had any sense, Flannery, you'd see the magic around you, as real as your damn clover. You'd know that it doesn't matter what the rest of the world says, in Boston or on your own front porch, because the magic is here, with you and me."

"No, Jack," she said softly. "I don't want to believe you. I can't."

"Come on, Mary Flannery. Where's your spirit? Let's get dressed up and go to their stupid party—together.

We'll show them that they don't matter anymore. We'll figure it out, sweetheart."

But Flannery shook her head. "I'm not going to their stupid party. I—I can't."

"I would be happy to escort you, Flan," Ken offered warmly.

"I'm not going to the stupid party," she repeated more loudly. "With anyone!"

"Fine." Jack tried to keep the anger he was feeling from creeping into his voice. "Maybe you're right. Maybe there is no magic. In which case, I have a deal to swing, don't I?"

"RuMex?"

"RuMex. I'm out of here, Flannery. I'll find a motel, I'll get my business cleared up within the next twenty-four hours. And I am out of here."

He didn't look back as he stomped out of the greenhouse and up the long yard to the pub. And it didn't take long to throw his things into a suitcase and throw his suitcase into his rental car.

But then he just sat there, with his hand on the key, and the key in the ignition. He couldn't go.

"Oh, hell." As he sat there, not turning the key, he realized what this daze, this inability to perform simple motor tasks, was all about. "I love her."

He felt like hitting his stupid, idiotic head against the steering wheel until he saw reason, but he knew even that wouldn't do any good.

"I love her. And I can't leave."

He pulled the key slowly out of the ignition and even more slowly unfolded his long body from the small convertible.

"Back to Inisheer," he said fiercely. "To straighten this out once and for all."

Chapter Twelve

Don't think about Jack, Flannery ordered herself, but she couldn't get the picture of his retreating back out of her mind. It was like watching the world through sunglasses, and then telling herself not to notice how dark everything looked.

"Flannery," Ken's annoying voice interrupted, "you're never going to get that new strain to propagate. Not in a million years."

One more moment in Ken's company, and she swore she would've burst into tears in sheer frustration.

"I don't think there's any reason for you to be here," she announced. Her voice sounded firm and sure, even if on the inside she was still raggedy from Jack's departure. "I think you should leave now, and I'd appreciate it if you didn't stop by again. Ever."

Ken's face fell. "But our research is so similar," he protested. "And we have so much fun together."

"We do?" After a short burst of laughter, Flannery shook her head. "No, we don't. Goodbye, Ken."

Ken started to launch another argument, but apparently thought better of it. Swallowing whatever it was he'd planned to say, he stomped awkwardly away, slamming the greenhouse door so hard that all the glass shook.

With determination, Flannery ignored his temper tantrum. Good riddance, she decided, as she strode back to the house with her head held high. Although she didn't want to think about Jack, and she didn't want to give him credit for being right about anything, she had to admit that he'd been on target on the subject of Ken. It wasn't fair to Ken, and it wasn't fair to herself, to accept an occasional date or even a ride to a conference with a man she didn't like in the least.

Ken was unpleasant, insensitive and cheap, and if she hadn't been desperately lonely, she never would've allowed him to step one foot into her life. But that was no excuse.

I chose this life. Now I have to live it. And if that wasn't a bleak thought, she didn't know what was.

Holding her emotions firmly in check, just in case she should run into some unwanted member of her family, Flannery let herself in the back door and slipped quietly up the back steps. Okay, she *sneaked* up the back steps. She preferred to think of it as a dignified retreat, but she knew better.

Finally, she was alone in her own room. As she tossed off her clothes and threw on her old familiar bathrobe, she wondered if maybe now, all alone, it was okay to allow herself to feel the pain.

And once she opened the floodgates, there was no turning back from a knock-down, drag-out case of the sorry-for-herself blues. She sagged against the sink, running cool water to splash onto her face. But it didn't help. She was still miserable. Maybe a bubble bath would cheer her up.

"If only Jack wasn't so impossible to deal with," she lamented out loud, wishing she had a bottle of something very strong, like good Irish whiskey, to drown her troubles in. She sat next to the bathtub and poured in half a bottle of bubbles instead. "He's impossible and infuriating and he knows exactly what to do to provoke me in the worst way."

She smacked the porcelain with one fist. If only he weren't from such a completely different world, a world that made her break out in hives. But he was. His was a world of exquisite women and expensive art, of skyscrapers and power brokers. And she just wanted to hide at Inisheer, to poke around in the dirt and grow four-leaf clovers.

She could have handled all their differences. "Really, I could," she contended, as she tossed her robe over the top of the hamper and sank into the steaming tub. If it weren't for the last "if only."

If only she could believe that he really cared.

Yes, that was the real sticking point, she decided, sliding all the way under the bubbles, trying not to give in to her misery. She wanted him to care for her, not just as a friend, a sparring partner, or a reclamation project, but about *her*, with all her faults.

"Maybe he does," she ventured. After all, he had gotten irritated with her on more than one occasion for being so hard to convince.

His voice echoed in her memory. *I've never in my life had more trouble getting it across to a woman that I like her, that I'm interested in her. Why do you find this so hard to believe?*

She didn't have an answer then, and she didn't now.

"Oh, Jack, should I believe you?" she asked out loud. "Why don't I believe you? What is wrong with me? You come along, and I need you so badly, and yet I won't let myself have you. Why?''

"I don't know," he said softly.

She sat up in the tub, and then immediately slumped back down under her protective covering of bubbles. "What are you doing here?"

"I came back."

"You came back." After rearranging her bubbles to make sure everything important was covered, she edged a hand out for her robe. Not quite close enough. Her nerves were so jagged today, she felt like lapsing into tears over the fact that she couldn't reach her robe. Forcing her emotions under control, she asked gloomily, "Why did you come back? Did you forget something?"

"Yeah, I guess I did."

"Oh, I see." She had allowed herself to hope for one tiny minute that he was really back, to stay. But no. She tried to lean out of the tub far enough to reach a towel on the rack, but it, too, was out of her range. Frustrated, she swore under her breath and dived back in the bathwater up to her chin.

"Here," Jack said innocently, plucking a soft white towel from the bar and unfolding it for her. "Allow me."

She didn't really have a choice. "But don't look," she commanded.

"Scout's honor," he told her, wiggling the towel.

As she practically leapt from the bathtub, Flannery suspected his eyes were not averted. Finally, safely ensconced in thick cotton, she inquired, "Were you ever a scout?"

He grinned. "Nope."

"I didn't think so," she grumbled.

Jack pushed open the door to the bedroom, ushering her in ahead of him. Still wrapped in the towel, she perched primly on the edge of the bed. "Well, what is it? What did you forget?"

A long pause, and most of her bedroom, separated them. And then Jack said, "You."

She stood up, almost dropping her towel in surprise. "Me?"

"You." One side of his mouth lifted in a crooked, vulnerable smile. "It's the damnedest thing. I realized I'm falling in love with you."

"You can't," she said, in a rough whisper that was the best she could do.

"Why not?"

She blinked several times, trying not to cry, not to throw up, not to explode on the spot. *He thinks he's falling in love with me?* What was she going to do now?

Jack's long stride brought him next to her in a matter of seconds. His hands rose, as if he were going to pull her into his arms, but then fell back at his sides. "Why not, Mary Flannery?" he repeated. "Why won't you let me love you?"

The dam burst inside Flannery. "Because I'm a rotten person and a chicken, and I won't do any of the things you want me to do," she cried. "Because I'm not the person you want me to be."

He tugged her forward, touching the bare skin of her shoulders with his hands, offering his own shoulder to cry on if she needed it. "Flannery, come on—"

"No, I'm serious." Even through the awful fog of misery, the wonderful feeling of Jack's fingers on her skin asserted itself. She wanted to rub against him and purr like a hungry kitten. She wanted to crawl into his arms and never come out.

Instead, she turned her head away and held herself very still. She had something to say. Although she didn't want to sound pathetic, she was afraid there was no way around it. "I'm not good enough for you, Jack, and we both know it."

"And here I was thinking I wasn't good enough for you," he said dryly.

"You were not." That idea was so goofy, she almost laughed. She probably would've if she could've accomplished it without crying at the same time. "Why would you say that?"

He shrugged, trailing one lazy finger along the curve of her neck and the angle of her shoulder, brushing at the soft waves that fell to her shoulders. Shivering in immediate response, Flannery closed her eyes.

"I know my own shortcomings," Jack said lightly, "and you told me once before you didn't respect me. I'm not very nice or very kind and I don't know a thing about how to tell a red clover from a white clover from a patch of Creeping Charlie."

"But, Jack—"

"No, no, I'm serious. If those are the things that are important to you, then I don't rate very high, do I?"

"I didn't mean it about not respecting you," she replied quietly. "I do, Jack. And I do think you're nice—whatever that means—and very kind." Focusing on the second button of his shirt rather than his face, she added softly, "I think you're the sweetest man I ever met. You have so much charm and so much . . . everything. I can't imagine who you wouldn't be good enough for."

He brushed the edge of her towel with his fingers. "Okay, you told me. Now it's my turn. I don't think you're a chicken or a rotten person. Flannery, sweetheart, I never want you to be anything other than what you are."

"Even if what I am is what you see right now?"

"The nearsighted botanist with a green thumb, right? Especially in this damn towel, yes, that's what I want," he said ferociously, tightening his hold around her, pulling her up against him.

Flannery was too stubborn to capitulate now, even though the feel of his hands on her body was heaven. "And what about the party?" she whispered.

"What about it?"

"You said before that I was hiding out because I didn't want to go. Are you going to be angry with me if I still don't want to?"

He paused, and she couldn't read the expression in his moody blue eyes. "If you really don't want to, I don't care." Again, he let silence punctuate his words for a long beat. Then he used one finger to tip up her chin. "But I don't pretend to understand why you want to hide your light under a bushel."

"What light?" she asked mockingly.

"Your light. The light in your eyes when you told me about Inisheer. Do you remember? All that stuff about the edge of the world and the mermaids. And when you saw the rainbow." Jack bent down so that his face was very close to hers, and his voice lowered to its huskiest register. "I saw the magic because you showed it to me. I've never believed in magic before, but suddenly, leprechauns and golden coins and a pub that rose like a phoenix from the ashes—it all seemed possible."

"That's Inisheer."

"That's you." As he barely grazed her lips with his in the smallest of kisses, she felt a renewed flicker of passion and the depth of her own desire. "So let's go to the party, huh? We'll have fun. We'll show your sister and her dopey husband what's what.''

''Ohhh, Jack.'' His kisses moved from her mouth to her cheeks, to the line of her chin, her eyelids, the tip of her nose. She couldn't breathe, let alone think, let alone say no. ''Yes, Jack,'' she whispered.

''You'll go to the party?''

''Oh, yes. I'll go.''

''Good.'' He smiled devilishly and reached for her towel. ''But first . . .''

''No,'' she demurred. ''Not now.''

But even as she said it, she curled into his hands, closing her eyes and letting the towel dip. Jack pressed her down onto the bed, her bed, with its tumble of quilts and Irish linen, spilling her hair onto the pillows. Parting the towel in the front, he placed gentle kisses along her collarbone, sliding his lips over her shoulders and down to the swell of her breasts.

But still she held on to it, not willing to let the last barrier fall. He cupped her breasts through the towel, rubbing the rough, soft fabric against her sensitive skin until she thought she would go mad.

''Come on,'' he whispered in her ear. ''Give me the towel.''

''No, Jack, I can't.''

''Yes,'' he persisted, ''you can.''

''No.''

He paused, bracing himself above her. His eyes were hooded, wary. ''Why not?''

''I don't know,'' she said in a very small voice. ''It just doesn't seem like the thing to do.''

''If you're not sure, that's okay. We can take it slow.'' Sliding to the side, Jack took her hand and lifted it to his mouth, pressing a small, soft kiss in the center of her palm. "But I want you to know, you can be sure of me."

"It's not you," she assured him. Beautiful, finely tuned Jack, with the face of an angel and the body of the devil himself? Sweet, kind Jack, who was willing to put his pride on the line and tell her he was falling for her, when she hadn't made any similar vows? "Oh, Jack. Believe me, it's not you."

"Flannery," he said awkwardly, "I know you haven't done this in a long time, and I don't mind at all, if that's what's bothering you. Actually, it's refreshing—"

"What?" She scrambled out from under him, clutching at her towel. As quickly as she could manage it, she pulled her jeans up off the floor and under the towel.

"What are you doing?"

Jack was still sitting on the bed with his shirt partially undone as Flannery wriggled into her clothing as best she could.

"I'm getting dressed," she said snidely. "What does it look like?"

"Aw, hell." Hands at his head, he dropped backward into the pillows. "What did I do now?"

"You think I'm no good at this, don't you?"

"No good at what?"

"You know, *this*." She pointed at the bed. "*That*. It. You know."

"Excuse me?"

"No, I will not excuse you. I know exactly what you think Jack, and that's been the problem all along." Buttoning her blouse, she tried not to get too flushed with righteous indignation. "I knew it. You almost blew it past me, but not quite."

"What in the hell are you talking about?" he shouted, banging a pillow into the brass headboard.

"You think that I'm some dried-up old maid and it's your duty to bring a little spice into my life, like we're stuck in a road show of *The Rainmaker* or something." She was hopping mad now, literally, as she stood on one foot to put her socks on. "Like your house in Boston, right. Like my pub! You see these dingy, neglected things, and you want to fix them up. Well, I'm not dingy and neglected, and I don't need your..." She searched for a word. "Your rain!"

"I don't know where you get these ideas," he protested. "You keep coming back to this dried-up old maid thing, and I don't have a clue why. Why do you think I'd think that? And what do you mean, my *rain?*"

"You know perfectly well what I mean," she snapped. "Why else would someone like you be coming on to someone like me? But you gave yourself away with that crack about me not having any experience. For your information, Mr. McKeegan, I'm no charity case. As you will recall, I was a married woman, and I know very well what goes on." Primly, she added, "As a matter of fact, I'm pretty darned good at...it."

He arched a black eyebrow. "Good at what?"

"At...it."

Jack's face was a study in insolence as he gazed at her for a long moment. "I find it difficult to believe you're all that good at it if you can't even bring yourself to say it."

"Well, it's not my fault if there's not a good word for it." She started flinging things out of her drawers, looking for her green sweater.

"It's over here," Jack said absently, leaning over the side of the bed to scoop it up off the floor.

"How did you know...? Oh, never mind." Irritated, she yanked it out of his hand.

"So what's wrong with 'making love'?"

She felt her face suffuse with hot color. "Excuse me?"

"The term," he said patiently. "You said there's no good word for your mythical 'it.' So I asked, what's wrong with 'making love'?"

"Oh, well, it's not always making love, is it? I mean, let's be realistic." Hastily, she pulled the sweater over her head. "If it's just for fun, or—" she took a deep breath "—just to, you know, put out a fire, it's hardly *love*. And saying, 'I had sex with someone' sounds like a survey, like Masters and Johnson or people who do that for a living. Or laboratory rats, for that matter. So then there's 'sleeping with someone' or 'going to bed with,' and I don't think either of those work at all. Beds and sleep aren't in the least necessary."

Jack made a funny choking sound, but Flannery persevered. "So what's left? I absolutely refuse to use any of the nasty words—they sound so crude."

"I, uh, think that's the idea," Jack offered helpfully.

She sent him a suspicious glance to see if he was making fun of her. "Well, not for me, thanks. But now you see why I call it *it*."

"I see a lot of things about you."

His voice was low and dangerous as he crawled out of the bed like a tomcat on the prowl. Before she had a chance to move, he was there, next to her and above her, staring down into her eyes. But he didn't touch her. Not anywhere. Not one inch of him touched her. Except his eyes, burning with smoky, hypnotic Inisheer blue.

"Let me tell you something, Mary Flannery. I learned this a long time ago, from hard experience. It doesn't matter what the hell you call it." His voice and his eyes lashed her, embraced her, and she tried to remember to breathe. "If it isn't making love, Mary Flannery, it's a waste of time. Making love, Mary Flannery, with your heart and your body. Otherwise, why bother?"

And then he swept by her and headed for the door.

"Jack," she whispered.

He turned. "What?"

"Is that what it would be between you and me? Making love?"

"Absolutely."

She felt his confidence reverberate deep inside her. "Okay," she said finally.

He cocked an eyebrow. "Okay, what?"

"Between you and me. Okay."

"Oh, so now you're not a charity case?"

Almost apologetically, she offered, "I guess I never was."

"Trust me. You never were."

"So, is it okay, then?"

He smiled again, a carefree, rakish smile that took her breath away. "Maybe later. First, we've got a party to go to. We'll see who the dried-up old maids are at this bash, but I'm betting they won't be dancing with me."

"Oh, I forgot about that stupid party."

"Yeah, that." Bending to her hand, he dropped a kiss on the back of it. "Put on your red dress, lady. We're going out."

"I don't have a red dress."

"Fake it." And then he winked at her and backed out into the hall. "See you later, sweetheart. Party time."

"NO, WE'RE NOT TAKING your hearse," he said firmly.

"It's not a hearse."

She wiggled self-consciously inside the stretchy black dress that was really much too tight and much too short. But Jack seemed to like it, if the heat in his gaze every time he looked at her was any indication.

"We're not taking it, anyway." Clasping her hand in his, he led her around to the front of the pub. "I have this perfectly nice little red convertible that I'm paying for, and we might as well make a jazzy entrance."

"Most of the guests will pull up in pick-ups and tractors," she warned him, only half kidding, as he held open her door.

"So we'll stand out."

"We'll stand out anyway, dressed like this."

It wasn't just her outfit, which was bad enough, in a showy sort of way. She didn't even know why she owned this dress; it was nothing like her usual style. But once, feeling naughty, she'd ordered it from the Victoria's Secret catalog on a whim. Every woman needed something black and clingy in her closet, didn't she?

With the tiny dress, sheer black stockings, spike heels and her hair all wild and unruly, she felt like somebody else, somebody in a bad music video. But this was the way Kathleen always dressed, and so did most of the teenagers in the area, so it would hardly cause a scandal.

Jack was another matter. He looked wicked and he looked wonderful. Dressed in a beautifully cut black suit, with a white silk shirt and vest, he was about as drop-dead gorgeous as these parts were ever likely to see. His hair was slicked back but still slightly spiky, very trendy. All he needed was a bimbo on his arm, and he would've blended in at any A-list party in Hollywood.

She'd never seen Jack this dressed up, let alone this hyper. Given all the arguing back and forth, she should have been the one suffering from a case of the jitters. But she felt relatively calm. Maybe it was that terrible, terrifying conversation about making love.

If it isn't making love, Mary Flannery, it's a waste of time. Making love, Mary Flannery, with your heart and your body. Making love...

Every time she thought about Jack's tantalizing talk, she felt flutters in her stomach and chills up her spine. So perhaps the reason she felt calm about the party was that she was petrified for its aftermath.

But not Jack. He was eager, energetic, bursting with life. In fact, he seemed hell-bent to have a good time.

"What's wrong with your clothes?" His gaze flickered fire as he took it off the road and trailed it down her body. "I like what you look like just fine."

"Not dried-up?"

"You look very juicy to me, darling."

Juicy? Where did he get those words? She tried to laugh, but it got stuck in her throat, and it came out as more of a smoky chuckle, something seductive and exotic, no sound that normal old Flannery made.

"It isn't me who's going to cause a stir," she said breathlessly. "But next to the other guys, in their overalls and feed caps, you're going to look like Cary Grant."

He glanced over at her, shocked. "They won't really be wearing overalls and feed caps, will they?"

"Oh, probably a few of them will. And then there'll be the lime-green leisure suits left over from 1972...."

"Flannery, this is a joke, right?"

She refused to comment. As they took the last curve into Crab Creek, Flannery felt a glimmer of anticipation. How would her sister and her ex-husband react to this femme fatale of a Flannery? And what about the rest of the town?

She pointed to a low cement-block building near the edge of town. "Get ready, Jack. That's the VFW hall, where the party is."

"It looks more like a bunker than a hall."

"Hey, every wedding reception in town is held here. If they're lucky enough to get the VFW and don't have to go all the way to the Elks Club over by Herodsburg."

"The big time, huh?"

"The biggest."

As he pulled the car into a gravel parking lot and parked it next to a passel of pickups, Flannery flashed him a smile.

"You do know how to polka, don't you, Jack?" she asked innocently. "And I hope you like beer out of a keg and Ritz crackers with Cheez Whiz."

She laughed out loud at the horrified look on his face.

"Welcome to the real world, Mr. McKeegan."

Chapter Thirteen

"Flannery!" Kathleen exclaimed, looking her up and down with an expression of disbelief. "I didn't expect you...or him. And especially not dressed like that."

"Hello, Kathleen," she responded quietly, and Jack squeezed her hand for support. "We're celebrating, so we thought we'd go with some real party clothes."

"It doesn't even look like you."

Flannery managed a wan smile. "Let's just say it's a new side of me."

"So what exactly are you celebrating?" Kathleen asked peevishly, as if to say *Don't you dare announce anything that might rain on my parade.*

Flannery and Jack exchanged amused glances.

"Being together," they said in unison, as well as if they'd rehearsed. They hadn't.

"Well, it's real nice you're here," Kathleen offered, although she didn't seem all that thrilled. "Terry's around somewhere, and I'm sure he'll be happy to see you made it, too." There was a pause. "I guess everyone in town will be shocked you showed up."

"Maybe so."

Too bad, she thought, and it was a freeing, exhilarating notion. She really didn't care. Let them all rehash the

O'Shea girls and their love triangle till doomsday. It didn't matter to her in the least.

"How are you feeling?" she asked Kathleen, because it was the polite thing to say, and she was bound and determined to be polite if it killed her.

"Oh, the baby, you mean? I'm great. Healthy as a horse. You know me!"

"No, I really don't. Know you, that is." She considered long and hard before she took the leap, a tentative leap of forgiveness across an eight-year chasm. Softly, she said, "But maybe someday we can do something about getting to know each other again."

"Well, gee, Flannery." Kathleen gave her a sideways glance. "Are you kidding?"

She still wasn't sure she was ready for this. "No, I'm not kidding. I don't know if things will ever be really comfortable again, but we'll see. Someday."

"Kathleen, Kathleen, is it true you're expecting, hon?" Inez crowed, crowding in behind them and effectively putting an end to the sisters' attempt at a conversation. "And don't you look thin as a rail. But that glow—it's unmistakable, hon!"

As Jack led Flannery out into a jumble of dancers, Inez said loudly, "Will you take a gander at them? I don't care what Flannery says, there's sparks between those two you'd need a fire engine to put out and still get enough heat to roast weenies a week later."

"With Flannery?" Kathleen retorted. "Not in a million years."

As Flannery ducked her head into his chest, Jack admonished, "Chin up, kid. There's nothing to be ashamed of."

"Kathleen is as self-centered and childish as ever. And everyone but her thinks we're having this hot affair out at Inisheer," she whispered. "God only knows what Inez is telling them she personally witnessed."

"Aren't we having a hot affair out at Inisheer?"

"No." Mischief caught her, and she added, "Not yet, anyway."

"Soon?"

"Maybe." As she smiled up at him, she realized that being in his arms was enough to make her forget she even had a sister.

"By the way," he said, giving her a twirl. "You lied."

"I did?"

"Yes, you did." Reining her back in from the turn, he held her close, very close. So close that the slubbed linen of his pants rubbed her leg and the raw silk of his shirt brushed her chin. "About what this party would be like. You lied through your teeth," he murmured in her ear. "It's a nice party. Nothing fancy, but nice. And you know, Flannery, I happen to like—" he peered over at the band on the small platform along one wall "—Chick LaRue and his Galloping Gigolos. Yeah, Chick and the boys are all right by me. And 'Stand By Your Man' is one of my favorites."

"Why is that no surprise?"

Flannery closed her eyes and let herself feel the twang of the steel guitar. It was hardly her favorite romantic tune, but she didn't care. Pressed up next to Jack, hip to hip, she didn't care about anything, except perhaps remembering to move occasionally when Jack did, so she could stay plastered to his body as they drifted around the dance floor through song after song.

After they'd done several revolutions of the room, enough time for Jack to take in all there was to the VFW hall, he remarked, "There's not one pair of overalls in the room, or one tractor in the parking lot. No Cheez Whiz, either.''

She lifted her head to smile into his eyes. "So they're on their best behavior tonight. They must've known you were coming."

Jack spun her around in the other direction. "Poor Kathleen," he murmured, glancing over at the door. "She looks bored."

"Uh-huh."

"And she keeps glaring at us, like maybe she's jealous that we're getting more attention than she is."

Her smile widened. "Uh-huh."

Jack swayed slightly to the music, bending her with him. "You're enjoying this, aren't you?"

"Uh-huh."

"So tell me, why is Kathleen standing by the door all night? Ready for a quick getaway?"

She shrugged. "She's greeting people, letting them swoon over her for being so noble as to have a baby."

"That's not very entertaining."

"She does have Terry's mother over there to talk to, if she gets too bored." Flannery tried not to gloat. She had always despised Terry's mother, a ponderous, pious old thing who had never forgiven any of them for the scandal of *d-i-v-o-r-c-e*.

"And Terry's mother looks like a real gem, too."

She couldn't stop the giggle that slipped out. "I'm afraid there'll be no dancing for Kathleen tonight. Terry doesn't like to dance, so he and his dad are probably off talking used cars somewhere." Fluttering her eyelashes at Jack, she gave in to the cattiness she was feeling. "Poor Kathleen. Isn't it a shame? I guess it's no fun being a wallflower at your own party."

"I don't believe I'm hearing this." He clicked his tongue in mock consternation. "Sister Mary Flannery, the martyred nun of Inisheer, enjoying someone else's unhappiness."

Her mouth dropped open. "That's a little harsh, don't you think?"

"Maybe. Sorry."

"Sister Mary Flannery, the martyred nun?" She pushed away from his chest, stopping in the middle of the dance floor. "Jack, I don't think I deserve that."

"Only a little," he said penitently. "Forgive me, Sister Mary Flannery, for I have sinned."

"Jack, you'd better stop this. I'm starting to get very annoyed with you."

"I said I was sorry."

Reluctantly, she slipped her hand back into his and let him pull her in close again, even though they were the only ones on the dance floor and Chick LaRue and his Galloping Gigolos were between songs. "But I'm not at all sure you meant that as an apology."

"Actually, you little sinner, I think it's a healthy sign to show some resentment toward Kathleen." He rubbed his chin softly against the top of her head. "It's about time, isn't it? After all these years, to vent a little anger at her?"

"Don't forget Terry. They both deserve it." She repeated, as if it were a mantra, "It really wasn't my fault. Well, hardly at all."

"Flannery," Jack started to say, "about Kathleen—"

"Uh, excuse me," a nervous voice from behind Flannery interrupted. "You're Flannery O'Shea, aren't you?"

"Yes, I am. Why?" She barely spared a glance over her shoulder at a teenager with a crew cut and a hopeful expression.

"I wondered if you wanted to, you know, dance," he tried.

"Thank you, but I already am dancing," she said politely.

No way was she leaving Jack alone while Kathleen was near and languishing unpartnered. So far this evening, they'd been wrapped in each other's arms on the dance floor for every single minute. And she wasn't planning on changing that strategy any time soon. "Maybe later."

From across the room, a middle-aged woman with a Doris Day hairdo screeched, "Virgil, you get away from that girl! You get away, do you hear me?"

"Yes, Mama," the boy said in exasperation. "That's a real hot dress, ma'am," he called back at Flannery, as he slinked off to ask some other lucky girl to dance. His grin was very shifty. "Real hot."

She wasn't sure whether to be complimented by the fact that he thought her dress was hot or insulted that he'd felt it necessary to address her as "ma'am." Not to mention the fact that his mother had called her a girl. It was enough to make a dried-up old spinster's head turn.

"Inez told me something about that boy, but I can't recall what it was," Flannery mused. "I think Inez said that he tried to poison some girl named Karla."

"Doesn't look like the poison type." Sliding her hair aside, Jack nuzzled her neck, ignoring the fact that the musicians were pedaling through an old Jimmy Buffet tune called "God's Own Drunk." It was hardly a neck nuzzling song.

"Ah, yes, but who does look like the poison type?" Flannery's head tipped back, and she almost let a small moan escape as Jack continued to press tiny kisses into the column of her neck. "You know, Jack, you could do it," she whispered huskily. "Like the too-handsome-for-his-own-good type who bumps off his elderly wife. Happens every day."

"I'm older than you are, Flannery."

"Well, I, uh, I didn't mean that we were, uh, talking about me and you."

"Good." He gazed down at her with a spark of hot mischief in his eyes. "I'm not ready to poison you just yet. Although I may get there if you don't shut up and let me kiss you."

"I don't want you to kiss me," she whispered.

He stopped dead, and a couple doing a vigorous two-step crashed into them from the side. Once they sorted that out, sending the two-steppers back on their way, Jack fixed her with an ominous look. He took her elbow firmly and guided her over to the very edge of the floor, near a couple of folding metal chairs being dismantled by three dirty, sticky toddlers.

"Could you kids go somewhere else?" Jack demanded.

One began to wail, but the other two grabbed the screamer and scurried away at the authoritative sound of Jack's voice, leaving nothing but chair pieces and a few ice-cream wrappers in their wake.

It was as if the grubby kids had never existed. Jack just stood there, staring down at Flannery. His narrow lips formed a stern line. "What's this all about? Why don't you want me to kiss you? If you start that nonsense about not being good enough again, I swear I'll strangle you."

"Not good enough? Ha!" she scoffed. "I'm too good for you. You told me so yourself."

"I knew that was a mistake." Still, he glared. "So what's going on?"

"When you kiss me," she said softly, "I'm going to melt into a puddle on the floor, right here, right now."

"And what's wrong with that?"

"If we start, Jack, I won't be able to stop it. I'll drag you out of your clothes and wrap myself around you like white on rice."

"My God, Flannery, don't say that kind of thing," he groaned.

"But it's true. And when I—" she steeled herself for the words she couldn't handle "—when I *make love* with you, I don't want to be in the middle of the VFW hall with half of Crab Creek watching."

His gaze softened. "Oh."

She nodded. "Yeah."

Enfolding her hand in his, Jack brought it to his lips and kissed it gently. Extremely casually, he pretended to stretch and glance around the room. "So, what do you think? Are you ready to, oh, I don't know, go somewhere else?"

"Like where?"

"Oh, I don't know." He stuck his hands into his pockets and backed away a few steps. "Hmm. Your place, maybe?"

"Inisheer, maybe?"

"Inisheer. Yeah, that sounds good."

He grabbed her hand and they raced from the VFW, giggling like children, ignoring the stares they got, jumping into Jack's convertible without opening the doors.

"I always wanted to do that," Jack declared. "Maybe I'll buy this car, just so I can hop in over the doors."

Flannery was struggling to pull her hem down to a more respectable level. "That wasn't easy in this skimpy dress, you know. Good thing it was dark. All the men hanging out in the parking lot were giving me the eye." Flashing a naughty glance at Jack, she added, "Which is a real change of pace for me."

"Maybe you ought to wear skimpy dresses more often." But his gaze fell to her legs in their sheer black stockings, and he cleared his throat gruffly. "Uh, on second thought, maybe you better save this kind of thing for special occasions. How about for my eyes only?"

"You know, it's funny," she mused, as she slid down and leaned back, letting her hair flow over the back of the seat. "I thought I would feel really dumb and awkward in this dress, like I'd be sorry I went out in public this way." She grinned wickedly. "But I feel *good.*"

His hand crept to her knee. "I can make you feel better."

Suddenly breathing became impossible. "Not while you're driving, you can't," she whispered.

"I could try."

"You could also wrap us around a tree, but what fun would that be?"

"Not a whole lot."

Reluctantly, he set both hands back on the wheel. But he glanced over at her every few seconds, and his eyes were so alive and hot, it felt like he was still touching her.

"Wait, Jack." She sat up a bit. "Where are you going? This isn't the way home."

"I thought I'd like to stop by Rainbow Springs first," he said easily.

"Not the pot of gold again!" She bit her lip, trying not to smack something in frustration. "Do you really want to go looking for that *now?*"

"No." His small smile was mysterious. "But what about the rainbow? Wouldn't that be a good omen for a momentous occasion like this?"

"Jack, it's dark," she reminded him, as he pulled the car off the road next to the springs. He held out a hand for her, and she took it, although she thought they were both nuts for being here at all. "Pitch-black. There can't be a rainbow in the dark."

"Sure there can." Gathering her close, he ambled out to the springs as if he had all night. Finally, right on the edge of the water, he brought their little hike to a halt.

"Are you stalling me?" she asked. "I thought neither of us wanted to wait anymore. I can't take much more of this."

"Shh." His lips were only a breath away from her ear, and he tightened his hold on her. "Do you see the rainbow?"

"It's dark," she said patiently. "Rainbows are reflections of light. Ergo, no light, no rainbow."

"But anything's possible here, so close to Inisheer."

He licked her earlobe, and she swallowed, going limp in the knees. But Jack held on.

"The magic gets stronger the closer you get," he continued, in that same haunting, tantalizing whisper. One hand held her fast at the waist, and the other stroked her cheek. "You know that, and I know that. There are certain places where the veil between this world and the next is so thin you can almost touch the other side, the fairy side. Like Inisheer, with the twin oaks. It's a fairy gate, remember?"

His words were unnerving. And they sounded very familiar. "Jack, have you been talking to my granddad? Did he tell you to say that?"

"No." He smiled. "This is all my own."

"But it's almost word for word what he says, about the division between this world and the next being thinner and more fragile here, about Inisheer being a gateway to the fairy kingdom."

"Maybe that's because it's true."

She stared out at the black water, cool and calm tonight, even though underneath it bubbled with the course of new water from all the tiny streams. "You think the magic is real?"

"I know you believe it, too, Flannery. You saw the rainbow, that first day you drove me here. Don't you remember?"

"Yes." She nodded. "Oh, yes, I saw it."

"And I see it tonight."

But when Flannery gazed up into the sky, all she saw was darkness. "No, Jack," she said sadly. "It's not here. It's dark. I know you want to believe in this, but sometimes you can't fight reality."

"Sure you can." Framing her face with his long, clever hands, Jack watched her closely. "Listen to me, Flannery. The light isn't in the sky. It's in you. I only found it when I found you. You've been pushing it down for so long now, you're afraid to let it out. But I know it's there. I feel it. And if you let it shine, the magic will light up the sky."

Everything she loved about Jack burned brightly in his moody blue eyes. Flannery reached up with one finger, tracing the outline of his narrow upper lip.

Without bothering to turn around, without bothering to look at the sky, she murmured, "You're right, Jack. There is a rainbow."

He bent down to kiss her, to cover her mouth with his, to meet her passion with warmth and sweetness and joy. As the blood in her veins turned to warm honey, as she went weak in the knees, she smiled into his kiss. "Oh, yes, I definitely see a rainbow."

Jack swung her up into his arms and carried her back to the car. It was only a few minutes to Inisheer, but she couldn't possibly get there soon enough. Her heart was pounding in her ears, and she had to concentrate to keep air coming in and out of her lungs.

She had never been more sure of anything, but she wanted to jump from the car, to run all the way home, just to have something to do.

The one mile to Inisheer felt like sixty. Flannery stuck her hand in her mouth and bit down, to keep from screaming with pent-up energy. She glanced over at Jack, and his jaw was clenched into a rigid line. His knuckles were white where he grasped the wheel; it looked like the thing might break in his hands from the power of his grip.

Finally, blessedly, Inisheer loomed. Jack screeched the car to a stop and vaulted to her side to pull her from the car. She didn't need any coaxing. Again, he lifted her into his embrace, carrying her.

As Jack shouldered open the bedroom door, it seemed very dark in there. He let her down carefully, but she was a tad wobbly as she came to her feet. Immediately, she slipped her shoes off, tossing first one and then the other to the far side of the room with a clatter that echoed in the escalating rhythm of her heartbeat.

Feeling self-conscious, she edged away to light the small, fringed lamp next to her brass bed. "Oh," she said suddenly, pulling her hand away. "Should I leave the light off?"

"No. Leave it on."

She walked back over to where he stood, and she reached out, slowly, setting one slim hand on each of his shoulders. Slipping her hands under the dark, cool fabric of his jacket, Flannery watched his face as she pushed it off over his shoulders and let it fall to the floor.

Only a tiny quiver, there, in his cheek, betrayed Jack's nerves.

He reached out, too, sliding his thumb against the stretchy knit of her dress, to the barely there sleeve, fitted off her shoulder. Looping his thumb under the fabric, he slipped it down farther, exposing another inch of skin to the rough brush of his fingers. And when the dress gapped, and the top of her breast, too, was bared to his gaze, he bent his head and pressed his lips to the soft, pale skin.

"Oh, Jack," she whispered.

There was a greedy catch to her voice, and it wasn't a sound she recognized as her own. Her hands trembled as she brought them to his shirt and his vest, trying to unbutton both at the same time, to strip them from him the same way her layers of defense were being stripped from her. But the silk was slippery, and her hands were clumsy. "Damn it."

"Slow down," he said softly, blowing cool air on her burning skin. But it only fanned the flames.

Quickly he divested himself of the shirt she'd had so much trouble with, and she sighed, spreading her fingers across his smooth, strong chest.

He caught her up against him, sliding his fingers up the spine of her clingy, curvy dress. "And how do we get rid of this?" he inquired. "There's no zipper, darling."

"No zipper?"

"No," he whispered, biting gently on her neck.

"Just slide it off," she suggested. She pulled her arms free from the sleeves to show him how easy it was. But without the sleeves, the dress wouldn't stay up, and it began to fall away from her hands.

"Let it go," he told her soothingly.

Pushing one hand through the waves of her hair, cradling the back of her neck, he pulled her close enough to find her mouth with his, to open it and slide in with hungry kisses. With his other hand, he tugged the dress down and out of the way, letting it slip to the floor in a small pool of black fabric. Her bare breasts rubbed his chest as he deepened, lengthened the kiss, and she thought she would die of desire.

Frightened of falling over, of swooning at his feet, she tightened her hold around his neck, and he gasped, pulling back slightly.

"Flannery, darling, I have to breathe."

He took in a few ragged puffs of air, edging back far enough that he happened to get an eyeful of what she was wearing. Or not wearing.

"Oh my God," he choked out.

She wasn't sure what to think. Maybe he only liked virginal white underwear.

"Oh my God," he said again. His eyes clung to the lower half of her body.

"Well," she said delicately, "does that mean you don't like the garter belt?"

"Flannery, my love," he said roughly. "I adore the garter belt. Now let's take it off, shall we?"

Flannery backed up, taking his hand and guiding him toward the bed, keeping her eyes fast on his.

His hair was tousled, and his eyes smoky, intense. His intensity only fueled the fire inside her, casting little trails of sparks down to her fingertips. She couldn't get her fill of touching him, holding him, running her hands over the hard planes of his glorious body. She was insatiable.

Just one smoldering look from those eyes, and her body responded deep inside. Without so much as a touch, she was tremulous, ready, ablaze.

At the edge of the bed, he sat first, still holding her hand, drawing her down to kiss him from above. Her hair draped down, brushing her face, his face, almost to his shoulders. Jack reached up to her, clasping her around the waist. Then he fell back onto the bed, dragging her with him, tumbling over and over into the tangle of bedclothes, trying to maintain the deep, wet connection of the unending kiss.

"I'm trying to take this slow," he said roughly, breathing unevenly as his hands slipped under her, feeling their way along the sinful scraps of black lace she wore. "But there's no way in hell I can do it."

"If you make it slow, I'll kill you," she whispered. "If I don't die first."

He snapped one garter, and her nerve endings sizzled from head to toe.

She nipped at his chin, wrapped her arms around his chest and pulled with all her might, tangled a leg around him . . . anything to make him go faster.

"I want to make love to you till we both drop from exhaustion," he said.

Snap went the other garter. Snap went her shaky grasp on reality.

He braced himself next to her, deliberately, painstakingly, easing off her stockings, brushing kisses on the back of her knee and the curve of her calf, until she was so limp with desire that she had no will to object or to thwart his languorous progress.

As his hands and his lips traced tantalizing patterns across her skin, his seductive whisper continued, drifting over her like soft spring rain. "I want to make love to you so completely, inside and out, that I'll know every inch of you better than I know my own name."

"Jack..." she said breathlessly. "What are you doing to me?"

He stripped off her garter belt, leaving her naked to his eyes. "Seducing you, Flannery."

But she could stand it no longer. Twisting, pushing him down into the cool linen sheets, she rolled over and on top of him.

"Who's seducing whom?" she asked, in a throaty whisper.

Her hands drifted to the top of his pants, where she unbuckled his belt and popped the top button with relish.

"Flannery," he murmured, trying to catch her hands, but she batted him away, fixed on disposing of his zipper and divesting him of his damn pants.

"Turnabout is fair play, Jack."

But she hadn't expected to peel away his pants and find...shamrock boxer shorts.

"Jack?" She sat back on her heels, gazing down at the boxer shorts in amazement. "But you've had your own clothes back for days, weeks. There was no reason to keep—"

"Shhh," he told her, "I liked these better. They remind me of you."

"Oh, yeah?" The sense of her own power was intoxicating.

And once he was as naked as she was, bare and beautiful from stem to stern, she offered a superior smile. Languidly sliding herself up and down his sweat-slick body, she planned to make him pay for making her wait, to prolong the hard, agonizing passion beneath her.

"Who's seducing whom?" he echoed, pressing himself up into her, finding her rhythm and matching it, pushing it.

She gasped aloud at the sheer sensation of it, at the tremors coursing her body, at the heightened, jangled, palpable tension arcing between them, like lightning between two rods.

It was impossible to hold back. "Now, Jack. Please now," she begged.

And, as her world exploded in fire, he spun her underneath him and thrust deep inside. She held on tight, meeting him stroke for stroke with more stamina and more passion than she knew she had.

Her eyelids fluttered closed, her mouth fell open as she struggled to breathe, and her voice rasped his name. And then Jack's control broke completely, and she heard her own name wrenched from his lips before he cried out and plunged over the edge into...

Ecstasy.

And when the waves subsided, when her mind had room for some thought other than simply "more," Jack curled an arm around her and dropped a soft kiss into the curve of her neck.

"You know, you warned me you were good at this." His smile was devilish in the dim light. "But, Flannery, my love, I had no idea just how good."

SOMEWHERE IN the foggy veil between the world of awareness and the world of dreams, Jack drifted aimlessly, not quite awake, not quite asleep.

As he pressed his head into the cool linen of a handy pillow, he caught, ever so faintly, in the very periphery of consciousness, the sound of an Irish fiddle, whipping up a mysterious, enchanted, unbearably sweet tune.

"The fairy music," he murmured. And he smiled as he floated into dreamland. "They're playing fairy music in the pub again."

Chapter Fourteen

The gentle rattle of rain against her windows woke her. It was a drizzly morning—soft and gray, a little fuzzy around the edges.

Flannery lifted her head, and there was Jack, already awake and grinning like the Cheshire cat. "You look proud of yourself," she said dryly.

"And why not?" Pushing pillows behind him, he sat up, letting the embroidered hem of the sheet slide to his waist. "I feel wonderful."

"You look wonderful." Flannery smiled up at him, wondering if it had ever felt this good to wake up. She was a touch creaky, but there was so much good will zinging through her veins, she felt like charging out and stealing from the rich to give to the poor.

But there was also one bit of business she needed to take care of first. "Last night, there was something I meant to tell you. But we got so..." She felt her cheeks flame. And just when she'd thought she was over all that schoolgirl stuff. "We got so carried away, Jack, that I never said it."

"Are we back to 'it' again?"

She offered a small smile. "This is a different 'it.'" Snuggling in a little closer, Flannery fiddled with the edge of the bed linen. "I love you."

His arm settled around her. "I know. But you don't have to say it, Flannery. It's in the way you look at me and the way you touch me." His lips curved into a sensual smile. "You touch me the same way you touch your clover. What more could a man ask?"

"But I want to say it," she insisted. "I'm sorry I haven't told you before, but I do love you, Jack. I feel like I have forever. I love you like crazy, like you just waltzed in and set up camp in my heart, and there's no way of dislodging you now." She felt dazed by the depth of it. "It's not something I thought I would hear myself saying again, in this lifetime, but there you have it. I love you."

As she tried vainly to hold on to her part of the sheet, he tugged her up his body and covered her mouth with his.

"Good morning, Flannery," he whispered. "I love you, too."

She shook her head, still not quite believing this was all happening. "You know, Jack, sometimes fate is so bizarre. It's as if you were dumped in my bed on purpose, and from the beginning it was destined to turn out this way. This is how it all started, you know, with you naked in my bed, wearing nothing but my favorite sheet, with my initials sitting in your lap."

Jack glanced down at the pool of Irish linen, and then back at her. "Your initials are in my lap? How very provocative. Well, your initials are not alone."

"They're not?"

"Nope." His mouth was so close to hers that she could feel his words puff against her lips. "Want to come over and see what else?"

As he hauled her up into his lap, wrapping her legs around his waist, she could feel it all right. All Jack, all man, all warm and alive and very, very naughty.

"Oh, Jack," she whispered.

"Uh-huh."

And he rocked her there in his lap, until she moaned and sighed and came apart at the seams.

"Tell me again that you love me," he urged. "Tell me."

Her words were rushed and indistinct. "I love you so much I can't stand it."

"I don't want you to stand it. I want you to be shivering and shaking and coming unglued in my arms for the rest of your life."

"I think that can be arranged," she murmured as she edged the sheet aside, leaving nothing between them but heart-stopping desire.

Once again, she tried to control the rhythm and the peak of the raging fire, but it soon burned completely out of control. And when they had spent themselves, and she was still gasping for breath, the brass bed began to clang and the whole room began to shake.

"I've heard of the earth moving, but this is ridiculous. What the hell is that?" Jack demanded. "Earthquake?"

"No," she said wearily, "just someone whaling the tar out of my back door."

"Ignore it."

But the pounding continued, and Flannery scrambled out of the bed, tossing on her robe as she crossed to the window to peer down below into the rain. "I don't recognize the car. Let's just forget it." She licked her lip as she gazed back at Jack, lying naked and supine, sideways across her pristine linens. "I vote we go back to bed and get some more, uh, sleep."

Jack just smiled.

"Flannery! Flannery O'Shea, I know you're in there, and this is important!" came roaring up from under the window, and Flannery stepped back, stricken.

"Kathleen," she announced grimly. "What do you think she wants?"

"Flaaaaannery!" Kathleen howled. "Granddad is missing. So will you please let me in?"

"When is your grandfather *not* missing?" Jack inquired, but Flannery frowned at the window.

"I should at least hear what it's about," she decided. Shoving up the window, inadvertently taking in a deep breath of cool, rain-soaked air, she shouted, "I'll be down in two seconds."

"And I'm right behind you," Jack muttered.

So, as soon as they could manage to cover themselves, with Flannery still in her bathrobe and Jack hastily clad in last night's clothes, they confronted Kathleen and Terry in the kitchen.

"He's gone," Kathleen said flatly, shaking out her umbrella.

"But he always runs around on his own. Sometimes I don't see him for days at a time!"

"This is different." Kathleen's gaze swept pointedly over her sister's disheveled attire. "I guess you were too busy last night to notice that he didn't show up at my party."

"Oh." She felt her face suffuse with hot color. "He wasn't there, was he?"

Kathleen pursed her lips. "No, he wasn't. And that's not like him at all. So something must be wrong, because I know Granddad would rather die than miss my party."

"Excuse me," Jack interjected, "but this is for real, isn't it? I mean, you're not here just to find out what happened between us last night?"

Kathleen's eyes flashed with fury. "A blind person could tell what went on between the two of you last night."

"Kathy," Terry tried in a warning tone, but she shook him off.

"It's disgusting!"

"This from a woman who slept with her sister's husband," Jack said coolly. "But then I guess you recognize disgusting when you see it, hmm?"

They traded a few more insults, and, just as it looked like Kathleen might try to skewer him with the point of her umbrella, Flannery stepped between them. "Take a time-out, will you? This is supposed to be about Granddad, not about any of the four of us." Catching Jack's arm, she declared, "Much as I love you for defending me, and much as I hate to agree with Kathleen, I do think it's very strange that Granddad didn't come to the party. And remember, he's old. We can't ignore something like this. So where do we go from here?"

"We start looking for him, of course," Kathleen grumbled.

"But where?"

That was, indeed, the question. A quick search of the house and the pub uncovered no Turlough Sullivan. Flannery sent Jack out through the downpour to the greenhouse while Terry poked around the other outbuildings and the garage, but there was still no sign of the family leprechaun.

"He could be anywhere," Flannery lamented.

"Well, what about Rainbow Springs?" Kathleen suggested. "Does he still have his hidey-hole in the cave there?"

"His what?" Jack and Flannery chorused.

"His hidey-hole." Kathleen lifted her slender shoulders in a shrug. "You know, where he always kept his junk when we were kids. The same place Great-Granddad did, around and behind the little caves in the front where we used to play."

"I—I don't know anything about a hidey-hole," Flannery managed.

"Sure you do," Kathleen persisted. "He said it was where he hid his pot of gold—you know, that old brass spittoon he stole from the courthouse when we were little."

As she saw Jack's eyes begin to darken, Flannery protested, "I swear I didn't know anything about this, Jack. You have to believe me."

"You kept telling me there was no pot of gold," he said savagely. "The very first moment I knew my contract was missing, I asked where he was likely to have hidden it. And you said you had no idea. And now—" he advanced on her "—and now it turns out you knew all along."

"I didn't! He never told me about his hidey-hole, I swear."

"Oh, come on, Flannery. You had to have known if I did. Granddad always liked you better than me."

"Where is this cave?" Jack inquired in a dangerous tone.

"Rainbow Springs." Kathleen smiled prettily. "Want me to show you?"

"Yes, I do. Immediately."

"Great. Terry can drive. And maybe Granddad will be there, and that will be the end of it." Steering both men toward the back door, she remarked, "What a relief, huh? I don't know why I didn't think of it before."

"Wait," Flannery called. "I'm coming, too."

But they were already gone. Damn it, anyway. As she raced up the stairs and shed her robe in favor of more useful clothing, she tried to gauge just how bad the situation was.

"It's not so terrible," she told herself, slipping a rain slicker and big yellow boots on over her clothes. "I really didn't know, and Granddad will bear me out. And, besides, there won't be anything in this mythical hiding place anyway, because if he never told me about it, how likely is it that it even exists?"

She felt a little better, but not much, as she slammed open the garage door and revved up her old monster of a Plymouth. Backing carefully down the long, gravel driveway, she was taking the curve at the bottom of the drive when she almost collided with an oncoming vehicle. Flannery groaned out loud when she saw who it was.

"Inez," she said sourly, rolling down her window, "what are you doing out here?"

"Dropping by a message for lover boy. As usual." A friendly grin split Inez's broad, square face. "Where you running off to, hon?"

"Rainbow Springs. I'm in a hurry, Inez. Can you move your car so I can back out? I would stay and chat, but this is an emergency."

"Oh, sure, hon." As soon as Inez repositioned her car, Flannery edged around her and into the road. Behind her, she heard the town gossip yell out, "Don't you want to hear the message?"

But Flannery gunned the motor and headed for Rainbow Springs. She had no time to waste on the likes of Inez.

There was no sign of the others at the springs, but she could hear their voices clearly enough, echoing out from the caves.

"Hello?" she called out, tiptoeing through ankle-deep water in the first tier of caves.

As far as she knew, the caves behind the springs filled with water and became completely inaccessible when it rained. She'd told Jack that, keeping him from searching during all those days it had rained, all those days he'd fussed and fidgeted at Inisheer because he'd wanted to be out looking for his contract or the pot of gold.

"I thought it was true," she muttered, sloshing through higher water as she followed the trail of their voices. The water was over the level of her boots now, flowing right in and soaking her feet. "For all I know, it is true, and I'm following those dimwits into death by drowning."

As the water climbed, she debated what she should do. Maybe they had taken a different route, and the tricky way the caves carried sound had confused her. "Higher than my knees and I'm going back," she said loudly.

The constant drip of water on stone was all she heard in response.

But then the small cave she was in led to a narrow passageway, a passageway she'd never known was there. And it rose at a slight incline, getting drier and drier as she edged down the corridor of rock.

The voices sounded louder now, and she knew she was nearing her grandfather's hidey-hole. With one hand on the rocky wall, she turned the final corner, and there it was—a pretty snug little cave all furnished and decked out in leprechaun style.

Kathleen and Terry hovered near the back of the cave, pawing through a few cardboard boxes, while Jack conducted a systematic search of a small desk built into the wall. The desk was heaped with papers and trinkets, most of the latter shiny. There was a brass pen holder, a golden apple paperweight and three or four pocket watches. A wicker rocking chair, probably lifted from someone's front porch, sat in front of the desk.

Her incorrigible grandfather had even found doilies and a green-and-white afghan to toss around, and colorful rag rugs to cover the chilly stone floor. The afghan was, no doubt, straight from Mavis Mueller's clothesline.

"Oh, Granddad," she whispered. "How could you?"

"Moreover, Flannery," Jack said accusingly, "how could *you?*"

"Now, you guys, don't fight," Kathleen said drearily. "Here's the spittoon I told you about." She held up a brass pot big enough to hold a good-size plant. It jingled when she proffered it. "You wanted to see it, right? I remember he was real excited when he found this at the courthouse, because he thought it was just right for his pot of gold."

"I don't remember any of this," Flannery announced resentfully.

"Well, here it is, anyway." Kathleen handed the thing over to Jack. "Come on, Terry, let's get out of here. Granddad's sure not here, so we might as well keep looking."

Dragging her husband behind her, Kathleen went trooping out of the cave, leaving Flannery and Jack to their own devices.

Jack folded himself into the wicker chair long enough to give the spittoon a thorough going-over. "More coins," he said, pouring a shower of gold out onto the desk. "A few brass and copper, but most of them look gold. And let's see, we've got three more watches, a locket and a bunch of papers down here at the bottom, wrapped in a plastic bag." His gaze narrowed on Flannery.

"Papers?" she asked weakly.

Jack pulled them out one by one. "It looks like the deed to the land the pub is on, a marriage license...and what do you know?" Jack's head snapped up, and his voice dropped into its most ominous register. "My contract."

"He did take them," she said in a hollow whisper.

"Of course he did." Leaving the other items in a pile on the desk, Jack whipped the contract back into the plastic bag and shoved it into his shirt pocket. "Just like both of us knew all along. Isn't that right, Flannery? Leprechauns and magic pubs—it was all a hoax to fool me long enough to squelch the RuMex deal."

Then he stalked out of the small cave without a backward glance.

"That's crazy," she tried, running after him, catching at his arm.

But he jerked his arm away and kept on walking, down the corridor and around the intricate path of caves, back through the knee-deep water and the ankle-deep water and out into the gray light of a rainy day.

Kathleen and Terry were long gone, but Flannery wasn't worried about them in the least. "Jack," she shouted, skating over slippery rocks and clumps of grass on her way around the springs. "You turn around and talk to me. This isn't fair."

But life was about to throw her an even less sportsmanlike curve. Because there under the weeping willow, as big as life, were J. B. Seton and his sidekick, Bucky.

Flannery faltered. Between her and the willow, she saw Jack also come to a sudden halt, as if he weren't sure how to approach the Seaboard Development brass. The two outsiders looked damp and miserable, with rain dripping off their big black umbrella, and puddles forming around their shiny black shoes.

"I assume you're looking for me," Jack's voice rang out.

"We certainly are," J. B. Seton returned in a very stern tone.

Bucky sneered, "Your forty-eight hours are up, Jacko. No word from you, so we caught the next plane."

Thunder rolled and lightning crashed high above them, as the storm began to pick up intensity. With raindrops pouring over her face and hair, running in rivulets down her bright yellow rain slicker, Flannery kept her chin up as she slipped in beside Jack. "How did you know where to find us?"

"This old broad at the general store told us to come here," Bucky tossed out. "But that doesn't matter much, does it? We're here, and we want the RuMex job sewn up. You blew it big-time, didn't you, Mc-Keegan?"

Jack started to slide his hand into his shirt pocket, but he hesitated. After a long moment, he sent Flannery a searching look.

She knew what was happening. *He had his fingers on the contract, but he doesn't want to turn it over.*

"Please, Jack, don't do this," she urged.

"Time's up, Jacko."

"Jack, I'm sorry, but Bucky is right. If you've failed again, I have to know."

"No, J.B., I haven't failed." Staring at them instead of at her, Jack clenched his jaw. And then he quietly pulled the plastic-wrapped packet of papers from his pocket and handed it over.

"Jack," she tried. But it was too late.

With one last massive rumble from the sky, the storm subsided, turning back into the gentle spring shower that had woken her that morning.

J.B. cuffed Jack on the shoulder and mumbled, "Good show," as he unfolded the papers under his umbrella and began to leaf through them. "Excellent, excellent," he declared. "Unfortunate we had to go to the wire on this, but an excellent set of negotiations on your part, nonetheless."

"Thank you, J.B."

"No, no, thank you, my boy." Seton rubbed his hands together in obvious anticipation of another great deal for Seaboard. "We'll just get these agreements back to the home office on the double, and then we'll all relax a bit, eh?" He turned to go, as Bucky jumped to keep the umbrella in place over his boss's head. "Coming with us, Jack? No need to stand out in the rain, is there?"

"I'll be coming later, J.B." Jack rammed his hands into the pockets of last night's linen trousers, oblivious to the fact that his clothes and his shoes were clearly being ruined in the downpour. "I have some things I have to clear up here first."

J.B. waved a dismissing hand and ambled off toward the limo waiting at the road. "We'll see you back in Boston then, ASAP. Oh, and Jack, get yourself cleaned up, will you? You look dreadful, my boy, not at all the Seaboard image.''

The Seaboard image, riding in the Seaboard limo, cruised smoothly away from Rainbow Springs, but Jack remained silent.

"You know you can't do this," Flannery argued. "You can't go back to Boston, Jack. I know you can't."

He shook his head sadly, sending a spray of water droplets out around him. "Why can't I?"

"Because it wouldn't be right."

The defeated look in Jack's eyes gave her a momentary flutter of panic. He wasn't going to leave over something as small and insignificant as that contract, was he?

"Jack," she persisted, pulling at his soggy sleeve, "you can't leave. The magic is here, remember?"

"There is no magic. You were right all along." He shrugged. "It was just a silly old man playing tricks and I got fooled because deep down, I guess I wanted to believe in something." Sighing, Jack tilted his head back into the rain. "Call it burnout or yuppie stress or a latent romantic streak—I don't know. I needed a vacation, and I got Inisheer and leprechauns instead. Lucky me."

"But you were lucky. You *are* lucky!" If he would only look at her, she was sure she could reach him, but he kept staring pensively into the sky. "Jack, listen to me. We found each other, and that's as lucky as it gets."

"You know, Flannery, you didn't need to lie to me. You could have saved us both a lot of trouble if you'd told me the truth about Turlough's hiding place from the beginning."

"But I didn't know," she said patiently.

He gave a short, unpleasant laugh as he looked over at her. "Yeah, right. You thought I'd toss the old man in the pokey, or maybe that I'd make a success of the RuMex deal, and you couldn't stand losing on either account, right?"

"Unlike you, Jack," she shot back, "I am not hung up on winning. That's what this all boils down to, isn't it? Jack McKeegan has to come out a winner or his pride will be hurt."

"No, that's not it," he interrupted, but she continued.

Practically taunting him, she proclaimed, "And if somebody pulls the wool over your eyes, even a harmless old man like my grandfather, then you can't stand it. He made a fool of you, so you're going to run back to Boston and let Inisheer get chewed up by RuMex's bulldozers, just to salvage your precious ego." She kicked at a pebble, sending it sailing into the springs. "You'll show us—our home will be a landfill for RuMex's next subdivision, but Jack McKeegan can feel like a big man again. Hallelujah!"

His voice was devoid of expression when he said, "If that's the way you want to look at it, fine."

"Fine."

"Fine."

They couldn't stand there in the rain forever, glaring at each other, so Flannery made the first move, marching across the field to get to her car. As soon as she took a step, Jack wheeled and started off in the other direction, heading for the trees.

"Where are you going?" she shouted.

"My car is at Inisheer," he returned coldly. "I'll walk, thanks. I know the way."

"Okay, Jack. Go." To his retreating back, she called angrily, "But we both know you'll be back."

He made no comment, just kept on walking.

Raising her volume, losing her temper, Flannery yelled, "Don't think this is over. Because it's not even close to over yet, McKeegan. Do you hear me, you blockhead? You will be back. Yes, you will. Because you love me!"

Jack's tall, slim form disappeared into a thatch of trees.

"You love me," she whispered. "And you'll be back. I know it."

Chapter Fifteen

Boston
September, 1992

Jack sat at his desk, drawing circles on an interoffice memo he was supposed to be reading. It was his new assignment, a big deal for a luxury shopping mall inside an old train station in Baltimore, but he couldn't have cared less.

Tipping back in his chair, he stared out his window into the corresponding window of the skyscraper next door. Out there, not too far away, the trees were turning. Out there, people were strolling along the shore, watching the waves come in at Martha's Vineyard, picking cranberries at Cape Cod, perhaps simply enjoying the warmth of September sunlight on the red bricks of Boston.

But not Jack McKeegan, who was in the bluest funk of his career.

"Jack?" Jennifer asked tentatively, edging in his door.

He rotated his chair back around to the front. "Yeah?"

"I wanted to be the first to tell you." She moistened her pretty lips. "J.B. just told me that I got the promotion. I'm really sorry, Jack. I know everyone thought it would be you."

"No, they didn't." He went back to the intricate design of doodles on his memo. "I'm not the fair-haired boy around here anymore."

"Well, not lately anyway."

"Yeah." He managed a cynical smile. "Not since, oh, March, maybe?"

"Not since St. Patrick's Day," she said sympathetically. "Look, Jack, if there's anything I can do..."

"Nope. There's nothing anyone can do." He lifted his shoulders in a fatalistic shrug. "I was a sucker and a chump, and I can't seem to get past that."

It seemed absurd that there was once a time he believed in leprechauns. *But it was my own fault, wasn't it? She tried to tell me not to believe.*

"But, hey, you shouldn't be standing around commiserating with me. You should be out celebrating your new job, Ms. Vice President. You deserve it, Jen. Congratulations."

"Thanks." She smiled mischievously. "Bucky is having a fit. That's a plus, anyway."

"Makes my day."

"Aa-hem" sounded gruffly from behind Jennifer, and she backed quickly out of Jack's office.

"Hello, sir," she said immediately. "Were you looking for me?"

"No," came the reply. And then the smooth head of J. B. Seton poked through the doorway. "Jack, I need to speak with you."

Halfheartedly, Jack sat up and pretended to be interested. "Come right in, J.B."

"It's RuMex again," the old man announced gloomily. "Sometimes I wonder if this RuMex deal will ever die."

"What do you mean, J.B.? They should be breaking ground even as we speak."

"Not anymore." J.B. grimaced, brandishing a yellow telegram in Jack's direction. "Read this, my boy, and you shall weep. It seems some sort of leaf..."

He consulted the sheet briefly, and then started again. "It seems some sort of leaf, a *Trifo*-something or other, has been discovered out there, all over the place. It's a hitherto unknown plant, a new version or a new strain or something, and the scientists are all hopping around, waving their arms and insisting RuMex go away, or risk endangering this... this blasted weed."

"Clover," Jack supplied. "*Trifolium*." He remembered hearing the fancy Latin term in Flannery's greenhouse, but he would've known even without the label. Flannery was still out there, manufacturing objections to the RuMex project, so he knew immediately what it had to be. "Four-leaf clovers."

"It doesn't really matter what it is," J.B. groused. "The Illinois EPA is in an uproar, and some idiotic yokel of a judge has issued an injunction, restraining RuMex from disturbing one little sprout of this *Trifo*-whatsit."

"So it's over, then. She wins."

It was almost a relief to know she had emerged victorious, that Inisheer and all its rustic charm would be saved, that he would never have to think about her or worry about her for the rest of his life.

Who's kidding who, Jack? As if this would stop him from thinking about her. As if this would end it.

Echoing Jack's thoughts, J.B. snapped, "Who says it's over? We still have a client, and there's still a deal to make. This project was squarely in your domain, Jack, from the onset. I feel certain we can still pull the fat from the fire, so to speak, regardless of these *Trifo*-weeds. If RuMex's headquarters can be salvaged, you're just the man to do it."

"Salvaged?" Jack ran a hand through the cropped ends of his hair. "How?"

"There must be something we can do!" J.B. thundered.

"If they're really dead-set on protecting the four-leaf clovers, I don't see what we can do, except move the site completely."

"Then move the site completely! Surely you can locate new parcels of land, close enough to these, but not so close as to interfere with the water table or whatever it is that's supposedly threatening that blasted weed."

J.B. paced off the distance between Jack's desk and the door, spun on his heel and traversed the same path again.

"Get on the horn, Jack. See how serious this injunction is, find out what's what. And then I want you back to that place on the double, and I want this straightened out." With his eyebrows drawn together darkly, J.B. demanded, "Do you hear me, Jack?"

"Loud and clear."

And for the first time in months, Jack felt like smiling.

THE FOG WAS AS THICK as an Irish wool sweater—the heavy, hand-knitted kind his Aunt Margaret had given him for Christmas every year when he was a kid.

Jack peered over the steering wheel, wondering if he were stuck in a time warp. When he reached Inisheer, would the green door beckon him inside to another inexplicable, impossible party, full of high-pitched fairy music and magic spells?

"Damn fog. You would know there would be fog again, just for me."

But he knew the area better now; even a fog of epic proportions didn't have the power to thwart him this time. Like a homing pigeon, he headed for Inisheer, not in the least confused or put off by the thick, drifting mist that blanketed his car.

"It isn't mysterious," he told himself sharply. "It's just fog. No tricks, no magic, just fog."

Nonetheless, when he finally saw the Inisheer sign, and he knew he was back at the edge of the world, he drove past the front door of the pub, taking no chances. His car wound its way to the back of the driveway before he pulled it to a stop. He would enter Inisheer the way he'd left it—by way of Flannery O'Shea.

His hand hesitated on the key in the ignition. Was he ready for this?

Ready as he'd ever be.

Swiftly he strode from the car and wrenched open the kitchen door. And there she was, standing over the stove, wearing the green sweater over her jeans, gazing at him as if she'd been expecting him.

"I didn't think it would take you this long," she said calmly.

Her serenity infuriated him. "You've been a busy little bee, haven't you?" he demanded.

She blinked. "Pardon?"

"You've been running all over the county, planting your damned clover on the sly, pretending it grew there all by itself."

"Why, Jack," she said sweetly, "if you mean the new strain of white clover that just happens to have been discovered locally, I can assure you it's completely natural. What gives you the idea that I planted it?"

Clenching his hands into fists, he advanced on her. "You couldn't just leave it alone, could you?"

Her green eyes widened and softened as he got closer. "No," she answered quietly. "I couldn't."

"You couldn't just leave *me* alone, could you?"

"No," she whispered. "I couldn't."

"Damn you," he swore, grabbing her around the waist and hauling her up against him. He ran his hands over her harshly, crushing her to him, reacquainting himself with the shape of her and the feel of her, burying himself in the inevitable shower of sparks, the blaze of chemistry that roared to life every time he touched her. "God, I've missed you."

Without a word, she wrapped her arms around his neck and pulled his mouth down to hers. She tasted hungry, needy, ravenous. She tasted marvelous.

Groaning, Jack returned the kiss, thrust for thrust, sliding to his knees on the hardwood floor, dragging her with him. He couldn't get enough of her mouth, of her skin. It had been too damned long.

They tumbled to the floor, ripping away their clothes impatiently, without regard for buttons or sleeves or anything but getting rid of the damn things. They needed to be together again skin to skin, before another second ticked off the clock.

The kitchen floor? he thought briefly, horrified that it had come to this. "The hell with it," he muttered. There was no time to go upstairs.

They couldn't stop touching and clutching at each other, and no embrace seemed hard enough or close enough. His mouth trailed over her breasts and her shoulders, her ears and her hair, until finally he could wait no longer. When she reached for him, guiding him, he plunged inside her, craving that last connection of their minds and their bodies. Flannery cried out his name and shattered in his arms, and he knew he was home.

Slick with the sweat of their lovemaking, he sat up and leaned against the oven. He cradled her to him, brushing damp hair back from her face.

"I'm still furious with you," he murmured, grazing her lips with soft kisses.

"I'm not too thrilled with you, either."

"You don't look like you're complaining."

She cocked an eyebrow at him. "Neither do you."

"I guess we'll both have to learn to deal with it."

"I guess so."

"I do have one question for you, though," he said lightly, framing her face with his hands. "What would you have done if they'd sent Bucky back here instead of me?"

There was a short pause. "Let's just say Bucky wouldn't have gotten this kind of reception."

"Oh, I see." He lowered his lips to hers again, drinking deeply of her sweetness, whispering, "So you wouldn't go that far to save Inisheer?"

"Not in a million years." Gently, Flannery put a finger to his lips. "I know there are other twin oaks out there, other fairy gates, other candidates to become the edge of the world. If Inisheer disappeared, I could find another one. But I'd never find another you, Jack.''

"You knew I'd come back? You were that sure?''

"I have to admit, I didn't expect it to take this long. I was starting to wonder if I'd have to come to Boston and drag you back here myself.'' Slowly, she pulled on her clothes, smiling as she handed over his pants and shirt.

"You would've done that?'' he asked, rebuttoning his shirt.

"Oh, yes,'' she returned. "Absolutely. Positively. Unequivocab—''

He stopped her with another kiss.

"Oh, dear,'' a lilting Irish brogue interrupted from the direction of the door into the pub. "It seems I've gone and done it this time.''

Flannery said primly, "Granddad, what are you doing here?''

"Well, I heard young Jack was back, and I wanted to tell him how much I approve of his scheme to put the pub back together. It's a grand plan, young Jack.'' Sully's eyes twinkled as he beamed at them both. "Now, I don't want you to be thinking I approve of the goings-on here right in front of my very eyes, but I'm trying to keep in mind that you're two young people in love and perhaps you've gotten carried away a bit. But you will be marrying my granddaughter, now won't you, lad?''

"Well, yes, if she wants to.''

"Uh, I do. I mean, I guess I do.''

Jack couldn't keep a grin from dancing across his lips. "Thank God,'' he whispered. She gave him back a misty smile, and he wanted to kiss her again, without the old man present.

But then it hit him. Warily, he gazed at Sully. "Wait a minute. How did you know I was planning to rehab the pub?"

"Because I'm a leprechaun, you dunderhead!"

"Jack, what do you mean?" Flannery interjected. "What's that about the pub? So you were really serious?"

"Well, it's an idea. I always wanted to, you know, just because it has a lot of potential." He felt awfully self-conscious all of a sudden. "Everything's all set to move the RuMex deal into Kentucky, but it's still not that far away from here really."

"You're moving RuMex's headquarters?"

"We didn't have a choice, darling." Crossing his arms over his chest, he sent her a cynical smile. "It seems some do-gooder discovered four-leaf clovers all over this area, within a five-mile radius of Inisheer. And Ru-Mex's irrigation plans, not to mention the waterfall they wanted out in front of their main building, would interfere with the water table, flooding some of the clover and drying out the rest. So, RuMex had to go. RuMex 0, Flannery O'Shea 1."

She grinned. "And what does the fact that they've relocated to Kentucky have to do with my pub?"

"Well, visiting bigwigs will still need places within a decent driving distance, places with entertainment, places to eat. I have the connections—my first three years at Seaboard, I did nothing but hotels and B and Bs—plus I practically grew up at Callahan's Daughter, so I know how to make a go of it with a first-class Irish pub, with authentic pub food, like the stuff you fixed me when I stayed here. Plus we could fly in fresh salmon, put Guinness on tap, really go for it."

"Is this for real?" she asked, her eyes round with disbelief.

Jack nodded, not sure of her reaction. Would she even want to own a pub? "I may be able to convince Seaboard to provide part of the start-up funds. If you like this idea, that is."

"I love it!" She was practically dancing with excitement. "Inisheer could be the way it was when my great-grandfather ran it, the way it was when my mother was a girl." She leaned up to kiss him, to throw her arms around his neck. "And you'll have a job here—you won't have to go back to Boston. That's the best part."

"And you won't have to support me with four-leaf clovers," he added dryly.

Flannery suddenly dropped back and looked around the kitchen. "Granddad's gone. Where did he disappear to?"

"Who knows?" Jack shrugged. "He is a leprechaun, after all. I guess he has tricks to pull, unwary strangers to con...."

"Poor, innocent granddaughters to match up with the unwary strangers...."

"Nope. Turlough is fresh out of granddaughters."

"Speaking of granddaughters..." Flannery said.

"Kathleen?"

"Exactly. After you met her in person, I figured you would tell me whether she was the one in the pub that night." She gazed up at him expectantly. "So, it was her, wasn't it? I mean, it was some kind of trick that she and my granddad played on you, right?"

"I honestly don't know."

"But, Jack, you have to know. Was it her or not?"

"Flannery, I don't know. The woman in the bar that night looked like your sister, but she also looked like your mother, in that picture I found." He really didn't want to start this all over again, but he supposed there was no way around it. "When I went back to Boston, I had plenty of time to come up with rational explanations."

"And you did? Come up with rational explanations, I mean."

"Yes, I did. There are magic stores that carry fake cobwebs, there are ways to blow dust around so a place will look like no one's been there for years, there are ways to lay carpet on grass so that cars don't leave tracks. Mediums and swamis—and people who conduct seances to bilk other people out of money—they've all been pulling that kind of scam since long before you were born. There are explanations that make hard, cold sense if you look deep enough."

"So you believe that's what happened—that my grandfather manufactured cobwebs and dust and laid carpet at Rainbow Springs?"

"Honestly?" Jack's voice didn't waver. "No."

"No?"

He gave her a cheeky grin. "No."

"But, Jack, then that means..." Flannery bit her lip. When she looked up at him, her green eyes were uncertain, confused. "If you say no, then that means you think it was magic."

"I do."

"Think it was magic?"

"Yes."

"But it can't be."

"Why not?"

"But you stopped believing. You went back to Boston." She peered at him anxiously. "I know that for a while you really believed in it, but that's when you were here, and we were falling in love, and everything seemed so magical, so special. I thought for sure you wouldn't believe anymore once you were away from here."

"I thought so, too." Jack ran a rough hand back and forth through his hair. "It's funny. I thought that when I left, the memory of this place would fade and I would be dead certain it was all a fake. That's why I went to the magicians and the ghostbusters—to convince myself that I'd been had. But I couldn't do it. I still believed in the magic."

"You did?"

"Hey, I would've gone to a shrink if I thought that would help." He caught her in his arms and smiled down at her sensible, magical face. "But it wouldn't help. Nothing would. Nothing but coming back and finding the magic again."

"And have you?"

"Oh, yes." Holding her tightly for a moment, he said softly, "Flannery, I was dead in Boston without you. I didn't want to be who I used to be, that hotshot John Patrick McKeegan, the rising star at Seaboard. I tried, but I'm not sure I even know who that person is anymore. Flannery, the magic is here—I know it's you."

"Me? But, why? There's nothing magic about *me.*"

"Oh, yes, there is. Because I don't have it by myself. But I'm not willing to do without it anymore." He swallowed, and his voice began to sound rough and husky. "If I stay here, will you share it with me?"

"Always, Jack. Always."

When she smiled up at him, he swore he saw rainbows.

"But there's just one thing...." she said softly.

"What's that, darling?"

She gave him a sideways glance. "If you really think my grandfather is a leprechaun, then what does that make me?"

He smiled. "That's easy, Mary Flannery. You're the pot of gold at the end of the rainbow."

ABOUT THE AUTHOR

Julie Kistler believes that it takes a curious mix of discipline
and creativity to think up new, fresh characters and plots,
to actually finish what you've started and then to send it off
into the world. Julie has always loved the fantasy world of
movies and books, and she feels that writing is a perfect
outlet for her creative talents. In *Flannery's Rainbow* her
imagination and romantic passion are at their best. She
truly captures the Irish spirit and brings to life a very special little man who calls himself a leprechaun.

JKCOR

Following the success of WITH THIS RING,
Harlequin cordially invites you to enjoy the
romance of the wedding season with

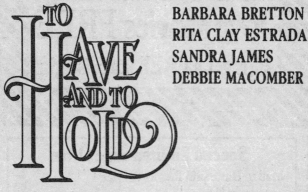

BARBARA BRETTON
RITA CLAY ESTRADA
SANDRA JAMES
DEBBIE MACOMBER

A collection of romantic stories that celebrate the joy,
excitement, and mishaps of planning that special day
by these four award-winning Harlequin authors.

**Available in April at your favorite Harlequin
retail outlets.**

Take 4 bestselling love stories FREE

Plus get a FREE surprise gift!

Special Limited-time Offer

Mail to Harlequin Reader Service®

In the U.S.	In Canada
3010 Walden Avenue	P.O. Box 609
P.O. Box 1867	Fort Erie, Ontario
Buffalo, N.Y. 14269-1867	L2A 5X3

YES! Please send me 4 free Harlequin American Romance® novels and my free surprise gift. Then send me 4 brand-new novels every month, which I will receive months before they appear in bookstores. Bill me at the low price of $2.96* each— a savings of 43¢ apiece off the cover prices. There are no shipping, handling or other hidden costs. I understand that accepting the books and gift places me under no obligation ever to buy any books. I can always return a shipment and cancel at any time. Even if I never buy another book from Harlequin, the 4 free books and the surprise gift are mine to keep forever.

*Offer slightly different in Canada—$2.96 per book plus 49¢ per shipment for delivery. Canadian residents add applicable federal and provincial sales tax. Sales tax applicable in N.Y.

154 BPA ADL2   354 BPA ADMG

Name _____ (PLEASE PRINT)

Address _____ Apt. No. _____

City _____ State/Prov _____ Zip/Postal Code. _____

This offer is limited to one order per household and not valid to present Harlequin American Romance® subscribers. Terms and prices are subject to change.

AMER-92   © 1990 Harlequin Enterprises Limited

HARLEQUIN®

A Calendar of Romance

Be a part of American Romance's year-long celebration of love and the holidays of 1992. Celebrate those special times each month with your favorite authors.

Next month, it's an explosion of springtime flowers and new beginnings in

APRIL

S	M	T	W	T	F	S
			1	2	3	4
5	6	7	8	9	10	11
12	13	14	15	16	17	18
19	20	21	22	23	24	25
	27	28	29	30		

#433 A MAN FOR EASTER
by Stella Cameron

Read all the books in *A Calendar of Romance*, coming to you one per month, all year, only in American Romance.
